BOOK YOUR PLACE ON OUR WEBSITE AND MAKE THE READING CONNECTION!

We've created a customized website just for our very special readers, where you can get the inside scoop on everything that's going on with Zebra, Pinnacle and Kensington books.

When you come online, you'll have the exciting opportunity to:

- View covers of upcoming books
- Read sample chapters
- Learn about our future publishing schedule (listed by publication month *and author*)
- Find out when your favorite authors will be visiting a city near you
- Search for and order backlist books from our online catalog
- Check out author bios and background information
- Send e-mail to your favorite authors
- Meet the Kensington staff online
- Join us in weekly chats with authors, readers and other guests
- Get writing guidelines
- AND MUCH MORE!

**Visit our website at
http://www.kensingtonbooks.com**

Beauty and the WOLF

MARINA MYLES

KENSINGTON BOOKS
Kensington Publishing Corp.
http://www.kensingtonbooks.com

KENSINGTON BOOKS are published by

Kensington Publishing Corp.
119 West 40th Street
New York, NY 10018

All Kensington titles, imprints, and distributed lines are available at special quantity discounts for bulk purchases for sales promotion, premiums, fund-raising, educational, or institutional use.

Special book excerpts or customized printings can also be created to fit specific needs. For details, write or phone the office of the Kensington Special Sales Manager: Attn. Special Sales Department. Kensington Publishing Corp., 119 West 40th Street, New York, NY 10018. Phone: 1-800-221-2647.

Kensington and the K logo Reg. U.S. Pat. & TM Off.

First Electronic Edition: June 2013
eISBN-13: 978-1-60183-099-9
eISBN-10: 1-60183-099-8

First Print Edition: June 2013
ISBN-13: 978-1-60183-210-8
ISBN-10: 1-60183-210-9

Printed in the United States of America

This book is for NICK.
You are my real-life hero and my forever love.

ACKNOWLEDGMENTS

The publication of my first novel is a dream come true and I am indebted to everyone involved. A huge thank you goes to my fabulous editor, **Peter Senftleben**, who gave me this opportunity and guided *Beauty and the Wolf* so beautifully; my agent, **Louise Fury**, whose good humor, energy, and expertise is beyond admirable; the masterful crew at Kensington; friends and fellow authors, **Beth Kendrick** and **Cathy McDavid**, who offered me tons of keen insight and advice; and my wonderful critique partners, **Terri Molina Dunham**, **Helen King**, and **Stacey Goitia**. (We've certainly had some good times at Denny's and Starbucks!)

Last but not least, I'd like to thank my amazing parents, **Mary Ann** and **Marino Morelli**. They taught me to never give up on anything—and I'm so glad they did!

The moon has the power to tear reason out of man's head by depriving him of human and cerebral virtues.
—PARACELSUS, sixteenth-century physician

When stars align at the hand of the Underworld God, a chosen few are but puppets on strings.
—Ancient Egyptian proverb

Chapter One

England, 1818

I am getting married today.

The realization bubbled to the surface of Lord Draven Winthrop's liquor-weighted mind. At the gong of the town clock, he shot up in bed and peered at his surroundings. The décor of the small space was unfamiliar, but the stench of stale ale and the sound of muffled laughter told him he was in a room over the tavern.

How had he ended up here—naked?

As he forced his cloudy vision to focus on the bedside clock, he gave another start. *Ten A.M. Bloody hell!*

In precisely thirty minutes, he was scheduled to exchange wedding vows with Miss Isabella Farrington. That didn't leave him much time to return to his estate, dress, and reach St. John's Abbey on the opposite end of town.

He stroked a hand over his face and stopped when he felt the rough fabric of a bandage. An image broke through the fog in his head. The wolf coming out of nowhere last night, toppling him from his horse, and lunging for him before he could get away. He'd gone for his revolver just as the wolf had sunken its teeth into his hand.

Draven reached for the bandage and peeled it back. The wounds were gone. *Am I seeing things?*

"Is the roguish Earl of Dunwich having second thoughts about getting married today?" The raven-haired beauty lying beside him propped herself up on one elbow.

He stared at her, trying to remember how he'd ended up in her bed. He had been on his way to the tavern for a drink. She was the barmaid who'd attended to his wounds; he remembered that much.

He also remembered that, despite her beauty, the pleasure in his balls had evaporated and he'd failed to perform for the first time in his life. While the girl's catlike blue eyes had shone with mischief and her creamy breasts had filled his hands like two, perfect mounds of silk, her lips couldn't match his fiancée's plump, glossy mouth. Nor did her nose twitch enchantingly as did Isabella's when he attempted a joke.

Good God. Was he developing feelings for the woman he was marrying? It was impossible. Love was something Draven didn't believe in.

"Are you having second thoughts?" she repeated.

His mouth went dry. Ignoring her question, he climbed out of bed to search for his clothes.

"If you're to marry, m'lord, I hope you won't lose your lust for fun." The barmaid giggled like a schoolgirl. "Perhaps you can come back to my room later so we can finish what we started last night."

He pointed an unsteady finger at her and smiled. "You're a tarty one. But I do not intend to disgrace my new bride."

"You mean to say the Earl of Madness is going to be a respectable man now?" she asked.

The mention of his public nickname made Draven cringe. It wasn't a secret he had spent time in an asylum when he was sixteen years old. Who wouldn't have come to the edge of madness after that horrible night in the woods—a night he could barely bring himself to think of? Being released had been a godsend, but it was a wonder he still had his wits about him—under the threat of the Gypsy's curse, that is.

Why couldn't he bury the reason for his incarceration along with the rest of his dark past?

He stared at his hand again. *Could there be truth to the blasted hex?*

Despite his drunken state and the overzealous barmaid, maybe the wolf attack happened. If it had—and if his curse came to life beneath this evening's full moon—what would he have gotten his new bride into so bloody soon?

Draven yanked on his clothes and left the tavern room in a hurry. Once he reached his estate, he managed to prepare himself for the wedding—though the preparation was done between rounds of whiskey shots. His late arrival at the abbey garnered him a barrage of contentious stares, but he couldn't care less. He faced the sour expressions of the guests with his shoulders pinned back. After all, he was Lord Draven Winthrop, infamous rake and nonbeliever in love. His reputation entitled him to carry on as if he was at the worst wedding in the world and that was damn near what was about to take place.

His gaze wavered to the back of the church. There stood his bride. Draped in an understated wedding gown of tiny pearls and lace, Isabella beamed as brightly as the flowers encircling her head. Draven gulped, and as sunlight fell upon his bride's sheer veil, he saw hope crest in her eyes.

With her shining auburn hair and fine features, she was a beautiful woman—even breathtaking. Why then did she represent a dark cupid about to pierce him with a fatal arrow? Draven was minutes away from losing his freedom, but that wasn't what was bothering him most. Under the threat of his curse, he couldn't afford to get too attached to his new wife. It was true that she'd begun to tug at his heartstrings, but he was marrying her for a specific purpose—and he intended to keep things to that.

The first strains of organ music bellowed and Draven's vision blurred. Isabella slid a foot forward and while she made her way down the aisle, he remembered the wolf bite he'd suffered last night. Suddenly he felt nauseous.

What if I transform into a werewolf for the first time tonight?

In that moment, Draven experienced a new emotion: fear. As Isabella inched closer, he knew this was all wrong—that he was putting her in danger—yet he accepted her hand when she presented it to him. Turning toward the priest with a knot in his gut, he heard something about Isabella honoring and obeying him, followed by something about him taking her for his lawfully wedded wife. Uttering words he couldn't be sure were correct, he swiveled to face his bride and groped for her hands. He lost himself in the warmth of her stare before she tilted her pert nose upward in anticipation of his kiss. Responding, he lifted her veil and cupped her small, cameo-shaped face. Then he brought his mouth to her lips. A tremendous spark ignited within him—and he was scared for the second time that day.

Disliking the feeling intensely, Draven forced his heart to freeze into the iceberg it had always been. And as he drew away from the kiss, he was left with nothing but cold insensitivity.

Isabella Farrington—now Lady Draven Winthrop, Countess of Dunwich—had only been married for seven hours but she was certain she'd just made the worst mistake of her life. Jostling inside the polished wedding coach that bore the Winthrop crest, she lunged forward in an ungraceful heap when it came to a stop.

Her groom shot her a callous look. "We have arrived."

Catching a glimpse of her new home through the window, Isabella pressed her fingers together to keep them from shaking. Draven's scowl prompted her out of the carriage and dread raced along her spine as she looked up at the imposing structure before her.

Set on a sloping bluff, the house known as Thorncliff Towers loomed over her like an enormous, vine-clad fortress. With its sky-high turrets, repressive stone façade, and arcane courtyard, it appeared as unwelcoming as Draven had been inside the carriage.

Her husband exited the coach behind her, a mess of a newly married man. Tugging on the points of his vest beneath his greatcoat of gold brocade, he indicated to the footman to open the front doors. Then, ignoring Isabella completely, he careened across the pebbled driveway in a cloud of port and cigar fumes.

Isabella watched him reach the portico before she gathered her skirts. As she scurried through the open doorway, she nodded to the aged female servant who greeted her. Then, turning her gaze to the manor's interior, she gave a shudder. Its décor was the epitome of melancholia and neglect. Worn carpets covered yards of scuffed parquet flooring while furniture upholstered in shades of gray filled a vast parlor. An enormous staircase, flanked by gryphon-topped newel posts, anchored the main hall and faced an unlit hearth positioned on another wall.

Draven stood beside Isabella in the foyer. Twilight's haze slanted through a window and illuminated his profile. From his straight, patrician nose to his darkly curled lashes that brushed the rise of his cheekbones, he *looked* like he could be her Prince Charming. But today her boorish groom had destroyed her dream of living a fairy tale.

Draven had appeared at the altar thirty minutes late, unrecognizable and completely foxed. After mucking their vows—who on earth was Laura?—he had either forgotten or disregarded her one request: a bridal bouquet of red roses. Following an embarrassing reception during which they were served cold finger sandwiches and cheap wine, he actually fell asleep in the carriage on the way to Thorncliff Towers. Mouth agape, he'd snored like a pig.

Now he gave Isabella an impatient frown as he gestured her up the stairs. She climbed the grand staircase in excruciating silence, highly aware of his hand pressed to the small of her back. Amid walls that seemed hushed by dark secrets, the contact—and thoughts of the intimacy soon to come—made her legs quake.

Maybe, she considered, Draven was still too drunk to mind her lack of experience.

Perhaps he'll fall asleep in the middle of our lovemaking.

But when Isabella turned around, his sharpened stare plunged those hopes into a dark abyss.

He took the lead once they reached the fourth story of the house. She continued to follow him until they arrived at a set of double doors.

"My bedchamber," Draven said without flourish.

She crossed her arms while he looked as though he would prefer to be miles away from here. *From her.*

"Isn't it traditional for a groom to come to his bride's bedchamber on his wedding night?" She couldn't hide her disappointment at his lack of gallantry.

"I sleep best in my own bed," he growled. "The sooner you come to know my preferences, the better off we will be."

Isabella didn't dare tell him he was more fun when he drank, especially after he had suggested she try the wine at the reception for the same reason.

With barely a look in her direction, he reached for the door handle.

"You have done nothing but humiliate me today," she said, biting back a full verbal assault. After all, Draven was her only hope for what she desperately needed: financial help for her downtrodden father. "The least you can do is carry me across the threshold."

Her husband eyed her for a moment, his dark eyes boring into her very soul. "Very well, but it is the last time I shall carry you anywhere."

Lifting her off the ground as if she were the lightest of feathers, he transported her through the doorway only to plop her on her feet at once. Then he marched to the window and gazed at the night sky awash with clouds. "You can change in there," he said, pointing to his dressing room without tearing his stare from the window.

Isabella hurried to the box-sized room. The faint odor of tobacco mixed with sandalwood clung to the air. Since she had refused the help of an abigail, she took her time removing her wedding gown and securing it on a hanger in the wardrobe.

Had Draven noticed that the dress was second-hand and frayed?

She set aside her shame and pulled on a cream-colored negligee he had supplied and stole a look in the mirror. She was a rather plain sight for a bride. With her auburn curls swept off her face in a simple chignon and her face free of rouge and lip-stain, she had put forth little effort this morning. *And why not?* Her mother, dead a year and two months now, hadn't been there to help—or hug—her as she prepared to marry a man she hardly knew.

Isabella had been introduced to Draven at a cousin's birthday fête six weeks ago and his unexpected appearance at the Farringtons' home in London the next day left her to wonder what a man like him could want with her. When he began to court her, he claimed that his title demanded he marry *someone*. Isabella, in return, had seen Draven as her last resort.

Isabella's eyes shifted to the very object responsible for her social eviction: *The cursed amulet of Princess Tousret.* The trouble began when word of her dark prophecy spread through London. In no time at all, suitors who'd previously shown her interest vanished into thin air. Further ruination occurred when she was released from her governess position.

Brushing her fingertips over the cool stone that hung around her neck, she told herself to think of her father. After all, she was doing all of this for him.

A noteworthy archaeologist, Sir Harris Farrington had spent the family's last half-penny on a trip to Egypt to find the amulet. He managed to unearth it, but the necklace wasn't nearly as valuable as it would have been if he'd found its counterpart, the bracelet of Amenhotep. To add to the disaster, Isabella's father had pushed the limits of the dig by sending three workers into a deep ravine to search for the bracelet. When the workers died, the gross mismanagement of the venture sunk Harris Farrington's reputation.

After that, finding a sponsor for future digs proved impossible.

Isabella ran a finger along the stone's thin, silver chain. When her father had given her the necklace for safekeeping, he had begged her never to don it. But she was a skeptic at heart and didn't believe in curses. She felt that the best way to protect it was to wear it, and now with the pin money Draven had given her as a wedding gift her father would be able to return to Egypt and search for Amenhotep's bracelet. It was an enchanted piece of jewelry thought to have the power to undo the stone's prophecy as well as restore her father's professional viability.

"What's taking so long?" Draven's gruff voice penetrated the wall.

"I'll be out in a moment!" The mirror bounced back the quiver of Isabella's voice and the paleness of her face.

Just breathe. To calm her nerves, she unraveled her hair from its tight chignon and smoothed the freed curls.

"I may fall asleep if you don't come to bed!" Draven's snarl caused her to jump.

Sucking in a breath, she entered her husband's suite. As Draven reclined in bed, the hunger in his obsidian eyes made her heart skitter. His smooth chest rose and fell beneath an opened, white shirt while the lights and shadows bouncing from the hearth enhanced his hollowed cheekbones. Stepping closer, Isabella couldn't help but notice how enticingly his black, shoulder-length hair glimmered in the firelight.

At the very least, she was grateful that Draven was handsome. She had even softened like a wet leaf during their brief wedding kiss. If only his dark nature and intimidating scowl didn't alarm her so.

He threw back the bed-sheet. A defined torso rising out of a pair of low-slung breeches made her avert her eyes.

"Join me," he commanded.

She turned away from him, braced her legs against the side of the mattress, and slid into bed. After drawing the counterpane beneath her chin, she stared up at the ceiling. She could hardly believe she was here.

"I must admit that I'm nervous," she said. "This will be my first time, well . . ."

The words hung in the air as heavily as if someone had used foul language in church.

Draven frowned. "If you weren't a virgin, I wouldn't have married you."

He rolled closer to her but when she locked eyes with him, his ravenous stare made her draw back. In a slow, sultry motion Draven tugged the counterpane down and traced her amulet with his fingertips. His touch on her chest was incredibly hot, as if his entire body were engulfed in flames. She, in contrast, shuddered icy jolts in her nervous state.

"Is this the stone that put gossipmongers in a dither?" he asked.

She nodded and looked down at the curio. It felt strange to have someone else touch it.

He cocked an eyebrow. "Do you ever take it off?"

"No."

"You're not afraid of its prophecy?" Draven looked puzzled.

She shook her head.

He retracted his hand. "What, exactly, does the legend foretell?"

Staring into his fiery eyes, she could hardly think. "Well"—she scrambled to gather her thoughts—"nearly three thousand years ago, the amulet belonged to a headstrong, Egyptian princess named Tousret. This princess made Amenhotep, a high priest from her court, one of her secret lovers. As punishment for her selfishness—and for this priest breaking his holy vows—the Underworld God saw to it that Princess Tousret was drawn to Amenhotep in the worst possible way: a fatal attraction as it were. The God's dark forces willed Tousret to stab Amenhotep before turning the knife on herself. Now any female who wears the stone even once is doomed to take the life of her true love before committing suicide."

Draven's eyes widened. "You are braver than I thought."

She blushed. It was the first compliment he'd given her. "The amulet is a part of my father. He risked his life to find it."

Draven fell into silence before he met her gaze again. "Lucky for you, I don't believe in curses."

The small tremor beneath his eye told Isabella he was lying.

"Still," he said, "the amulet symbolizes too much dark history for my taste. Next time, I want you to remove it."

Next time? She was barely managing this round of intimacy.

Desire darkened Draven's eyes and Isabella gulped. He leaned closer, his mouth hovering over hers. She pinched her eyes shut and folded her hands over her stomach to prepare for his kiss.

He stopped. "There is no reason to be prim and proper with me. You're no longer a governess."

Isabella's eyes flew open at his condescending tone. It took all the restraint she could muster to hold her tongue.

Draven shoved the counterpane to the foot of the bed and studied the outline of her body. He drew her to him. Her breasts pressed against his chest, igniting a crackle of energy between them. Isabella's throat caught and in a surreal moment, he clamped his mouth over hers. When his tongue forced its way past her lips, Isabella's blood moved in wild rushes—and control over her emotions slipped from her grasp. She closed her eyes in silent ecstasy, surrendering to the deepness of his kiss and to the excitement it stirred in her.

The jab of Draven's knee between her thighs snapped her back to reality. Chiding herself for reacting to him with such passion, she composed herself.

His hand swept over her breasts and when it descended to the flat plane of her abdomen, Isabella stiffened. She found it difficult to breathe under the pressure of his mouth and she had no idea to which side she should tilt her head. As his arousal grew solid against her leg, her pulse leapt at the foreign feel of it. Rolling on top of her, Draven's shirttails draped over her negligee and, as he traced her lips with the ease of an expert, Isabella remembered his previous kisses. She'd known him to be tender, at least in those moments, so she began to relax a bit. Then he began pawing her. Reaching down, he pried her knees apart and slipped his hand into the open space. When he rubbed her core in rough motions, her limbs froze. Her groom was a devastatingly handsome man but she was only willing to acquiesce to him at her own speed.

"Forgive me," she said. "I've heard that creating a child can be a wondrous experience. It's just that—"

She blinked against a bright light. Shifting her gaze to the window, she saw that a full moon had emerged through a pair of parted clouds. As the ivory cast spilled across Draven's face, he pulled away from her with eyes that flashed a profound fear. "I must inform you that I have no intention of fathering any offspring," he said.

The admission couldn't have knocked Isabella more off balance. "I . . . I don't understand."

Draven bolted out of bed. His entire body began to shake. "I have personal reasons for not wanting a child. But what you need to know is that we will use a modern form of prevention."

She pulled herself to a sitting position. "You choose this moment, our wedding night, to inform me of this? Didn't you think I should have a say in the matter?"

As the veins in his temples bulged and pounded, she recoiled against the headboard.

"Something is happening to me," he said, spinning away from her. All at once, his shirt split up the middle of his back and fell to the floor. Then, with his face hidden from view, he picked up a chair and hurled it through the window.

Isabella whipped back the bed-sheet, her hand pressed to her mouth in horror.

What is happening?

Fearing for her safety, she rushed inside the dressing room and locked the door. Through her sobs, she heard a loud cry then more breaking glass. A minute later, all was quiet.

She grabbed Draven's wool coat and draped it over her negligee. Turning the doorknob over with a quaking hand, she forced herself to peer into the bedchamber. Wind whistled into the room through the shattered window and the fire in the hearth had all but died out. But Draven was nowhere to be found.

Seizing the chance to flee the room, Isabella escaped into the corridor and raced downstairs. She'd known this loveless marriage was a bad idea, but now she was truly frightened. Refusing to stay at Thorncliff Towers a moment longer, she ran for the stables. And with every step she took, she vowed never to return.

Chapter Two

Two years later

The black post chaise bounced to a stop in front of Dunwich's coaching station. Huddled on its rear bench, Isabella didn't notice. She was too busy dreaming up adjectives for the man she loathed with every fiber of her being.

Mysterious. Cruel. Selfish. Despicable. Deceptive. *Mad.*

"Madam," the driver called above a brewing storm, "this is your stop."

She looked out the window. In the distance, Thorncliff Towers hovered ominously over a wall of trees like an imposing fortress. It was a foreboding sight, but what struck terror in her heart was the thought that Draven was waiting for her inside.

Isabella had returned to London without knowing what had happened to her husband on their wedding night. Instead of initiating a divorce during their time apart, he'd tried various tactics—some outrageous yet all from a distance—to convince her to return. As time went on, her lack of response must have caused him to abandon his persuasive efforts.

How will Draven receive me now? All she knew about his current state of mind was that he had shut himself away from the world under a cloud of depression.

Ironically, things hadn't been much better for Isabella. The Farringtons had slipped into tremendous debt following the accident Harris Farrington suffered while searching for Amenhotep's bracelet. Isabella helped her disoriented father return to London after the disastrous landslide, and in caring for him, she'd been forced to ration their food and seek a governess post again. Unfortunately, no one was willing to hire a countess who had scandalously abandoned her wealthy husband.

Those torturous months had hardened Isabella. She survived as best she could, but like a slow-festering wound, the Farringtons' poverty became intolerable and that destitution compelled her to make a change.

"You must return to Draven," her weakened father begged. "Since he obviously has no intentions of divorcing you, he is the only one who can help us now."

After her cousin, Fiona, offered to take in her disabled father temporarily, Isabella finally agreed. But she decided that she would return to Draven armed with a plan. She couldn't afford proper medical care for her father, but if she became the mother of a genuine Winthrop heir, she would obtain indefinite financial security. Having Draven's child meant that her husband—with his instability and wrath—wouldn't be able to toss her aside so easily.

There is only one problem, Isabella thought as the carriage hitched a curve. Considering Draven's refusal to have children, she must become accidentally impregnated in the throes of passion.

The driver opened the door and as he held out his hand, an unexplained force propelled her into the thick fog. The portly driver, who had informed Isabella that he would go no farther than Dunwich, heaved her portmanteau to the ground. After he resumed his seat at the box, he threw her an empathetic look and sent the horses off with a snap of his whip.

The carriage streamed away and she received a shower of mud from its rear wheels.

"Of all the damnable luck!" It felt liberating to swear in the solitude of the empty street. She yanked a handkerchief from her reticule and wiped the mud from her face.

Glancing around, she wondered if Draven had received the letter she sent three weeks ago. If he had, where was his carriage?

Isabella's agitation escalated as the storm broke. Seeking shelter from the rain beneath the station's portico, she waited and waited. When there was still no sign of the Winthrop coach, she tugged on the brim of her bonnet and hurried inside. The main room stood as silent as a graveyard at midnight and contained no one except a man behind a counter.

Shivering, she took a step forward. "Good evening, sir. Do you have a driver available to take me to the Winthrop estate?"

The elderly man leaned forward. "Perhaps. May I ask who you are, madam? I know everyone in this small village."

"I'm Isabella Far . . . I mean, I am Countess Winthrop." She hadn't used her married title in such a long time. The words tasted bitter in her mouth.

"You don't look like a countess," the spindly clerk said as he eyed her disheveled appearance.

"For heaven's sake! Would any woman in her right mind claim to be married to the volatile Earl of Dunwich if she were not?"

"No," he conceded.

She forced an anxious lump down her throat. "Sir, if you please. I've been traveling all day from London. Do you or do you not have a driver available?"

"On this miserable night, your ladyship? It's nearly nine o'clock in the evening and you have no lady's maid to accompany you."

Isabella gripped her reticule. "Regardless, that is my request."

Concern clouded the man's pale eyes. "There is a driver available, but I wish you would wait 'til morning, m'lady. The roads haven't been safe to travel at night." He leaned even closer and she held her breath to avoid his stale odor.

"Not safe?" she asked.

"Nay. A wolf has been spotted in the forest."

"That's impossible! There are no native wolves left in England."

"Not an ordinary wolf. A *werewolf*," he said, his voice catching.

She looked at him as if he'd just sprouted wings. Werewolves were the stuff of dark fairy tales and she liked to think she was too old to believe in them now. Determined to keep to the schedule she'd penned in her letter she said, "I cannot wait until morning."

"Very well, your ladyship. Sebastian, ready the coach," the man cried over his shoulder.

While Isabella purchased a ticket of passage, a balding man wobbled past her to gather her luggage. She bid the clerk a hasty good night, followed the slow-paced Sebastian, and climbed into the carriage with exasperation on her lips.

The team of horses took off at full gallop. As the animals heaved the coach up the cliffside road, Isabella's fingers quivered around the hand strap. A clap of thunder roared over the coastal waters of Suffolk and her nerves propelled themselves to an unprecedented level.

Take a damper! She traced the outline of the amulet before securing her hands in her lap. If she hoped to face Draven with any sense of dignity she must try and order herself.

She peered out the window as the carriage charged forward at breakneck speed. When a pair of stone columns topped by ominous-looking gryphons streamed by, she realized she had entered Winthrop property. The thought drew Draven's smoldering stare that much closer.

Remembering her plan to seduce her estranged husband, she unclasped the top buttons of her dress and shimmied her ample cleavage upward—as she had seen a disreputable woman do once. She was wholly uncomfortable with being a Jezebel, but she was willing to do it in the name of seduction. And what better opportunity to seduce Draven than on the night they were reunited?

The carriage rattled on and the oppressive house Isabella had spent but a short while in came into view. It looked more eerie than she remembered. The rambling structure loomed over a bevy of turbulent waves like an abandoned lighthouse. At the very apex of Thorncliff Towers, thick stones formed individual thorn-covered spires, undoubtedly inspiring the estate's name. The estate seemed to scrutinize the coastal town of Dunwich with cold insurgency while its shadowy, unkempt grounds coaxed Isabella's neck hair to stand on edge.

The coach sped over a final grade like an angry black raven. Still rumbling violently, it entered a courtyard bordered by clipped hedges where it rolled to a halt.

The smell of brine filled her nostrils as the driver opened the door. She stood and craned her head forward in order to take in the sheer size of the house. Her upward gaze skimmed the pattern of stones and came to rest on a window in the house's south turret. Lightning flashed and though her vision was obscured by the downpour, she could have sworn she saw a male figure watching her from the window. The jaunt of the man's head and the broadness of his shoulders were familiar but as quickly as the lightning flashed, the figure disappeared.

Was Draven watching me?

Plagued by a prickling of nerves, she accepted the driver's hand and forced herself to make contact with the ground. Her half boots sunk into the muddy earth.

"Bloody rain!" She rather enjoyed spewing her second profanity of the day.

Trudging through the mud, Isabella made her way to the marble-coated portico where she located the bell pull. The squall hissed angrily behind her. She gave the cord a tug and waited. The latch flipped over and the portal creaked open to reveal a grim and pervading darkness.

Chapter Three

While Draven slept, a scattering of dark clouds gathered to release a full-blown storm. Thunder boomed and jostled him out of his slumber. As rain pelted the window, he rolled over in bed with a groan.

Isabella.

Thoughts of her frustrated, saddened, and aroused him. He had yearned for her like a dying flower needs water during their separation, but he was thankful that she hadn't seen him transform on their wedding night. The wolf bite he received the night before they married had condemned him to the dark side. Since then, he'd become doomed to change into a bloodlusting wolf beneath every full moon—for all eternity.

On the nights he shape-shifted, Draven prowled the limits of Dunwich, forcing himself to feast on cows and farm animals instead of seeking human blood. Although he hadn't killed anyone in his canine form yet, restraining himself was proving to be pure hell. He kept the monster at bay by locking himself inside his suites for twenty-odd days every month—eating, working, and sleeping in complete solitude.

That solitude reminded him of a place he never wanted to visit again. The asylum.

Detesting himself, Draven slid his feet to the floor and padded to the mullion-paned window. He pushed a hand through his hair as he stared at the road leading away from the estate. Isabella could be arriving any minute. Unless, perhaps, she had decided to stay in London after reading his response to her letter. Of course, his correspondence may have missed her altogether. *Bloody unreliable post.*

But knowing what he did of his wife, he surmised that she had received his letter and chose to ignore his warnings not to come. That is why he had refused to send a coach to gather her in Dunwich. The last thing Draven needed was the scent of Isabella's blood filling the hallways of Thorncliff Towers . . . tempting him. Provoking him.

Ironically, he had written Isabella multiple letters at the start of their separation—begging her to return. Because he never received a reply, he came to the conclusion that she was too scared to come back. He could hardly blame her, yet he couldn't chance a public transformation while he traveled to London to fetch her.

At that point, he'd been forced to send someone after her. The fearsome ruffian Draven hired had arrived on Isabella's doorstep as instructed, but she had refused to accompany the strong-arm back to Dunwich. Draven realized then that nothing short of kidnapping Isabella would ensure her return.

As his bloodlust grew more urgent, he had sequestered himself away from the world.

A knock at the door worsened his mood.

"Who is it?" he roared.

"It's Rogers, sir. Are ye in need of anythin'?"

"God's balls, Rogers! I told you: I'll ring for you."

"But ye haven't had yer supper, m'lord—"

He fisted his hair. "Bloody hell, man. I said 'go away'!"

"As ye wish, m'lord."

When the valet's footsteps faded, Draven pushed open the window and breathed in the cold night air. A strong draft raked over his body as he studied the rain descending in sheets over the house. It was a depressing scene—one that matched his sense of self-loathing. There was no denying he was a *vârcolac* now, as the Romanians called them. *A werewolf born from the depths of black magic.* He had learned that an all-powerful *rauna* curse held its victim captive until that unfortunate soul offered proof of his penance. It was an identity he—and all his male heirs—were bound to unless he could change his selfish ways and gain compassion. In the meantime, if Draven tasted human blood—even a drop—he would stay a beast forever, with no chance of seeing his human form again.

He'd always blamed the crime he committed in that Gypsy camp for sealing his fate, but now he was beginning to realize that the instigator was his bullheaded arrogance.

He pulled the window shut with a scowl but the crunch of wheels over gravel caught his attention. Pressing his face to the cold glass, he saw a coach come to a halt in the center of the courtyard.

"Isabella . . ." he murmured.

Heart thundering, Draven watched his wife materialize from the coach. As she tipped her bonnet back, he was reminded of how beautiful she was. Thick, auburn locks haloed her oval-shaped face and her dusty-pink lips curled charmingly at the corners. She was a natural beauty whose indescribable radiance had seized him the instant they'd met at that dull party.

When he had spotted her amid a sea of guests, he had presumed that she was far from a dowdy matron beneath her conservative dress. His suspicion had been confirmed on their wedding night. With her outrageous mane freed from its chignon and her delicious curves on display beneath her silk negligee, Isabella had done more than impress him. She had beguiled him.

Of course, there was another, less chivalrous, reason Draven had proposed to her. He'd come across a newspaper article telling of the cursed amulet Sir Harris Farrington found in Egypt and subsequently passed on to his only daughter. The article had inspired Draven to travel to London to seek out Isabella. He figured that if his curse ever came to fruition and his beastly alter ego grew out of control, it would be her fate to stop him. By becoming part of the Egyptian prophecy that destined Isabella to kill her lover, he had gained "insurance" as it were.

He marched to his desk, jerked open one of its drawers, and withdrew the newspaper article in question. After giving it a quick glance, he crumpled the article and tossed it into the roaring fire.

He wanted Isabella to kill him—put him out of his misery—but she was doomed to take her life afterward. Thus, he had been incredibly selfish to marry her . . . and his continuation of their marriage was just as self-serving. Why couldn't he prove that he'd grown a heart by divorcing her and be done with it?

If he ever hoped to rectify his curse, Draven knew he must seize this chance to show compassion. That involved driving Isabella back to London. Back to safety.

As he resumed his place by the window, lightning illuminated the sky in a sudden burst. Isabella raised her glance to where he stood. He reeled away from the casement and held his breath. Had she seen him staring at her?

He coaxed his head toward the portal again and watched her sink into a puddle of mud. In two days' time, a full moon would peak. Its threat was stirring his thirst for blood—and his sexual appetite—to a frightening crescendo. That meant Draven must convince his wife to leave as quickly as possible. And he knew precisely how he was going to do it.

Praying that he would be able to resist the scent of Isabella's blood and the attraction she provoked in him, he ventured out of his suites for the first time in twenty-six days.

Chapter Four

Isabella waited in the doorway while the rain dropped in deafening sheets behind her. The manor's housekeeper, a woman she remembered as being colder than the Arctic Ocean, stepped into the light.

"Welcome back, Lady Winthrop." The housekeeper glimpsed Isabella's low neckline and raised an eyebrow in disapproval.

"Thank you, Mrs. . . ."

"Eaton."

"Thank you, Mrs. Eaton." Isabella took in a breath. She hadn't been at Thorncliff Towers long enough to learn any of the servants' names. Gathering her collar together for momentary coverage, she offered the housekeeper a small smile. "You . . . you aren't surprised to see me?"

"Nay. His lordship informed the staff that you might return tonight."

Draven did receive my letter. Infuriation heated Isabella's cheeks but she managed to control the anger in her voice. "The coach driver will be handing over my portmanteau."

Mrs. Eaton nodded curtly.

Isabella was relieved when the housekeeper backed away to allow her entry. Shaking the wetness from her blue shawl dress, she crossed the threshold. Once she reached the edge of the foyer, she took a moment to survey the room she remembered so well.

Nothing had changed. The antique furniture and fixtures were still shadowed in monochromatic shades of gray and the parquet floors continued to cry out for a good polishing. Her gaze swept the grand staircase as it curved upward. *To Draven's suites.* Isabella pressed a fingertip to her lips. She could almost feel the sensual scorch of her husband's mouth and the warmth of his large hands roaming her body.

Shocked at the heat the memory still provided, she forced her eyes back to the darkness of the lower level. She noticed that the candle sconces along the walls were still and that the fluted oil lamps on the entry table remained dark. Was this nonchalant welcome representative of how Draven would receive her?

Isabella laced her fingers together tensely only to shake them loose. As much as she tried to be more carefree, it was difficult for her. Her mother's prolonged illness coupled with her passing had robbed her of any gaiety. And the promise she'd made to Mum on her deathbed—that she would always take care of Papa—had forced her to abandon her own wants and grow up in a hurry.

Perhaps a cooing, rosy-cheeked baby would restore her joy. She longed for a child—and in this dreary, loveless place, she would certainly welcome a precious son or daughter with her entire soul.

Once the coach driver deposited her belongings on the foyer's parquet floor, Isabella removed her mud-soaked boots and followed Mrs. Eaton down a corridor. A room to her left caught her eye. Paneled in warm cherry wood and bordered by hundreds of books, it was a well-stocked library. The sight came at her like a rush of fresh air. She adored reading.

An elderly manservant stood inside the room. He was the only member of the household staff she'd been introduced to. After all, he was Draven's valet who accompanied his master everywhere.

"Welcome back, m'lady," he said.

"Thank you, Rogers."

He seemed pleased that she recalled his name. "I'm here to lock up the library. The master don't want no one in here."

Isabella started to question him, but the valet gently closed the door in her face.

She followed the straight-backed housekeeper down a long stretch of wall. As she passed a hanging mirror, she stopped and glanced at her reflection.

How am I supposed to seduce Draven in this pathetic state?

She managed to rub the last smudge of mud from her cheek and smooth a frizzled curl, but she'd only made a small improvement. It would take at least a dozen salon attendants skilled in coiffures and couture to make her resemble the countess she was supposed to be.

Isabella hastened to the end of the hall where a pair of curtains exposed a comfortably furnished parlor. Illuminated by the patchy light of a fireplace, the room displayed an inviting ambience the others lacked.

The housekeeper stood just inside the room. "Ye'll be comfortable in 'ere while we see to yer luggage, yer ladyship."

"Thank you, Mrs. Eaton."

The woman nodded icily and Isabella began to regret that her father had not accompanied her.

"Yer chambers are the first set of rooms on the second floor. Gwyneth is yer abigail," Mrs. Eaton said. "She will be visitin' yer suites to introduce herself."

"Very well," Isabella said.

"Oh, and the countess wishes to have a word with ye before ye retire for the night, m'lady."

Draven's mother is here? Isabella let out a groan. Helena was the last person besides her unscrupulous husband she wanted to see.

When Mrs. Eaton left the room, Isabella sat on the divan and removed her travel-stained bonnet. Her stomach rumbled. She had forgone supper during a travel stop in order to pay for the last leg of her journey. Pressing her hand against another hollow gurgle, Isabella listened to a clock in the corner tick away in the silence of the room. The unnerving sound made her wish she were anywhere but here.

Beckoned by the crackling hearth, she strode to the fire. She dried herself in front of the flames and studied the details of the unfamiliar room. Above the mantel hung a portrait of a strapping man standing beside a black stallion. Her pulse accelerated as she raised herself on the tips of her toes and peered up in the dim light. *Could the subject of the painting be Draven?*

Indeed it was. The smooth olive skin, the firm jaw, and the muscular shoulders were just as she recalled. Swept back in a collar-length queue, her husband's hairstyle, though it rebelled against the short curls fashionable today, enhanced his angular cheekbones and full lips. He was inarguably handsome, but it was Draven's black eyes that rocked Isabella to the very core. In the brief time they'd spent together, she had been unable to pinpoint precisely what they housed.

Anger?

Determination, perhaps?

Or were they void of emotion altogether?

For a moment she tried to envision her husband's stare as it had devoured her with a sizzling chemistry on their wedding night—before everything had gone horribly wrong.

The swish of the curtains breached her thoughts.

"So, it's true." Lady Winthrop pinned Isabella with a stare. "You have returned."

Chapter Five

Isabella frowned. "Yes, your ladyship."

Flickering light jumped from the hearth and cast strange shadows across the noblewoman's face. "You may call me Helena, as I permitted you to do the day you married Draven."

Although she was attractive in her own right, Isabella's mother-in-law looked nothing like her son. Rather, Helena resembled a fair-skinned, ill-tempered queen. The countess's strongly arched eyebrows and flared nostrils gave clues to a challenging character while her chestnut hair richened against the paleness of her complexion. And like a royal studying one of her subjects, the noblewoman took in the sight of Isabella with eyes that spoke a thousand criticisms.

"You look thin," Lady Helena finally added.

Isabella made no reply. She only hoped the rumbling of her stomach couldn't be heard from where Lady Winthrop was standing.

"Your return here came as a surprise to Draven and me. We thought we'd never see you again."

Isabella squared her shoulders. "I had time to rethink my decision to leave your son."

"Good, considering how you've disgraced yourself," Helena replied. "You are aware that vicious gossip does not fade easily into the woodwork."

Isabella turned back to the fire and spread her hands above the flames. "I, for one, couldn't care less what people think."

"I beg to differ," Helena said. "Your concern over how Society viewed you led you to marry Draven in the first place."

She spun around, the warmth of the fire forgotten. "What do you mean by that?"

The dowager's lips quirked as if she were enjoying herself. "When your father and I discussed your union to Draven, he claimed that he didn't wish to leave you alone during his trips to Egypt. But we both know the real reason Sir Harris wanted to marry you off, don't we? Considering that you were twenty-six years old at the time, not to mention your serious nature, he feared you would never attract a suitor in the *ton*—let alone contract a marriage. I gathered you felt the same way."

Isabella clenched her fists. "I had interested suitors, but no proposals. Those men knew I wasn't ready to leave my father."

Helena smiled smugly. "Did I forget to mention the most prominent reason your father was in a rush to marry you off? *Your amulet.*"

Isabella's hand flew to the stone at her neck. "This amulet gave me the chance to learn which suitors were weakened by superstition," she said proudly. "But that's of no consequence now. Draven proposed—and wasn't it you who arranged our meeting in the first place?"

The countess walked the length of the room in full majesty. "I did no such thing."

"But Draven said—"

"Of course I had no objection to him marrying you," Helena told her. "I assume you've heard the rumors that my son is mentally ill."

Isabella's heartbeat faltered but she kept her reaction contained.

"As those rumors raced around England," the dowager said, "they made me wonder: what kind of sophisticated and thoroughly particular noblewoman would agree to marry Draven if he were truly mad?"

The insinuation that she was neither sophisticated nor particular boiled Isabella's blood. "Your opinion cannot hurt me, Helena. Draven married me and that is that."

Helena ignored her retort. "After what transpired between you and your husband, I'm surprised you are wearing your wedding ring."

Isabella glanced down at the wide filigree wedding band she had kept stowed in her jewelry box until today. With sparkling sapphires set in pear-shaped petals of platinum, the ring had impressed her during the initial days of her engagement to Draven. Now it meant nothing.

She sent her mother-in-law a cool stare. "Is there anything else you'd care to point out?"

"I see from your inexpensive frock that you have run out of money," Helena observed.

Isabella touched the worn fabric of her travel dress. So her struggles betrayed her. "Draven and I discussed that my pin money would be used to send my father to Egypt," Isabella snapped. "Now that money is gone."

"Your situation will improve now that you have returned. But I doubt that your decision-making skills will improve as well," Lady Winthrop scoffed.

Isabella ground her back teeth together. She had no desire to continue their verbal joust. "I've had a long day. If you'll excuse me, I will retire to my bedchamber."

"Before you drift off to sleep, my dear, ponder this: how do you think Draven will react to you now that you have returned? You dishonored him. Perhaps it will take some time for him to warm up to you, if he ever does."

Didn't Helena know that her son was a heartless devil?

"I would like to know if you are still in residence here." Anger seeped into Isabella's voice.

Helena sucked in the staleness of the room. "I am. I suppose I could live in my Mayfair home, but I prefer not to face my friends in London with the scandal you've cast upon Draven and me. Besides, I reasoned that my son needed me after he'd been abandoned by his wife."

"To say that I'm indifferent to your presence here would be lying, Helena. Good evening," Isabella said.

The noblewoman shot her a haughty glare as she swept out of the room.

Screeching winds and battering rain vibrated off the rooftop as Isabella reached her suites. Clicking the door shut behind her, she scanned the room and its furnishings. An enormous four-poster bed dominated the space while a lace-skirted vanity stood adjacent to it at an angle. Along the opposite wall, a sturdy chiffonier marked the entry to a private washroom—a luxury Isabella appreciated.

Anxious to relax, she located her portmanteau and the tray of food Mrs. Eaton had sent up. She ate quickly, downed the cordial, then exchanged her damp traveling dress for a nightgown. Refusing help from Gwyneth when the girl knocked on the door, Isabella loosened her hair into a braid and slipped beneath the counterpane of the four-poster with a sigh.

She would have to find Draven tomorrow.

The storm rattled the windowpanes to a strangely soothing melody. As she started to fall asleep, a gust of wind swung the unlocked window frame into the room. When the frame struck the wall with a tremendous bang, she leapt out of bed and rushed toward the window. Wind and rain thrashed her body. Isabella leaned her weight against the heavy frame, but she was unable to close it.

Her nightgown clung to her body, making her breasts peak uncomfortably beneath its cold fabric. Frustration rose in her throat. To her surprise, a hand snaked across the bottom ridge of her bosom and jerked her out of the storm's path.

She pushed the wet hair from her face and turned to see who had come to her aid. A combination of prickly terror and animal attraction tingled her spine as she found herself staring at her estranged husband. And he didn't look happy to see her.

Chapter Six

Draven looked like a wild man.

Well over six feet tall, he hovered above Isabella like a titanic wave. An abundance of long, jet-black hair framed his diamond-shaped face while his shirt flowed alluringly over muscled shoulders. Unbuttoned, the shirt revealed the burnished chest and rippling torso Isabella hadn't forgotten.

After drinking in the sights of his narrow hips set off by low-slung breeches and the fascinating planes of his unshaven face, it dawned on her that Draven's eyes had taken on a strange shade of red. It lent him a look of uncensored madness.

Fear building inside her, she stood motionless. Draven slipped his hand from her waist, moved to the window, and shut it. Turning back in her direction, he surveyed her from head to toe. His untamed eyes settled on Isabella's breasts and she realized her garment must be completely transparent. Reminding herself that she meant to seduce him, she made no move to cover herself, though her heart was banging incessantly against her rib cage.

"Th-thank you for helping me," she stammered through chattering teeth.

He acknowledged her exposure with one arched brow. When he parted his lips, she braced herself for the rich tone of his voice.

"How ironic," he said. "We meet again in the same wardrobe in which we parted ways."

Memories of that night flashed before Isabella in rapid succession.

Draven commanding her to join him in bed.

Her self-consciousness in the sheer negligee she wore.

His hot mouth on hers and his hand prying her legs apart.

The hint of remorse in his eyes as he informed her they would never have children.

And his mysterious disappearance.

She lit a candle branch as she groped for something equally clever to say. Drawing a blank, she forced a smile instead. "You're not wearing a dressing robe. I suppose you were sleeping when I arrived this evening."

Draven made no reply as he continued to stare beyond the window at the darkness. It seemed like an eternity before his titillating, aristocratic voice poured forth again. "There is no sign of the moon tonight, thank God."

She frowned for it seemed an odd thing to say.

Taking a wide, defiant stance he turned his stare in her direction. Eyeing Isabella with insolence, he dragged bent fingers through his dripping hair. She watched the muscles of his stomach flex and release at the motion, and when her gaze returned to his hypnotic face, she realized he'd caught her staring at his torso. Her face burned.

"Why have you returned?" His tone was sharp.

"As I said in my letter, my father and I have fallen upon hard times."

A trace of annoyance surfaced in his tone. "And as I said in my reply, you are not welcome here."

"What reply? I have received no correspondence from you for a year."

"Cursed post," he glowered. "As slow as a snail."

"In this letter, did you insist I not come back?"

He nodded, his fathomless eyes boring into hers. "Don't you remember that I deemed our marriage a mistake?"

"Why then, have you made no effort to end it?" she challenged him.

Fury flushed his face. Unable to provide a response, he remained silent.

"Regardless, I am here," she said, "and I will not flee this place again. Nor will I be sent away under your command."

He thrust her an icy stare, but this time she did not avert her eyes. Her plan was not proceeding the way she'd envisioned, but she refused to make her disappointment known to Draven.

"What can I do to make you leave?" he said with a simmering anger.

"Nothing," she said flatly.

His hands curled into fists by his side. Isabella studied his face and she thought she saw a devious light flicker in his eyes.

"If you insist on staying," he said, "I will accept your return under two conditions."

Pride straightened her stance. "What is the first condition?"

"That you remain here always. There will be no leaving this manor."

"But my father—?"

"He may visit for a day or two at a time."

"Are you saying that I am a prisoner here?" Her body trembled at the thought.

Draven cast her a grave expression.

Tears rose in Isabella's eyes. "I can see you are no less cruel than you were before."

"I heard about what happened to your father." His nostrils flared as he spoke. "There is no helping him if you don't agree to remain here."

She twisted her wedding band, her gut clenching as she deliberated. After a moment she nodded solemnly and said, "I assume the second condition is that we never have children. But I was hoping—"

He interrupted her. "The stipulation that we never have children remains part of our arrangement, yes. But now I no longer wish to share your bed at all."

"W-what do you mean?" He'd just snatched away her remaining hope that she may become accidentally impregnated in the throes of passion. Her head reeled.

"You heard me," Draven thundered. "During your departure, I've undergone an affliction of sorts and I no longer trust myself in your presence."

An *affliction?* Was this a confession of his madness? He did look different to her. The shadows circling his eyes and his rumpled appearance signaled a spiral into melancholia. Perhaps he'd fallen completely apart after she left him, just as the fresh gossip about him claimed.

"Are you ill?" Isabella resisted the urge to feel his head for a fever.

"That's the simple explanation, but a satisfactory one."

"Have you seen a doctor?"

"I've seen many doctors," he admitted. "Each one gave me the same diagnosis: my affliction is incurable. Therefore we shan't speak of it again. Nor shall you inquire after what happened to me on our wedding night."

"You won't tell me?" she asked.

He shook his head.

"This is terrible!" She turned away, battling to suppress the rejection he'd stabbed her with.

"What did you expect?" he asked. "A shower of rose petals to greet you? Although you abandoning me did not cause my affliction, your actions disgraced me. Now we are to live as strangers. We will meet at mealtimes and nothing more."

Isabella gave him a hard look. "I disgraced you after you deceived me and terrified me, by God."

"God had nothing to do with it." He stepped closer and she could feel his warm breath on her face.

"Despite the fact that we have nothing in common, I agreed to marry you under the assumption that we would have children," she said.

"And money did not figure into your reasoning?" His tone was relentless.

She looked at her feet.

Waving the thought away with obvious disinterest, he made for the door. She put a hand on his arm to stop him. She had agreed to the first of his conditions—to remain here forever—but his second requirement changed everything and she would not stand for it.

"Hear me out," she said in a steely voice. "It is still my dream to be a mother. Now that you have severed all intimacy between us, you have destroyed that very hope. My lord, you leave me no choice but to offer you an ultimatum. You have two days to agree to grant me children or I shall be forced to leave this house and take a lover. It is up to you. You may plant the seed of your own son or daughter or you can help me raise a bastard."

His face turned as red as blood on white linen. He caught Isabella by the wrist. "You just made a promise to stay here. Furthermore, how dare you make me choose such a thing? You don't know what you're asking."

Isabella yanked her arm away. "Then why don't you explain it to me?"

Draven's eyes blazed. "I cannot tell you the reason I shan't produce an heir, but know this: in two days, under the shadow of a full moon, evil will stalk this entire countryside."

"Don't change the subject," she ordered. "If I don't get the answer I want in two days, I will return to London."

"I'm warning you, Isabella."

"Another warning? I know what you're trying to do. But scaring me will do no good," she said. "I have no belief in ghosts or goblins."

"But do you believe in *werewolves?*"

The very notion made her heart flutter. Since childhood, the image of a werewolf had frightened her more than any other macabre creature. "There are no native wolves left in England which means werewolves can't exist here." She repeated the words her mother had always reassured her with.

"You're wrong," he said. "The wolves are gathering. You see, their alpha appears beneath every full moon, bringing with it an unquenchable thirst for blood. Last month, this beast killed a group of livestock in a violent frenzy. It is the other reason you mustn't leave this house."

"You must be joking."

"I rarely joke."

"Thank you for your words of caution, but you are talking to a very intelligent woman."

"Good," Draven replied, "because intelligent people trust no one."

He made for the door, brushing her shoulder in the process. Isabella put a hand to the spot he'd touched. Her skin was hot, nearly burned from the contact. She followed Draven to the doorway and watched the shadows envelop his enormous figure. Once he had vanished, she changed into a dry nightshirt and sought the comfort of her bedcovers. Still quaking, she pulled the thick counterpane to meet her chin.

That night, slumber evaded her for when she squeezed her eyes shut, her husband's brazen stare penetrated the darkness. The image terrified Isabella even more than the idea of a werewolf.

Chapter Seven

Draven left Isabella in a rush of anger and took the stairs that led to his apartments two by two.

Who does that woman think she is? How dare she make me choose between fathering my own child and raising a bastard!

He peeled off his wet shirt and threw it on the floor. He'd meant to scare her away with his punishing stipulations, but, damn it, she had thrust her own outlandish demands upon him instead of falling into his trap.

Thunder exploded dangerously close to the house, yet Draven hardly flinched. He was too busy spewing expletives about how miserably his plan to make Isabella leave had backfired. It had done no bloody good to strip away the possibility of intimacy with her. Or to steal away her freedom. Or to rob her of motherhood—or even frighten her with the idea of a werewolf.

Even his claim that he was plagued by a strange affliction had not fazed her.

He had tried to do the right thing in expelling her from the house, but she had twisted matters into an infuriating knot.

As Draven marched to the top landing, he chided himself. He

should have known better than to think his attempt at compassion would work. Selfishness had tainted every inch of it. The reason he'd tried to get Isabella to leave was self-serving: if her scent triggered him to kill her, he wouldn't be able to tolerate the guilt that came with committing another murder. Killing that Gypsy girl, though her death was accidental, was something that haunted him day and night. And he refused to bear any further remorse.

Now he had another problem. In light of Isabella's blasted ultimatum, what was he to do?

Draven reached his bedchamber and went in search of a drink. Sloshing brandy into a snifter, his temper continued to percolate. His wife was an enraging woman and her independent spirit maddened him as much as it stirred his libido. The vision of her exposed in her wet nightgown had heated his body. His cock had hardened and he'd been forced to tear his stare from her erect breasts and her alluring triangle of nether hair—which hadn't been easy feats.

What's more, the coppery fragrance of Isabella's blood had stirred his wild side just now. His blood felt like molten lava in his veins and his mouth was watering with a thirst he'd never known before. *Could the temptation lead to violence?*

No, Draven decided, he couldn't risk withdrawing his stipulations. If Isabella refused to be scared away, he might be in the same room with her at mealtimes but nothing more. He needed to prevent all physical contact between them—and for her own protection, she was forbidden to leave the grounds of Thorncliff Towers or she might encounter Draven in his canine form.

Without bothering to dry himself off, he sunk into his favorite armchair by the fire. Ignoring the discomfort of his unsatisfied arousal, he downed a mouthful of brandy as Rogers entered the room.

"Are ye ready fer yer medicine, yer lordship?" the valet asked cordially. When he spied the brandy in Draven's hand, the servant dropped his smile and made a tsking sound. "Sir, ye know it's unwise to mix lithium and alcohol. Now we can't give ye yer dosage 'til tomorrow!"

"Just as well." Draven scowled. "That medicine can go to hell. It hardly does anything for my mood swings. What do those doctors know?"

Rogers's brows furrowed. "More than we do, sir."

The valet dragged over a footstool and propped Draven's heels on top of it. Draven accepted the towel and dry shirt the manservant had folded over his arm.

"Have ye had a chance to greet 'er ladyship?" Rogers asked.

"Yes. And our reunion was disastrous. Isabella came back to help her father, but she is being excessively demanding about it."

" 'Demandin''?" echoed the valet.

"You know as well as I that I cannot risk fathering a child under my curse."

"She doesn't know that, sir."

"I'm aware that she doesn't know, damn it! Regardless, she had the gall to suggest that she's willing to take a lover because I am denying her."

Shock passed over Rogers's face. " 'er ladyship can't mean it, sir."

"She doesn't mean it," Draven said with certainty. In fact, he possessed knowledge that confirmed his wife's innocence.

A man of wealth and power, he had hired someone to watch over Isabella during their estrangement. By covertly trailing her, he had discovered that infidelity wasn't her style. Isabella did nothing inappropriate with a man named Joseph Gossington—an insolent character Draven wanted to strangle with his bare hands. He had kept Gossington at bay by arranging for the would-be suitor to be incapacitated for a very long while.

Of course the planned attack hadn't been the proper thing to do, but "proper" was a formality Draven had thrown out the window long ago.

Still, if Isabella learned of his distrust, she would be infuriated.

Rogers cleared his throat. "If ye don't mind me sayin', sir, be gentle with 'er ladyship. For if she leaves this house again, ye may lose 'er forever."

By God, that was something Draven hadn't thought of. His relationship with Isabella had dwindled to the weakest thread, but he was determined to preserve it. That meant he must stall Isabella's ultimatum without revealing his darkest secret.

No one but Rogers knew of Draven's harrowing past and the loyal valet didn't intend to expose the fact that he was under a hex. Not only would revealing the background of his curse put his title in jeopardy, it would give Isabella ammunition to prove that his blue blood was tainted. She would surely have grounds to divorce him in that case.

Of course the more immediate question was: would Draven as the hunter, become the hunted?

He suspected that Isabella's arrival tonight had set the wheels of her Egyptian prophecy into motion. She was certainly exuding a newfound strength and courage. And considering Draven's own experience with black magic, he wondered if her transformation was the first step toward his destruction.

While Draven couldn't be certain of that, there was one thing he was sure of. If he hoped to change the course of his curse, he must gain back the upper hand with Isabella while he tried to keep her prophecy from playing itself out.

Bombarded by his thoughts, he slouched in the chair, shoulders wide, knees shot outward. After Rogers departed, he raised the crystal snifter to eye level. The titian hue of the brandy reminded him of Isabella's curls on display through her wet pantalets. A stirring burned his loins and his cock rose again. He'd been faithful to his wife during their time apart and now his body ached for pleasures of the flesh. Inhaling Isabella's sweet, warm scent and caressing her skin, even if it had been through her nightgown, had mounted Draven's hunger.

Visions of her crested breasts and curved hips rose in his mind again. Deciding there was no harm in desiring his wife from the privacy of his room, he closed his eyes and reached deep inside his breeches with his free hand.

Chapter Eight

Isabella willed her eyes to open in the gray light of dawn. Befuddlement seized her but it only took the sound of rain at her window to remind her that she was in a god-forsaken prison.

She rolled over and stuffed the goose-down pillow beneath her cheek. Her reunion with her sour-mannered husband had gone poorly, to say the least. Not only did it prove that she and Draven were still at odds, it also gave credence to his rumored insanity.

How dare he insist I stay at this house without the possibility of intimacy!

Frowning, Isabella touched her toes to the cold floor. She padded to the window and threw back the heavy, brocade curtains. Dreary daylight glared back at her. She watched as three seagulls soared through the depressing weather. As they floated away from the steep cliffs in a graceful glide, their lonely caws filled the silence.

She peered farther down the coastline. There were no signs of civilization anywhere near the manor, making the estate an ideal place to hide away from the world.

Did Draven really expect her to stay at Thorncliff Towers forever?

He had seemed serious when he spat out the words last night—words that stung like a whip. And when he snatched away any chance of physical contact between them, it shook her to the core. Did he not desire her in the way a husband should desire his wife? She had little experience with men, but the lust in his eyes and the way he kissed her on their wedding night told her otherwise.

Isabella fingered her amulet as she turned away from the window. She knew that giving Draven an ultimatum was an enormous risk, but it wasn't as though she had planned to present it. He had provoked her and in the midst of her anger, the words had rushed out in a raging stream.

What will his reaction to it be?

She could only hope that pride would prevent Draven from allowing her to seek a lover.

Moving to the basin, Isabella studied her reflection in the mirror. Her dense hair fell about her shoulders in gentle waves and her complexion appeared dewy from the moist, coastal air. With her decent bone structure and a pair of nicely bowed lips—her mother's lips— her looks drew numerous compliments.

Why is Draven treating me as if I have the plague?

Of course, Joseph Gossington was a man who had treated her quite differently. A tall, muscular gentleman with gleaming blond hair, Joseph had been introduced to Isabella at her cousin's house two months ago. She had felt his eyes on her the entire evening. Because he had talked and flirted with her unabashedly, their time together sent tongues wagging all over London. Several weeks later, they met again by sheer happenstance in the market. During a walk to a local café, he had snaked a secretive hand around her waist and in a mesmerizing tone, mentioned her estrangement from her husband. He even offered to supply Isabella with carnal pleasures, if she so fancied.

Joseph's sparkling sea-blue eyes could easily have seduced her but she didn't react to him at all. Instead, her thoughts flew to Draven. Of how his touch had seared her skin like wildfire on their wedding night. Of how his deep kiss had blurred her senses—and how his ominous eyes would intrigue her until the end of time.

I need to focus on the dilemma at hand.

Stealing a look at the table clock, her stomach clenched. She was scheduled to meet Draven and Helena for breakfast but she'd be damned if she would eat with a man who had ordered her to become a prisoner.

After she asked Gwyneth to bring her a tray of eggs and toast, she busied herself with arranging her belongings inside the chiffonier. A tremendous banging began at the door.

"Isabella. You are my wife and you will come down to breakfast this instant!"

"I'm not hungry," she called back.

"You *are* hungry or you wouldn't have ordered Gwyneth to bring you a tray," Draven thundered.

"I just lost my appetite."

"You will eat with me or you will receive no food!"

"Very well. I'm perfectly content to sit here and stare at the walls."

A silence passed. Then she heard, "I . . . I'm sorry I was such a brute last night."

She said nothing.

"I didn't mean to take away your freedom, Isabella," Draven said. "It's just that I want you to listen to me. I am still your husband."

"A husband who denies his wife intimacy. Under those circumstances, you will never be anything but a monster to me," she said.

A growl, more animal than human, rattled the walls as Draven's footsteps pounded away.

A few hours passed and Isabella couldn't ignore her hunger pains any longer. She summoned Gwyneth to help her into a worn empire-line dress of pale green before she started for the breakfast parlor.

Arriving at the airy room, she found that the dining table had been set with one egg cup, one oval serving dish layered in potatoes, one plate, and one teacup.

How had Draven known I would finally emerge?

Enveloped in silence, she sat down and unfolded her napkin. A large portrait gracing the east wall caught her attention. The painting showcased a gentleman dressed in a handsome riding habit. Wearing a sophisticated ascot, the man sat atop a beautiful white Arabian with his hand planted on his hip. Sporting wavy sable hair, chiseled cheekbones, and impeccable posture, the regal figure resembled Draven in the drawing room portrait. However, this gentleman possessed clear, blue eyes that leapt out at Isabella with straightforwardness—contradicting the madness she witnessed in her husband's black ones.

Could this be Draven's father? She strained to read the name plate that accompanied the painting.

"Cyril Octavian Winthrop 1791"
Earl of Dunwich

So this was the father her husband had known for only a short time. During their courtship, Draven told Isabella that Cyril Winthrop died from an illness, leaving him at sixteen to deal with a daunting title and his mother's coldness.

Isabella peered closer. The resemblance between father and son was obvious. In fact, everything about the nobleman's face reminded her of Draven except for his eyes and the shade of his skin.

Helena's eyes were also blue and her skin was so pale that it bordered on alabaster.

So where had Draven gotten his dark complexion and black eyes? The more Isabella knew of him, the more he became an enigma of the most complicated and vile sort.

She dug into the food. It was cold but to her, it tasted magnificent. Downing the meal too quickly, she became nauseated. Her body was on the verge of malnutrition and she'd lost a considerable amount of weight. She had been watching over Phillip, her cousin Fiona's youngest son with, alas, no salary. At Fiona's house, Isabella often feigned fullness in order to take the food home to Papa.

Now she needed to ease her body into eating substantial meals again.

Feeling drowsy, she sat back in her chair and in the stillness of the room, she was relieved to be without Draven. Why was he trying to control their relationship with no degree of compromise? She must steer clear of him while he pondered her ultimatum.

Fatigued from the heavy meal and lack of sleep, Isabella decided that some outdoor exercise would rouse her energy. She made her way to the back of the house where she maneuvered down a flight of stairs. The manor resembled a maze but she knew she would never forget the escape route she had used on her wedding night.

As she neared the kitchen, she passed Gwyneth on the stairs.

"Oh, m'lady!" the abigail cried. "Can I help ye? This 'ere is the servants' stairwell."

"I didn't know," Isabella fibbed. She had rather hoped no one would see her.

"Where are ye headed?"

"To the fields behind the house. I'm going to take a walk."

"If ye change yer mind and decide to go on horseback, be careful," Gwyneth whispered. "The horses tend to be nasty."

"Thank you, Gwyneth," Isabella whispered back.

She continued on until she emerged into the bright sunshine. Thankful that the rain had stopped, she strolled across a wide veranda then veered off along a pebbled walkway. To her left, a neglected garden screamed for attention. Encircled by a low wall, the small space was centered by a stone statue formed in the shape of a Grecian goddess. Upon further inspection, Isabella saw that the garden contained crispy, brown flower beds and sparse bushes. Had it once boasted willowy orchids, plump wisteria, or rich, red roses?

She liked to think it had.

She gazed beyond the unkempt space and spotted a charming gazebo rising out of the mist. The structure's white paint was badly chipped and faded and the land surrounding it looked untended.

All in all, Isabella reflected, Thorncliff Towers didn't lack potential. It just needed some tender care.

Raising her skirts, she meandered toward the horse stables. A figure on horseback moving through the woods caught her eye. Her heart stopped. It was Draven. *Why was he stealing into the forest?*

"Good morning, your ladyship."

Isabella whirled around at the unfamiliar voice.

A lad of fourteen or fifteen materialized from the stables. With warm, brown eyes, defined cheekbones, and hair as black as Draven's, the boy possessed enough exotic features to make younger girls swoon. He had a saddle slung over one shoulder and was carrying a large, flat brush in his other hand.

"Good morning," Isabella said.

"My lady." He did a small bow. "I'm Viktor."

She smiled though she was distracted.

"Are you planning to go for a ride, your ladyship?"

On horseback? The idea made her nerves race. "No. I was just going for a walk."

The lad seemed relieved. "Glad to hear it. His lordship gave me strict orders that you are only to ride with him. He also instructed that you not wander far." The boy set the saddle and brush on a patch of grass then rubbed his shoulder. "There is a wild wolf roaming the countryside."

She felt her face go white. "Yes, I've heard the rumors."

The sun peeked through a cloud and the stable boy shaded his eyes with his hand. "You're safe on the grounds during the day. The werewolf only appears during a full moon."

Werewolves. Mention of the creature stirred a deep-seated fear Isabella could thank her uncle Morton for. On her eighth birthday, her father's twin brother had come for supper carrying a children's book filled with dark tales. Propping Isabella on his lap, he read her a story about a man who'd gone mad before he turned into a wolflike monster. Terrified, she had slid off Morton's lap and sought refuge behind her mother's skirts.

Now that she was grown, she chose to scoff at the existence of werewolves because she wouldn't allow herself to be frightened like that again.

She raised her chin in the boy's direction. "There are no such things as werewolves."

He picked up the saddle and swung it back over his shoulder. "I don't mean any disrespect, my lady, but *something* destroyed the neighboring livestock. Whatever it was had supernatural strength—and I assure you that in my culture, supernatural forces exist."

"Your . . . culture?"

He nodded. "I am a Gypsy."

"Whatever are you doing at Thorncliff Towers?"

"Master Draven was kind enough to let me stay and work here after he caught me stealing food from the kitchen. It's not something I'm proud of, but his lordship gave me a second chance."

Isabella frowned. It didn't sound like Draven to be so kind. She wondered what had actually motivated him to help the boy. "Has anyone been hurt by this phantom werewolf?"

"No one has been attacked," replied the boy. "But if I were you, my lady, I'd be glad that I was forbidden to go into the forest alone."

The lad's warning quelled her desire to take even the shortest of walks. Turning on her heel, she hastened back to the house. As she neared the back door, Isabella realized that living at Thorncliff Towers was going to be like visiting a carnival. Stomach-surging surprises at every turn.

Chapter Nine

Draven maneuvered Lucifer through the forest toward Dunwich.

When Rogers informed him that three Gypsies were seen milling about town this morning, his blood began to race. Apparently the vagrants had become separated from their tribe and Draven didn't want to miss this chance to speak with them. Although he was still dealing with his disdain for Gypsies, he wasn't going to chase them away this time. Rather, he was jumping at the chance to query them about his curse.

Emerging from the woods, he coaxed his stallion down a sea-hugging path. The wind off the slate-gray North Sea whipped his face and seeped beneath his frock coat, but he didn't mind. He loved this countryside because it surrounded what had been his father's home.

How Draven viewed the town of Dunwich was another story. With eight churches to its credit and an abundance of God-fearing citizens to fill them, the town judged him and his lack of involvement through righteous eyes. Knowing that he was already being judged by Satan's wrath, the churches' holiness was the last thing Draven needed.

Once he reached the center of town, he was greeted by the usual display of contemptuous looks. Ignoring the heated stares, he dismounted, secured Lucifer, and wandered about in search of anyone resembling a Gypsy. A man and a woman huddled together in the shadows of the tavern caught his eye. A girl, no older than fifteen, hid behind the couple, her eyes fixed on a mangy cat nestled in her arms. She reminded Draven of the unfortunate Gypsy girl he'd encountered long ago and his gut clenched.

He approached them. The man and the woman looked startled.

"We don't want no trouble, your lordship," the woman called out.

Draven fastened his hands on his hips. Memories of what happened the last time he stood face-to-face with a Gypsy woman stole his breath away. "Don't worry, madam. If you answer a question for me, I shall give you no trouble."

Pride surfaced in the woman's eyes. She wrapped a shawl around her head and held it to her chin with gnarled fingers. "What is it you want to know?"

He motioned for the trio to move around the corner of the building for privacy. "Are you part of the Szgamy tribe?" he asked.

"The Szgamy tribe?" Horror darkened the woman's eyes. "No. They are very powerful Gypsies. Extremely magical."

"Yes. I found them on my property once," Draven said.

"You did more than find them," she accused him.

He looked at her with amazement. With her stooped posture and cragged face, she reminded him of a witch in a storybook. "How do you know that?"

"I have the sight. I know something happened when you encountered the Szgamy tribe."

She waited for Draven to go on but he hesitated. "I unintentionally hurt a young girl and the tribe's matriarch cursed me," he finally said.

The woman shuffled a little closer to him. Her husband tried to stop her, but she shrugged him off. "You are plagued by a *rauna* curse, my lord."

"Yes, damn it. A *rauna* curse."

"And you want to know how to reverse it."

"Is there a way?"

The woman spread her hands wide. "No, my lord. Unless the person who cast the original spell on you deems that you are worthy of its freedom."

"I know that much." Draven scowled. "But is there a time line attached to the spell? None of the books I've read provide a straight answer."

The woman sucked in a breath. "There is no 'dead-line' for a *rauna* curse's victim to show redemption, if that's what you mean."

Draven exhaled with relief.

"Regardless," she said, "you must understand that this kind of spell becomes exaggerated over time."

"I beg your pardon?"

"Listen carefully." The woman lowered her voice. "The hex punishes its victim by exaggerating the faults that person had before they were cursed. For instance, if someone drank heavily before, they will drink uncontrollably now. If they were cruel before, they will become *devastatingly* cruel."

Draven braced himself. "And this is done to make it harder for someone to change their shameful ways?"

"Correct. So you must ask yourself, my lord: what has become exaggerated in your life since you became cursed? The answer will reveal your greatest fault."

"I see." His voice rattled uncontrollably. He withdrew a small pouch of gold coins from his greatcoat and handed it to the old woman as a show of gratitude. "Thank you."

He spun on his heel. As he made his way back to Thorncliff Towers, he couldn't get the woman's words out of his head. Mulling over his many faults took a while, but the answer to her question finally sprang up like an evil-looking wind-up toy. Over and over again, he had bedded women without feeling. He had treated them as objects only to cast them aside. He'd even been with another woman, a barmaid at the tavern, the night before he married Isabella. In his foxed state, he had allowed the sultry tart to attend to his bite—among other things.

My rakish sexual appetite is my greatest fault and now it is spiraling out of control around Isabella.

Draven pulled Lucifer to a halt. Peering beyond the edge of the jutting cliff, he could hardly breathe and his head pounded. He'd been given years to become a better person. To convert. To gain compassion. And what had he done? He had blazed across the countryside flaunting his roguish ways before cutting himself off from the world as a selfish recluse.

In that moment, he was struck with a cold, hard fact—one that he'd been unwilling to face before. He had been an insufferable brute all of his life, which meant he could never change. Even if he wanted to. He needed Isabella's help.

If she were here to stay, she could provide a way to stop this madness. And if she wanted a child, then, blast it, that's what she would get. He must seduce her into trusting him enough so that she would follow the fatal path of Tousret's curse.

Damn the fact that I might impregnate her.

Because his bloodlust was growing every day, it was essential that he make love to her soon. Their intimacy would set the amulet's curse into action. Once he got Isabella to fall in love with him and they consummated their marriage, she would kill him. The tricky part would be ensuring that his wife did not take her own life after she ended his. He knew he couldn't live knowing that would happen.

Draven guided Lucifer away from the cliff and rode swiftly back to the manor. As he glanced at the setting sun, he realized that he'd missed lunch and now he was going to be late for dinner. No doubt Isabella was sitting at the table waiting for him, a frown upon her pretty face.

He entered the house through the rear door and pounded into the dining room. There was no sign of his wife. He sat and waited but his patience quickly thinned. Once he realized that Isabella wasn't coming, he hastened up the stairs where he encountered Gwyneth. The maid told him that his wife was eating supper in the privacy of her bedchamber. Glowering, he rapped on her door.

"Who is it?" she called out.

"It's your husband. Let me in."

"I'm not decent."

"I've seen you in your drenched nightshift and the image has left little more for my imagination to feast on," Draven said curtly. "Pray don a wrapper and open the door!"

As Isabella swung the portal open, he entered in a rush. Breathing deeply, he paced the length of the room before he wheeled around. She studied his flushed cheeks and his windblown hair before she resumed her seat by the fire.

"I've been waiting for you in the dining room," he said. "Why didn't you come to supper?"

"Why didn't you appear for nuncheon?"

His eyes formed slits. "It isn't polite to answer a question with a question."

"Nor is it polite to leave your wife alone at mealtimes."

His nostrils flared at her impertinence, but deep inside he was moved by her beauty and by her boldness.

She shrugged. "Perhaps you scared me into solitude with your talk of werewolves."

"I'm growing tired of this game, Isabella. Please answer my question."

"Very well, since you said 'please.' " She crossed her fork and knife over her plate. "I assumed my presence at mealtimes would have no effect on you whatsoever."

He squared his hulking shoulders. "Whatever gave you that impression?"

"Is that your attempt at a joke?" She cocked her head to the side.

"I told you: I rarely joke."

"If we are only to see one another at mealtimes," she said, "maybe it's best if we didn't see one another at all."

"That would make me very unhappy." Looking her directly in the eye, he smiled awkwardly. "I . . . I apologize for the homecoming I gave you. I was angry that you abandoned our union, but I admit that I was the one who led you to that decision. Now I am glad you have returned."

She stood and moved closer to him. "There you go again."

He gave her a perplexed look. "What is it I've gone and done?"

"Your words and your expression speak something different."

The loveliness of Isabella's amber eyes flushed heat through his veins and his sex reacted.

"What are you talking about?" he asked.

"Your face doesn't convey the same apology as your words."

"Confound it!" He began to pace again. "I didn't come here to be analyzed, like some patient in that blasted asylum."

The color drained from her face.

Control your temper, Draven told himself. *You need Isabella.* Months ago he had tried to kill himself, but the knife wound to his heart had healed instantaneously. Now he was relying on his wife to stop him.

He halted in his tracks then took a step forward. "I didn't mean to—"

"Why did you come here?" she challenged him.

"To tell you that I request your presence at breakfast tomorrow morning." He forced a dry thump down his throat. "I could not join you for the first two meals of the day due to circumstances beyond my control."

"Will you be joining me for breakfast on the morrow?" she asked.

"I shall."

A heavy silence hung between them while he summoned a kinder tone. "You have my word. If I am forced to miss any more meals in the future, I will send word to you through Mrs. Eaton—or Rogers."

She shot him a dubious look.

"Would it please you if we shook hands on such a promise?"

Draven extended his palm forward. When Isabella grasped it, her fingers quivered beneath his firm touch. He leaned in and whispered, "Have you been faithful to me these months, my dear wife?"

"I have." Isabella raised her chin.

"Then you have no potential lover waiting for you in the wings— a lover willing to grant you children?"

Red blotches spread across her chest and her palm grew moist.

"As I thought," he said. "You were bluffing about conducting a liaison." Lowering his gaze to the ruffle that bared the swell of her breasts, he wet his lips.

"I was not bluffing!" she cried.

"You were because you wouldn't disappoint me by being a harlot."

She snatched her hand away. "You know nothing of what I will or will not do. Furthermore, my ultimatum stands."

Draven drew back. She was making things bloody difficult. He wanted to bed her, feel her soft curves beneath him, but he wasn't going to let her treat him like a puppet on a string.

With a swirl of his coattails, he turned to leave. "I will knock on your door and accompany you to breakfast tomorrow morning. I expect you to be ready."

"I will never do as you command," she raged.

Glaring, Draven slammed the door to avoid being hit by the candlestick Isabella thrust in his direction.

Chapter Ten

*A*nger makes nary a good bedfellow.

Waking from an abominable night's sleep that testified to the adage, Isabella rubbed her eyes. As she willed them to focus on the somber haze that filled the room, her anger over Draven's insolence returned full force.

Perhaps, she thought, a bath would soothe her fury.

She padded to the washroom where she located the servant's cord. As she waited for Gwyneth to arrive with warm bathwater, she busied herself by smelling an array of fragrant bath salts that surrounded the tub.

The freckle-faced abigail arrived in no time with two buckets of water. Isabella resisted the urge to help the girl when she struggled to dump the water into the tub. After Gwyneth took her leave, she pinned her mass of curls atop her head and slipped out of her nightshirt. Gripping both sides of the bathtub, she dipped into the bayberry-scented water. Her stress melted away momentarily as she leaned her head against the polished porcelain and captured a cloud of frothy suds in her sponge. Purring like a kitten, Isabella released a rich cascade of water between her breasts.

A feeling of unease skittered across her neck and raised goose bumps on her arms. Clenching the sides of the tub, she glanced around but noticed nothing out of the ordinary. Still, she was unable to brush aside the feeling that someone—or something—was watching her. She turned to look in a standing mirror that sat on a nearby ledge. In the reflection, she saw a human eye between the stones of the wall. Donning her robe, she rushed into the hall and ran headfirst into Draven.

He looked dashing in a finely cut, blue waistcoat and snug-fitting breeches tucked into a pair of polished Hessians. Although his well-groomed appearance contrasted with the tousled, fiery man she had encountered last evening, defiance still shadowed his face.

Pulling the cords of her robe into firm knots, she stared up at him. "Were you watching me, my lord?"

"Watching you do what exactly?" was his arrogant response.

"I was taking a bath just now and I saw someone watching me between the stones in the wall. If it was you, I thought you weren't interested in seeing me without my clothes."

"My dear wife, I am the first to admit my longing for female company at this secluded mess of an estate," Draven said, "but I am no Peeping Tom. My guess is that some young hall boy has become fascinated with you. If I find him, I'll have his position without recourse."

"I don't see a hall boy about," Isabella said. Giving him a hard frown, she mumbled something else under her breath.

"Pardon?"

"I said: you would never admit to spying on me."

He shrugged nonchalantly. "Believe what you want."

Isabella wrapped a hand around her damp neck.

"You're creating quite a puddle out here," Draven remarked as his expression softened. "Let's dismiss this unpleasantness, shall we? Why don't you get dressed since I'm here to accompany you to breakfast?"

Refusing to be charmed by him, she lifted her chin. "I never agreed to that. I'll meet you in the breakfast parlor, although I have little to say to you until you are willing to discuss the ultimatum I presented you with."

Draven's eyes narrowed. In a stiff motion, he tucked one hand behind his back and bowed. "I will go ahead, if you wish."

Feeling no need to impress her unpredictable husband, Isabella stepped back into her suites and slipped into a simple muslin dress. She exited her chambers once more then retraced the complicated hallways and staircases she had conquered yesterday. When she entered the sunny breakfast parlor, the clink of china and the smell of baked bread greeted her.

Helena was seated at the head of the polished table. The noblewoman merely nodded her head in Isabella's direction before resuming the preparation of her tea.

Isabella decided not to complain about Helena taking the seat designated for the mistress of the house. After all, she didn't care to start an argument this early in the morning. She did, however, make a mental note to speak with Draven about his mother's presence here when breakfast was over.

Accepting the chair Rogers pulled out for her, she stole a look at her husband. He'd chosen a chair at the opposite end of the table from Helena. The intenseness of his gaze allowed Isabella to see that, in the illumination of morning, his eyes appeared colder than ever. Black as a chalkboard, they possessed no spark of warmth. She glanced down and fussed over her tea, but his stare continued to vex her nerves.

As the trio ate, the subdued noise of breakers washing over boulders provided the only sound. Isabella tried to raise her teacup without her hand shaking as her husband continued to scrutinize her.

"I have taken the liberty of having some dresses made for you," he said. "They will be delivered in a few days."

"I'm sorry if my wardrobe displeases you," she said, meeting his gaze.

"Not at all," Draven replied. "I think you look lovely."

A scalding warmth rose in her cheeks. She tore her eyes from his and looked down at her food.

"Your notorious pendant is rather stunning." Helena spoke up.

"Thank you." Isabella brushed her fingers over the smooth surface. Radiating a spectacular blue color, the thin, rectangular lapis bore carved lines of Egyptian hieroglyphics. Symmetrical inserts of coral and onyx highlighted the ancient engravings.

"I, for one, have never heard the story of the prophecy in full detail," Helena said. "Pray tell?"

Sucking in a breath, Isabella considered sealing her mouth shut and running from the room. But Helena was showing a rare moment of civility, and better yet, their conversation deterred her from acknowledging Draven's narrow stare. She proceeded to recount the curse of the stone as succinctly as she could.

When she was finished, Helena offered no visual reaction to the story. "Don't tell me you believe in this curse."

"Of course not," Isabella replied. "But I cherish the amulet greatly since it was a gift from my father."

"Word has it that your father never recovered its counterpart, the bracelet of Amenhotep," Draven chimed in.

"That's right." Isabella slid him a glance. She was surprised that he'd taken an interest in her father's work.

"And what power does this bracelet supposedly possess?" Helena queried.

Isabella took a sip of her tea then returned the cup to its saucer. "Amenhotep had the bracelet made so that the other priests from the court—his loyal friends—may bless it. Filled with the power of good, the bracelet was created to oppose the forces of black magic. Amenhotep was about to put it on, to protect himself, when Tousret stabbed him to death."

"What a dreadful story," Helena said. "I would never wear anything so morbid."

"You mean you would never be brave enough to," Draven said. "Personally, I think it's fascinating."

Both Isabella and Helena flung him a disbelieving stare.

His chair scraped the marble tile as he stood. "Adequate breakfast," he said. "Now I'm off for a good ride. Care to join me, Isabella?"

She bit back her surprise. Hadn't Draven claimed they would see each other at mealtimes and nothing more?

"I don't own a riding habit," she protested. If he was ready to discuss the ultimatum she had given him, they could hardly do so while they rode.

He made a clucking sound with his tongue. "I'm sure that frock paired with an overcoat will do. Remember I have ordered you a bevy of new dresses if that one gets ruined."

She cringed inwardly for riding was one of her least favorite things to do. "But it rained this morning. Surely the moors will be soaked with mud—"

"Don't tell me a sensible woman like you is afraid of a little mud? I suggest that, since we are stuck here with one another, we should try and be civil."

She said nothing.

His gaze was direct as he tried another tactic. "Still, if you're inept on the back of a horse—"

Isabella looked down her nose at him. "I'll meet you at the stables in a quarter of an hour."

Draven breezed from the room and her stomach fluttered. She'd been aware of his fixating stare at breakfast but whether or not he meant for her to notice it, she wasn't sure. She only knew it belied his attraction to her and she was going to take this opportunity to seduce him.

Chapter Eleven

Isabella was the first to admit that she had very few adventuresome qualities. Clumsy at anything involving motion, she'd fallen from a horse when she was a girl and hadn't ridden since. She had watched little Phillip receive riding lessons every Wednesday afternoon, but that did her no good now.

Trying to ignore her quaking nerves, she hastened to her room and grabbed a pelisse from her wardrobe. As she tugged it on, the image of Phillip pulled at her heartstrings. With china-blue eyes and hair the color of saffron, the eight-year-old boy possessed a temperament as sweet as his angelic appearance. Regardless of her plan to produce a genuine Winthrop heir to secure her position with Draven, her personal ache for a child was beginning to consume her. She had become a governess because she loved children, because taking care of others was in her nature. It was something she'd always done and a secret part of her had been anxious to wed Draven so that they may start a family.

Isabella maneuvered down the steep flight of stairs at the back of the house. The stairwell was designated for servants but it was the quickest way to the fields.

Nearing the kitchen, she was enticed by the scent of a soufflé baking in the kitchen's oven. The smell made her realize she'd eaten very little during breakfast. After her ride with Draven she would ask Mrs. Tidwell, the head cook, for an early nuncheon.

She took another step toward the kitchen but voices stopped her in her tracks. Isabella peered around the corner and listened.

"I wonder if her ladyship plans to eat any more meals in her room," Mrs. Tidwell said sharply. "My food doesn't taste nearly as good after sittin' on a tray."

"Lord knows," Gwyneth answered between the clanking of dishes. "But I hardly blame 'er. Her ladyship doesn't seem very 'appy to be back."

"I hope the master doesn't scare her off again," the cook said. "She's a right angel, returnin' to 'im in the first place."

"I 'ope she stays too," Gwyneth added. "His lordship gave me a lift from kitchen-maid to abigail. If the countess leaves, I'll be right back where I started."

"Right proud of any position, ye should be. My mother, God rest her soul, always told me: be respectful and hold fast to the position ye're given."

Gwyneth dropped her voice to a whisper but Isabella could still hear. "I'm not one to gossip, but I overheard somethin' shockin' in the hallway. It was her ladyship accusin' Master Draven of spyin' on 'er during 'er bath."

Mrs. Tidwell tsked. "They're a married couple but they don't act as such. And I'd say his lordship is capable of much worse than spyin'. Did ye know that Master Draven spent three years in an asylum after his father died?"

Gwyneth sucked in a breath. "My word!"

"Not that I like ta gossip either," the cook continued, "but I heard it was somethin' besides his father's death that put him there."

"Ye don't say! Well," Gwyneth stated, "he's 'andsome enough to make me knees knock but he seems a bit off. I hear 'im wanderin' the halls at all hours before 'e locks himself in the library. Then there's 'is doses of lithium. . . ."

"He'd scare me dead away too!"

The two women shared a giggle.

"I just wonder if the missus knows about his lordship's madness," Mrs. Tidwell said after their laughter subsided.

Gwyneth sighed. "She'll find out soon enough. Well, can't spend all mornin' jabberin' in the kitchen. I'm off to tend to 'er ladyship's room."

My God, Isabella thought. Even the servants suspected Draven of being a lunatic. *I'm about to seduce a madman.*

She set herself into motion as Gwyneth passed her on the stairs.

"M'lady!" The girl went rigid.

"Gwyneth." Isabella smiled. "I'm off for a ride."

The girl remained silent while her cheeks went pink. "Remember what I said about those horses."

"I remember," she said gently. "Now please tell Mrs. Tidwell I'd like an early meal when I return."

"Yes, m'lady."

"Thank you, Gwyneth," she said.

Isabella continued on until she reached the fields beyond the manor house. They were a mess, just as she had anticipated. To add to her irritation, she discovered a wicked-looking horse standing on a small slope in front of the stables. Massive in size and nasty in disposition, the creature bore a silver saddle that complemented the richness of its pewter coat. Frowning, she accepted the horse's reins from the stable lad she'd encountered the other day.

"His name is Dante," Viktor said.

Isabella wound the leather reins around her hands nervously. "Of course it is."

"Pardon me, my lady?"

"Oh, it's nothing."

"Good luck with him."

"Thank you." She paused. "Where is my husband?"

"Master Draven will be out in a moment. He prefers to ready his own horse."

As she waited, Dante fumed and snorted in Isabella's direction. There was no doubt in her mind that her husband had hand-selected the horse to make her look like a fool.

Taking his sweet time, Draven emerged with the reins of his magnificent black horse clasped in his gloved hands. He swept toward Isabella without uttering a word. Erect in posture, Draven displayed an alluring confidence as he dropped his horse's reins and came to assist Isabella into her saddle. He clamped his strong hands around her waist and she fought the urge to lean back against his chest. Still, he was close enough for her to feel his breath at her earlobe and the sensation shot right through her.

After Draven mounted his stallion, they were off. Under clear skies of blue and over thick pockets of mud they thundered with a liberating fury. As her husband moved alongside her, it became apparent to Isabella that he was an accomplished rider. In fact, an impressive show of his straight back and experienced hands made him an attractive horseman.

Twittering in her own saddle and clinging desperately to the bridle, Isabella followed Draven over the moist marshes, down through the woods to the edge of Dunwich and back.

"Do you ride every morning?" she asked breathlessly once they'd guided their horses to a stop at the foot of a dangerous-looking cliff.

He met her stare with interest. "I intend to start. After you've spent any length of time at Thorncliff Towers, you will want to escape its dreary atmosphere as well."

Isabella pushed a curl from her eyes. "I don't know if my legs could stand this kind of riding every day."

"That's a shame. I hoped you would join me outdoors every morning."

She gave him a smile. "Am I not an enemy to be avoided?"

"Please forget what I said yesterday, Isabella. I acted impulsively and out of anger. I regretted it all evening." Draven flashed a devastating grin. "Can we be pleasant with one another?"

Hope sprang in her chest. Considering her husband's good mood today, persuading him to make love to her might not be as hard as she thought.

"I suppose there's no harm in joining you for a ride every morning," she said.

He crossed his hands over the saddle horn. "Good."

"Perhaps we can spend some time in the library afterward."

"I would love to, but following my ride, I seek the solitude of my suites."

"What keeps you holed up there all day?" Isabella asked as her breath misted in the morning chill.

"I am in the process of starting a shipbuilding business. Before he died, my father spoiled me by purchasing property in the Canterbury docks." Draven inhaled the fresh air. "Keeping my mind on business helps me maintain a sense of sanity in this dreary place."

"I thought I was the only one who thought this estate was dreary."

She watched the front of his hair flap about in the wind. With a charming tilt of his head, he smiled at her and the way his face transformed wrapped pleasure around her spine.

"We should dismount and sit awhile," he said. "I'm sure the horses would like to graze."

He swung himself to the ground then skirted his horse to help Isabella down. A breeze from the shoreline fluttered over them once they settled on the swaying grass. Isabella plucked up the last flower to survive the autumn chill and spun it in circles by its stem. "Speaking of Thorncliff Towers, doesn't it bother you that the house is so remote?"

Draven shrugged. Most of his shoulder-length hair had fallen from its queue. Isabella resisted the urge to touch the shimmering strands.

"The public at large has never been very kind to me. One could say I prefer solitude," he said.

"What about friends?"

"What about them?"

"Do you have any?"

"Not really." His voice caught slightly. "From way back, even my schoolmates thought me odd."

Empathy pinged through her. "I had the same problem. When I was growing up, my nose was always stuck in a book. The other children teased me for being so serious."

"They say serious children grow into serious adults," he teased.

"I suppose that's true. But I became even more solemn when my mother died."

Draven dropped his smile. "I'm sorry."

She shrugged but inside the hurt came back. "At least I have my father."

"Presuming you have more friends than I, you must prefer to be among people."

She nodded then looked into his eyes. "I hated being alone when my mother died and my father was in Egypt."

"But it taught you to be independent. Correct?"

"Yes," she answered as a sense of vulnerability crept along her spine. "Out of necessity, I'm not a submissive type of woman."

Draven examined her as if she were a science experiment. He had begun to pry into Isabella's deepest recesses and she wasn't at all comfortable with the intrusion.

"It appears that you've always placed the care of others before yourself," he said.

"Perhaps. When my mother was alive, she suffered from poor health. I attended to her quite diligently, but I don't deserve a medal. I was raised to believe that sacrifices are sometimes necessary."

"And now that you are here, you find yourself in an ironic situation," Draven said as he hung his elbows over his bent knees.

"What do you mean?"

"You're a wealthy countess and you're still making sacrifices. Sacrifices such as being married to me." His eyes twinkled engagingly.

She laughed. "At least my wardrobe will improve."

He laughed as well. Then he paused. "You also have more authority than you've ever had. Come now. What will you change about Thorncliff Towers now that you're its countess?"

Highly aware that Draven had shifted closer, Isabella chose her words carefully so as not to offend him. "The estate looks a bit neglected but it's the garden that bothers me most. It's crying out for some color. Rosebushes, perhaps? Red roses are my favorite flower."

"And I forgot to supply you with a bridal bouquet made from those flowers, didn't I?"

"Yes," she said as her cheeks warmed. It appeared that he hadn't forgotten completely.

He reached out and squeezed her hand by way of an apology. A brief silence accompanied the electricity that passed between them. They sat studying the waves cresting in the distance. The silence exaggerated the warm touch of Draven's broad shoulder against hers.

"Well"—Draven cleared his throat—"I'm pleased that you have an interest in Thorncliff Towers. Perhaps drawing up an improvement plan is something we can do together."

"I'd like that," she said.

Draven cast her a sly smile. "In fact, we can do quite a few things together, assuming you drop your ultimatum."

Things like what? Make love?

If he was willing, she must try and seduce him right here and now. The sun broke through a cloud mass, showering them with heat. Isabella forced herself to hold his gaze. She unbuttoned her lace collar in slow motion and moistened her lips in what she assumed was an inviting gesture. "I won't have to abide by my ultimatum if you invite me into your bed," she whispered.

Draven raised a winged brow. Remaining silent, he removed his greatcoat. As he leaned closer, off came his frock coat. Then in slow tugs, he unbuttoned his shirt.

Isabella ran a finger down her neck, lower and lower inside the fabric of her dress, until her hand rested at the rise of her breast. Draven stared at her. It was his turn to wet his lips. They locked eyes and he reached over to take the daffodil from her hand. Her heart sped.

Securing the flower behind her ear, he bent over her as she leaned back on her elbows. "You're very beautiful, Isabella. A beacon of goodness in my eyes."

Her soul stirred at the compliment.

"And you could be a wonderful husband, if you'd try," she murmured.

"Do you know what I think?" His voice purred with eroticism.

"What?"

"I think you are as aroused as I am." His fingers stroked her arm before they reached the nape of her neck.

Will he kiss me?

Draven's stare shifted from her eyes to her mouth. Cupping the back of her head, he bent forward and seared her lips with a slow, scorching kiss. Isabella's heart thudded like a caged animal's. As sensual energy roared through her, she let out a moan.

She never suspected seducing Draven would bring her so much pleasure.

He gathered her to him with urgency. His tongue plunged its way past her lips while her body shuddered. Swelling against him until the sensitive tips of her bosom heaved against his open shirt, Isabella longed to feel his hand at her breasts. Fondling them. Kneading them. And she wanted to feel his hard, smooth body intertwined with hers.

Draven forced her head closer with a firm yank. The fervor between them escalated as he bore her down and shifted his weight on top of her. His fingers sought her tangled hair while he devoured her neck and throat with his lips. He traced her leaping pulse with the tip of his tongue and Isabella's eyes fluttered shut. She wanted him to do much more than kiss her.

As if he had read her thoughts, Draven ran his hand along her bodice until it reached the mound of her breast. With the ease of an expert, he found its nub through the fabric and tweaked it until she groaned with ecstasy.

He gave her another hard kiss and she could feel his shaft grow monstrously erect against her leg. As he bunched up the fabric of her dress, his breathing came in ragged spurts. He slid a hand up her thigh. Hot and completely aroused, Isabella sucked in a sharp breath. Her folds flooded with moisture in anticipation of his fingers reaching her center.

Like a silent thief, Draven's fingers stole inside her pantalets and combed her soft curls. Carefully but very firmly, he located her damp petals. As he captured her mouth, his fingertips caressed the sensitive skin of her flanges and while his hand moved in tighter circles toward her center, she spread her legs so that he could delve a finger inside her.

At the feel of it, Isabella swore she could see the gates of heaven. "Oh, Draven—"

Draven's hard prick continued to press against her leg but at that moment, his mouth turned cruel. He extracted his finger only to grope her breasts in a painful grip.

"My Bella—" he murmured gruffly. "My beauty."

She commanded her inner voice to be quiet and enjoy the moment. If she didn't stop him, perhaps they would make love here under the cloudless sky. It's what she wanted. Yet Draven's frenzied actions reminded her of his rough behavior on their wedding night.

He continued on in impatient motions but she recoiled. Panic seized Isabella. She tried to jerk her head away from the crush of his mouth but he wouldn't let her. Grunting, he yanked her chin back in his direction and bit down on her lip. She screamed and slapped his face. He rolled off of her while she sat up and put her fingers to the bleeding wound.

Draven's eyes widened at the sight of her blood. "Christ—"

"How could you?" she screeched.

He clutched her hand, blood and all, and brought it to his nose.

His body began to tremble while his eyes flashed an unnatural shade of red—as they had on their wedding night.

Isabella bolted to her feet and stumbled to her horse. "I must clean this off."

"Wait!" he ordered.

The fierceness of his voice stopped her. Her legs quaked.

"I'm sorry, Isabella, but I warned you not to come back."

Giving him no answer, she hurried onto Dante's saddle and galloped away in a blaze of terror.

Chapter Twelve

Temper flaring, Draven handed Lucifer's reins to Viktor. He saw Isabella disappear into the house as he approached it. *Good thing.* If she hadn't run away when she did, he may have ravaged every inch of her.

What the hell is happening to me? The Gypsy spell was getting the better of him without the appearance of a full moon.

Guilt gripped him as he marched toward the steps that led to the shingle beach. The feel of Isabella's freed locks against his freshly shaved skin and the confectionery taste of her lips had spawned his wildness in the light of day. Worse yet, he had sliced her mouth open, spilling blood that smelled salty and bittersweet—different than the blood of the animals he'd conquered. And much more enticing.

He cringed to think he'd allowed Isabella even the slightest glimpse at his inner demon.

She must think me deranged.

His lack of power against his other half churned his stomach, as did the shame that accompanied it.

Straining to order himself, Draven shoved his gloves into the pocket of his frock coat and breathed in the moist, billowing wind. A group of waterfowl squawked overhead as he reached the beach.

The breeze that swept over the small bay calmed him momentarily. He crossed the pebbled beach and watched the cold seawater rise into whitecaps. The warm colors of sunset that glimmered above the bay reminded him that a full moon would rise tonight. He scowled. For Isabella's sake, he hoped that she had safely locked herself away in her suites.

Isabella put a hand to the windowpane and watched Draven storm to the beach below the manor house.

Had she made a mistake in trying to seduce him? He'd become violent, cruel. Was he capable of anything but aggression? *Will he ever make love to me gently?*

If she was so determined to have a baby with Draven, she needed to find out all she could about his so-called "affliction." Considering the possibility that this condition may affect their child, she must know what lay ahead of her. After all, what kind of person smells someone's blood?

She was a wreck. As she managed to force her jittering nerves aside, a plan formed in her mind. Maybe she should look for clues in Draven's suites that would explain his bizarre actions.

Touching her bleeding lips, she made her way to the south turret. The essence of Mrs. Tidwell's words replayed in her head as she arrived at the doors that marked her husband's chambers. *Draven is capable of much more than spying. He spent three years in an asylum following his father's death.*

The possibility that Draven was mad alarmed Isabella. Although it didn't negate the rumors of him being a murderer, it would explain his violent demeanor.

Letting out a shudder, she entered his suite and bolted the lock behind her. She struggled to breathe as she pressed her back to the door. Her encounter with Draven on the knoll seemed like a nightmare, an unsettling blur. When he brought her blood-smeared hand to his nostrils, he had convulsed without control and a shadow of evil had passed over his face.

What will he do if he catches me going through his personal things?

Suppressing the fear churning inside her, Isabella rushed to the dressing room. The space smelled of sandalwood and tobacco, just as she remembered. She ran her hand over a mahogany-topped bureau displaying Draven's personal effects. A shaving brush stood within a matching mug and an ebony-coated razor lay beside it in its wrapper. Behind a Truefitt and Hill toiletry jar rested a herringbone comb.

She closed her eyes and inhaled her husband's lingering scent. Sliding the tip of her tongue over her lips, she wondered if she'd missed her only chance to know Draven's hard body against hers.

Gathering a clean handkerchief, she pressed it to her injured mouth. She crouched down and began to search her husband's wardrobe. There on the bottom shelf sat a plaid blanket. She removed it and saw nothing behind the folded material on the same shelf. But when she returned the blanket to its original position, a brass key tumbled from its folds. Isabella picked it up and flipped it over in her hand. *What did it unlock?*

She tried the key at Draven's desk to no avail. Would it give her entry into the mysterious library?

She moved to the window Draven had leapt through on their wedding night. To her dismay, it faced the courtyard and not the beach. She wondered if her husband had reentered the house yet. If not, perhaps she had time to try the key in the library's door before he returned.

She decided to take her chances. Rushing to the manor's first level, Isabella slipped the brass object into the lock. She sucked in a breath and turned the knob. It opened! After stepping quietly into the dark, circular room, she clicked the door shut behind her and threw back the curtains. Then she set about searching for anything that might enlighten her about Draven's family history.

A writing desk stood in the corner of the vast library yet held nothing of importance. Shelves of novels and various textbooks yielded nothing noteworthy. She was about to search the drawer of a side table when Draven's booming voice shook the walls.

"Rogers, I'm going to my chambers and I don't want to be disturbed."

"Will ye want supper brought up later, sir?"

"No."

"As ye wish, m'lord."

Isabella heard Rogers's footfalls on the back stairwell while Draven's boots pounded on the main staircase. Her pulse raced. There was only one place she hadn't searched: a decorative chest hidden behind a three-setting sofa. Stretching a hand forward, she pulled on the latch. *Locked.*

Her hopes sinking, she looked about for something she could use to open it. Hastening to the writing desk, she extracted a letter opener. She returned to the chest and fumbled with the sharp object, cringing when it made noise inside the lock. She was ready to abandon the task when she heard a *pop.* The chest's lid swung into the air by its hinges, releasing a whiff of musty air. She peered inside and saw that deep in the shadows sat an ornate notebook. A journal of some kind.

Isabella sat on a nearby stool and ran her fingertips over the binding. On its cover was an embossed symbol of a moon. After she flipped the cover open, she thumbed through the pages at a rapid speed, glancing through illustrations of lunar phases, schedules of forthcoming full moons, and recipes for herbal remedies. Intrigued, Isabella stopped at the most recent entry penned yesterday.

> *October 12, 1820*
> *The scent of Isabella's blood beneath her skin is driving me mad. I've become transfixed. The flow of her blood naturally makes her pulse throb. As her pulse rises and falls against the cream of her neck, I long to run my mouth along it and gently bite down.*
> *Damnation!*
> *Why has she returned here? Simply to torture me? No. She has done the honorable thing by resuming our marriage. Therefore I must be a gentleman and do the same. How I wish I could tell her of my curse. But she would surely leave me again. In my silence, I will have protected relations with her. I hope I can stop myself from hurting her, for God knows, I care for her deeply.*
> *Will I ever tell her of my affections—or of my Gypsy hex?*

The entry made little sense. Isabella's heart beat in triple time. What hex could Draven be referring to? She was happy that he planned to make love to her, but his attraction to blood still alarmed her.

Her hands trembled and she felt light-headed. Draven's words offered proof of his violent thoughts but it also gave her a glimpse at his emotions. Tears sprang to Isabella's eyes. By the torment Draven recorded here—and considering the reference he'd made to a Gypsy hex—it was obvious he hadn't been fully cured before he left the asylum.

The rumors of his insanity must be true.

She flipped backward through the book. Stopping at an entry marked "*rauna curse,*" she read more.

> *July 15, 1819*
>
> *Learned details of a* rauna *curse. It is a spell cast over someone who possesses full Gypsy blood—or a half-breed. It's meant as punishment for dishonoring one's heritage. Ironclad. The only way to have it revoked? I must show genuine redemption.*
>
> *If I don't, I'll be foredoomed by tasting even a drop of . . .*

She turned the page, but Draven hadn't continued the entry.

A drop of what? She was dying to know. To add to her confusion, she knew Draven had no Gypsy blood in his veins.

He must be more delusional than I thought.

Cupping a hand over her mouth, she raised herself on unsure feet. She bent to replace the journal when a hand clasped her shoulder.

Chapter Thirteen

Isabella's heart slammed against her ribs. When she whirled around to meet Rogers's gentle face, relief brought her shoulders forward.

The valet slid the journal from her hands. "M'lady, ye shouldn't be lookin' at things that don't belong to ya."

"I know. I'm sorry." She fought to regain her composure.

"Not to worry, yer ladyship."

She offered him a smile.

He returned it. "I 'ave good news, m'lady. Yer father just sent word that 'e has arrived in Dunwich."

"My father?" she cried. "That's wonderful!"

"I'll take ye to him, m'lady."

"Thank you, Rogers."

The manservant glanced down at the journal and ran a weathered hand over the moon symbol on its front cover.

Isabella started to explain why she had been snooping but the valet interrupted her.

"Beggin' yer pardon, m'lady. His lordship may enter here at any moment. I think it best if ye leave 'ere this instant."

"Of course." She tried to step around him.

He put his hand out. "The key?"

She gave it to him, disappointed that she'd no longer have access to the room. Rogers returned the notebook to the chest and locked it. Still, there was no doubt in Isabella's mind that he would find another hiding spot for it soon.

"I guess I'll be on my way," she said. She hastened to the door but stopped at the threshold. "Do you know anything of the Gypsy curse his lordship referred to in his journal?"

He shrugged his shoulders. "Can't say as I do, m'lady. I'm the sort 'a man who only believes in things I can see or touch."

She nodded.

The hunched figure took a step forward. "And I see one thing for certain, yer ladyship."

"What is that, Rogers?"

"There is love for ye in Master Draven's stare."

Isabella was at a loss for words. She stared down at her hands and decided to change the subject. "Has the Winthrop carriage been readied?"

"By me personally, m'lady."

She wasn't about to ask permission from Draven to fetch her father. "I'll just refresh myself in my room."

"I'll be waitin' outside, yer ladyship."

Isabella picked up her skirts and hurried to her suites. What would she say to her father when she saw him in Dunwich? Her thoughts were as convoluted as a twisted tree trunk. Nerves racing, she moved to the mirror. Her reflection stunned her. Blood crusted her upper lip and her entire mouth was swollen from the mad kisses Draven had thrust upon her. Her mane resembled a rat's nest complete with thin blades of grass lodged in her snarled curls but oddly enough, the wild daffodil Draven had secured behind her ear remained.

Lord above! What had Rogers thought of her disheveled appearance? Years of learning to hold his tongue must have kept him from commenting on it.

After Isabella wiped away the stains that coated her face and marred the muslin day dress which doubled as a riding habit, she began to move about the room in tense circles. Draven had stunned her with his aggression. Yet it was that same urgency, combined with the journal entry asserting that he cared about her, that proved he didn't trust himself in her presence.

The fear she used to feel at her husband's wrath was now hardening into a distinct purpose. She wasn't going to let anything prevent her from finding out the true nature of Draven's affliction.

After re-pinning her hair and rinsing the last of the mud speckles from her forehead, Isabella left her suites and boarded the awaiting carriage. The vehicle clattered toward Dunwich and the solitary ride soothed her.

The carriage stopped in front of the coaching station a half hour later. Her father was waiting on its wide, front step, balancing on a cane. She flew out of the carriage and flung her arms around his neck. "Papa, I've missed you terribly!"

"Isa," he murmured into her hair.

She never wanted to let go but eventually Isabella pulled away to study her father's face. The kindly, chartreuse eyes were just as she remembered and the wave in his silver hair caught the sunlight as it always had. Leaning forward, she welcomed his signature fragrance of peppermint.

He smiled. "My darling—or should I address you as Lady Winthrop?"

"Papa," she said with reproach.

"Gracious. That was quite a journey from London. It's astounding how remote this village is."

"Frighteningly so." She paused. "Oh, I'm so happy to see you."

He chuckled. "You've already said that."

"I can't believe you traveled alone."

"You aren't the only one. When I told Fiona I was coming here, she made the same face you're making."

She clasped his hands. "Well, never mind that."

His smile vanished. "The question is: are you well, my darling?"

"I'm fine," she lied.

"Are you sure?" He eyed her deep scratch.

Isabella ran a finger over her lip. "Draven and I went for a ride this morning. You know how clumsy I am on a horse."

"You fell off?"

"Is it any surprise?"

He took her hand and patted it. She felt badly for lying to him, but she was too confused by her own thoughts to reveal anything at the moment.

"Let's walk, shall we?" Limping against his cane, Harris started down the path toward the sea.

Isabella picked up her skirts and followed. Treading over clusters of white and pink pebbles and pockets of sparse vegetation, she listened as her father relayed the conversation he'd had with his chaise driver about Dunwich.

"A most charming place, but in a dire state I understand."

" 'A dire state'?" she repeated. She was ashamed to think she hadn't bothered to learn anything about the place her husband governed.

"Yes," he said. "Apparently the Winthrop family refuses to help stop the erosion of Dunwich's land mass."

"Erosion?"

"It's quite a shame. This place used to be one of the biggest merchant ports in England. Until a devastating tidal surge washed most of it out to sea." He was clearly upset. "The town's location invites battering tides and fierce coastal storms. The beaches are eroding at an alarming rate."

"It's disappointing that Draven hasn't offered to fortify them. I shall discuss it with him since I should have some influence as countess."

"Will Draven listen to your opinions?" her father asked.

"I hope so." She halted. "Papa, I'm glad you changed your mind about coming here."

He stopped walking as well. "You don't understand. Something changed my mind for me."

Puzzled, Isabella raised an eyebrow.

"This letter arrived the day you left for Thorncliff Towers."

Her hands trembled slightly as she took an envelope from him and opened it.

Isabella,

I will not mince words. I was shocked to receive your recent correspondence. As you well know, two years have passed since you fled from me and from the wretched temper I displayed on our wedding night. My curiosity about your well-being has been satisfied through the gossip mill that reaches even this remote, fog-laced coastline.

In response to your letter, I must begin by telling you that "if only" are two words that haunt me. If only you had stayed, I would have eventually relayed to you why it is I refuse to have children. If only my temper hadn't scared you away dur-

ing our blasted argument. If only I didn't have to tell you not to come back to me.

It is much too dangerous for you here now. Something vile has happened to me . . . something that you do not deserve to be company to. If only—there are those words again—a shameful act from my past wasn't pushing me to the darkest recesses of evil.

I beg you, stay away at all costs.

Draven

Isabella looked into her father's face. Lines of distress creased his forehead and his frail eyes were overflowing with concern. If he had arrived an hour ago, before she had read Draven's delusional words coupled with his astonishing admission of affection in his journal, she would have coddled her bloody lip and left Thorncliff Towers without looking back. But now things were different. She couldn't leave Draven. Not in his mental state.

She looked at the letter again, studying each word as if she were deciphering a riddle.

What shameful act was Draven referring to?

"You can tell me the truth, Isabella," her father said. "Your lip. Did Draven strike you?"

She gasped. "No! He's done nothing of the sort. I told you it was an accident." She needed to protect Draven until she could find out everything about his past.

Harris breathed in a stream of fresh air. "Considering the ill will between you, I was hoping this letter was just a lot of nonsense drudged up by Draven to keep you away."

She feigned a smile. "Now that I've returned, we are getting along quite well."

Her father took her gently by the shoulders. "Are you being direct with me, Isa?"

"I'm sure you could tell if I were lying," she said lightly. "You've always had that ability."

He studied her for a moment then released a sigh. "Very well. But I don't appreciate Draven Winthrop playing games with my girl."

Playing games? That was the grossest understatement Isabella had ever heard. She slipped her arm around him and led him back to the center of town.

"Since you don't seem to be in danger, I'll be heading back to London," he said.

"You will not," she said, clasping his elbow. "It's too much traveling for one day."

He smiled. "I am rather tired. But I don't want to intrude."

She clasped his elbow. "I insist you stay at the manor. There is plenty of room."

He frowned. "I won't be in the way?"

"Not at all. You are family—and family is never in the way."

They made their way back to the carriage and Isabella instructed Rogers to return them to Thorncliff Towers.

Her father settled against the plush velvet squabs and smiled at her. "Tell me all about your reunion with the earl," he said.

Isabella's knees quaked beneath her dress. *What should I say?* If Papa knew any more about his son-in-law's dark side, he would surely insist that she leave him.

"At first it was awkward, I must admit. But civility has grown between us."

"Civility, eh? Sounds like true love." His eyes teased her.

She swatted him playfully on the arm. "You're incorrigible."

Harris looked out the window at a row of thatched-roof cottages. "You know, it's the oddest thing. Inside the coaching station, two men were discussing the existence of a mad wolf."

She said nothing. He glanced at her.

"Judging from your pale face," he went on, "I see the rumors in town have reached you too. I understand several animals were killed by this beast."

"They were probably killed by a wild dog, not a wolf. Anyway, what I am truly afraid of is Helena." She joked to lighten the mood.

His eyes darkened. "Helena? Is that old witch visiting your household? Turn this carriage around at once!"

She laughed. "Helena isn't visiting. She's in residence at Thorncliff Towers. It's another thing I need to discuss with Draven."

"That's my Isa! Always thinking. Always organizing her future."

She smiled.

He reached over and patted her hand. "No worries. I'm certain there is an explanation for what killed those cows."

She broke eye contact with him and studied the landscape rolling by.

"I have an uncanny ability to read your mind, you know," Harris said.

"Do you?"

"Yes."

She smiled. "What am I thinking?"

"You won't admit it, but the story Uncle Morton read to you when you were a child stayed with you."

She cringed. *Why must I be reminded of it again?* "Speaking of Uncle Morton, did he visit you at Fiona's home as he promised?" she asked.

Harris flushed a deep shade of pink. "I shouldn't have planned a meeting with him at all."

"Why?"

"Morton never showed up. After making some inquiries, I learned he's been thrown in the Fleet."

She gasped. "What happened?"

"Morton was a buffoon, as usual. He stole money from his employer."

"How awful," she said, recoiling.

Fleet was a debtors' prison. It was alleged to be the worst place on Earth. The prisoners were left to rot in its stench, unless their debts were paid, which Isabella surmised, wasn't very often.

Harris shrugged. "My brother has gone and done it this time. But I suppose it's high time he paid for his mistakes."

She and her father lapsed into silence. Never before did she remember a falter in their conversations before his disappearance. In the awkward moment, she reached for the amulet and rubbed it between her fingers.

"That's a lovely necklace," her father said. "Where did you get it?"

Isabella flung him a confused look. "You gave it to me, Papa. This is the amulet of Tousret. You were searching for its counterpart, the bracelet of Amenhotep on your last dig. Don't you remember?"

He sank back in his seat. "My memory hasn't fully returned. I'm sorry."

He went silent again and Isabella felt an ache in her heart.

Will Papa ever return to the man he was?

Chapter Fourteen

Night fell over Thorncliff Towers with a palpable hush. Draven watched a veil of tattered clouds push across the sky. The masses parted, revealing a perfectly round moon, and his nerves jumped. The appearance of a full moon had fascinated him once, but now it struck fear into his heart like a keen-edged sword.

He stood behind the horse stables, completely nude. What was the sense in donning clothing that would be ripped to shreds?

After pacing the length of the small structure, Draven stopped in front of the stable's back door. The sound of his erratic heartbeat rose above the hissing wind.

For nearly half of his life, he'd been disturbed by the knowledge that he was unloved and unwanted. Raised by a string of governesses, he had longed for the attention of his preoccupied father. Helena, of course, was rarely to be found.

During those years, he wanted to be somebody different. Now, ironically, he was. He was a monster.

Ivory beams of moonlight shone upon him, encircling Draven in a glow of light. A flash of heat surged through him, burning its way up from his toes. His body trembled and as much as he battled to control it, to conquer it, the painful metamorphosis started.

Cries of agony escaped his throat as his fingers and hands extended into sharp claws. A layer of black fur coated his skin and his nose extended into a hideous snout. His body bucked as he crouched to the ground as a creature bigger than a tiger.

In one agile motion, Draven leapt into the night. After scaling the soft earth of the headland, he stalked across the lawns of the estate and headed for the opposite side of the house.

He needed to see Isabella. No doubt she despised him for frightening her, but something beyond his wolf form yearned to witness her goodness, her genuine nature. And he needed to implant her in his memory—so that he didn't lose more of his humanity.

Isabella's bedchamber faced the open sea. It wouldn't be the easiest place to reach but he knew he had to try, no matter the risk. Using every ounce of his primal strength, he pounced from the soft ground up to a jutting balustrade, then higher until he reached the narrow balcony of her bedchamber. Panting from the effort, he leaned his head forward and peered through the large windowpane.

Isabella!

Draven hid in the shadows and watched as she strolled through her bedchamber wearing nothing but her Egyptian amulet. In graceful strides, she carried her smooth, petite curves toward the chiffonier. Her full breasts swayed gracefully, riveting him, inviting him. Isabella gave a twist to light a candle branch and offered him a glimpse of her firm buttocks in the incandescent moonlight. In his beastly form, Draven could smell the scent of her blood from where he stood and his mouth grew wet.

Isabella slipped into a dressing gown and took a seat before her vanity. When she withdrew a single pin from her hair, her auburn locks tumbled about her slim shoulders and fell between her breasts. Unaware that she was being observed, she proceeded to comb her curls with long, elegant strokes.

Heat spiraled through Draven's loins. He ached to touch her. To tell her how he felt. But it was as if she were miles away, behind a wall of glass so thick it could never be penetrated.

A bolt of lightning slashed across the sky, its bright light flooding the narrow ledge. The sudden flash caused Isabella to shoot a glance out the window. When her eyes met his, she screamed and recoiled.

Draven froze. The human part of him wanted to go to her and hold her. He was desperate to tell her not to be frightened of him, that he would never hurt her as long as he had control over his actions. On the other hand, the canine part of him wanted to devour her in savage bites.

Isabella inched tentatively toward the window. She pressed her face to the windowpane and gazed at him. The fact that she hadn't fled washed encouragement and relief over Draven. He'd tried to scare her with tales of werewolves earlier, but now that she had seen him, things were different.

He pawed the ledge that supported him, and dipped his head out of respect. He would give anything to stay with his stare drawn to hers, but he couldn't deny his burning hunger anymore.

Isabella placed one hand on the window. Thunder exploded behind Draven and rain sliced the night sky. With a final look her way, he sprang from the balcony and landed unsteadily on the wet railing of the next balcony below. Unable to keep his balance, he slipped and fell to the ground with a series of yelps. He heard Isabella open the window of her bedchamber. His gaze surged upward and he saw her face materialize in the pouring rain.

Will she come after me?

Afraid that he might become unhinged by the scent of her blood, Draven grappled to his feet and limped off into the shadowy darkness.

Isabella raced toward Draven's bedchamber in a blind rush. She reached his door high in the south turret and pounded on the wood.

"Draven! Wake up. I saw it! I saw the black wolf!"

Her nerves thrummed as she waited for a reply. Maybe he couldn't hear her voice over the pelting rain and deafening thunder.

She rapped louder.

Mrs. Eaton appeared, bleary-eyed. Rogers was directly behind the housekeeper, grasping a candle branch.

"What's wrong m'lady?" Mrs. Eaton asked.

"My husband. Do you know where he is?"

"I'm sure he's asleep in bed," she replied.

"No, I've knocked loudly and there is no answer."

The housekeeper looked puzzled. "Then I wouldn't know, yer ladyship."

"Master Draven is out for the night," Rogers said a bit too carefully.

Isabella crossed her arms. "In this weather? I doubt it."

Rogers stiffened. "He told me he was goin' to the tavern."

Rogers's loyalty to Draven was admirable but at the moment she found it quite annoying.

"I don't believe you," she said.

"I'm sorry, m'lady," the valet answered.

Harris appeared, tying the sash of his dressing robe. "What's all the fuss?"

"Papa! Draven has disappeared. And the black wolf. *I saw it!*"

"You saw it?" His brows dipped together. "I don't understand—"

"It was balancing itself on my balcony. I looked out my window and the wolf was staring at me. It had razor-sharp fangs and bristling fur—" She slumped against him.

Harris squeezed her tight. "It's all right, my dear. Where is the wolf now?"

"It fell then limped off." Isabella choked out the words. "I hope it's too hurt to attack Draven."

"Draven is outside in this storm?" her father asked.

"He isn't in his room," she said.

"I'm sure your husband can fend for himself, Isa." Harris took her by the shoulders and led her down the hall. "Now, let's get you back to bed."

"No. I couldn't possibly sleep now. Draven may be in grave danger."

"What are you going to do?" her father asked. "Sit outside Draven's door until he returns?"

"Wait for him? Yes!" Isabella's eyes lit up. "That's precisely what I'll do."

Rogers looked alarmed. "Are ye certain, yer ladyship?"

"Yes. Please bring me a chair."

The valet left the hallway. Moments later, he returned with a chair from one of the nearby bedchambers. After he secured it against the wall, Isabella settled into it with a determined expression.

Chapter Fifteen

Dawn's light brightened the hallway as Draven rounded the corner. He was tired and his leg ached. Though he wore fresh clothes, his face was dirty and streaked from the rain. If he could get to his suites without anyone seeing him, no one would notice the discrepancy in his appearance.

What a hell of a night that was. He wanted nothing more than to fall into bed.

Striding down the corridor, he looked up and saw Isabella. *What the devil is she doing in that chair?*

"Draven!" Terror shook her voice.

Was she still scared of him after the strange episode on the knoll? Had she recognized him in his canine form?

He limped forward and she rushed into his arms.

"You look pale. Aren't you well?" he asked.

"I'm fine. But I was worried about you." She tilted her head back and he could see the tears that stained her cheeks.

"You were worried about me?" He paused. "How long have you been sitting here?"

"All night."

Guilt shot through him. What torment was he putting her through?

Wrapping his arm around her shoulder, Draven directed Isabella back to her chambers. Once he'd tucked her into bed, he drew the counterpane up and kissed her on the forehead.

"Draven, I was so concerned," she said again.

He sat beside her and clasped her hand. She had waited all night for him to return, but he couldn't tell her the truth about where he'd been.

"Why were you concerned?" he asked. "I couldn't sleep. I rode Lucifer until the weather turned foul. When I tried to turn him around, I fell off my horse."

Thank God I hid a set of clothes inside the stables.

"Then you didn't see it?" Isabella grasped the cuff of his waistcoat.

"See what?" Draven asked.

"The black wolf. It was watching me from outside my window."

"Are you certain?"

Her voice shook. "You were the one who warned me about it and it's real. And menacing. And diabolical looking."

"Were you frightened?"

"Yes, I thought it was going to crash through the window," she said. "Until—"

"Until what?"

"Until I looked into its eyes. You might think me silly, but the creature's eyes were human."

Draven bounced off the mattress and took a clip around the room. "That isn't possible."

"They were real," Isabella said. "And they were watching me."

He wrapped his hand around the back of his neck. He was desperate to tell her the truth, but the truth would frighten her beyond repair. "You cannot be certain."

"I am certain. That's why I was so worried when I couldn't find you."

She began to cry. It was the worst sound he'd ever heard.

"Shush now," he urged as he sat on the bed again. "You need to rest."

She dropped her head onto his thigh and snuggled against it. The contact warmed him. Her eyelids dropped and she sighed as he stroked the soft rise of her cheek.

"Isabella, can you hear me?" he asked.

"Mmm," she responded as her sniffling stopped.

"I'm sorry for hurting you on the knoll. I'm not myself lately."

"It doesn't matter," she said in a voice thick with sleepiness. "I could tell the wolf needed me. Just like you do."

Isabella slept until late the following morning, something she had never done before. After she dressed, she went to the spot where the wolf had fallen to the ground.

As she stood there, she remembered the creature's razor-sharp teeth and demonic posture. With ears that rose in points and winged away from its snout, the beast had looked ravenous enough to eat her alive—and forceful enough to crash right through the window and do just that.

Why didn't it attack me?

Oddly, it seemed that the creature had been trying to communicate with her. She could have sworn it tried to speak to her through the piteous expression in its eyes.

The thought jolted sympathy through her, as did Draven's disappearance last night. She was completely relieved when she saw him appear. What's more, Draven had been so gentle and patient with her last night. It was a side of him she'd never seen and she was surprised at how passionately she had responded to it. Their relationship was teetering on the edge of closeness, but she wanted to know all about the Gypsy's spell he had made reference to in his journal. How could she prod the information out of him without revealing that she knew his spell existed?

She must speak with Draven. Only then could she set herself on a path that might help him.

Isabella rubbed her arms against the chilly air and strode back inside the house. Her growling stomach directed her to the breakfast parlor. When she arrived at the table, she was disappointed to find no one but Helena present. Unfortunately, her mother-in-law had seen her so there was no chance of Isabella escaping back to her bedchamber unnoticed.

"Good morning." The countess dipped her chin in greeting.

"Good morning," Isabella said, still standing. To her surprise, she noticed a rare show of concern on the noblewoman's face. "Is something wrong?"

"Haven't you heard?" Helena replied. "The beast was sighted last night prowling the outskirts of Dunwich."

Isabella clutched the top of a chair. "Did the villagers destroy it?"

"No. Apparently they shot at it but they missed. I'm certain the entire village is terrified. I hope they catch and kill this monster," the dowager fretted. "It destroyed a stray cat and three cows from a neighboring farm."

Isabella swallowed an anxious lump. "It's too dangerous for my father to leave right now. I must warn him about going into town at nightfall. Have you seen him?"

"We spoke early this morning, before he left for Dunwich," Helena informed her.

"What did he say?"

"He intended to send correspondence to his old friend, Benjamin Rayburn."

Benjamin Rayburn. The name brought back fond memories for Isabella. Uncle Ben, as she had referred to him in her youth, worked as a solicitor in London. He had been more of an uncle to Isabella than her father's twin brother, Morton, ever was. It warmed her heart to know that the two men were corresponding.

An awkward silence lingered between herself and the countess. "Where is Draven?" Isabella asked.

At the mere mention of her son's name, Helena's face darkened. "How should I know? He's more mysterious than a night owl. He spends the majority of his day dreaming of shipbuilding and rarely addressing me."

Isabella pressed her lips together as Helena continued. "I know he's your husband, but he raises my blood pressure." The noblewoman dropped her fork onto her plate with a clatter. "He's careless and thoughtless and self-centered."

"Draven seems to have some redeeming qualities," Isabella offered.

"Redeeming qualities? Such as a smoldering arrogance you obviously find attractive?"

"That's not what I meant."

"Allow me to give you some womanly advice, my dear. A black cloud hovers over Draven. He will destroy all those who stand in his path." With that, Helena dabbed the corners of her mouth with her napkin and bid Isabella a curt good morning.

Astounded, Isabella sat alone in the room. The patter of rain drew her to the windows. She wiped the condensation away and peered out. Fog, brewed from the choppy sea, was rolling inland. She watched the rainfall for a few more moments before she gathered enough courage to begin her search for Draven. She was about to leave the room when Rogers emerged from a swinging door, muttering that Alice should be clearing the breakfast dishes instead of him.

"Rogers," she said, "would you be so kind as to tell me where his lordship is?"

The elderly man released the dishes onto the table with a clank. He turned to Isabella with a ghastly look " 'E's in 'is chambers, but Master Draven strictly forbids anyone to disturb 'im while 'e works, m'lady."

"Not to worry"—she smiled sweetly—"I'll knock first."

"I know it's not me place, but if I were ye, I'd not mention the journal ye came across yesterday."

She gave him another gentle smile without promising anything.

He shook his head and resumed his chore with a troubled look in his eye.

Rogers's words stayed with Isabella as she climbed the grand staircase. She raised her hand to knock on Draven's door but fear stopped her. Would her husband be infuriated if she interrupted him?

She turned to go when a voice inside her urged her not to be afraid anymore. Afraid of werewolves and her own husband. Afraid of never being loved and cherished as a wife. Afraid of never becoming a mother. She was here for answers about Draven's supposed curse and answers were what she would leave with.

She rapped on the door and waited for a response.

"Not now, Rogers!" a voice boomed.

"It's not Rogers," Isabella called.

A brief moment passed without any sound. She held her breath and opened the door. Draven was sitting at his desk. He shot her a disapproving look.

"Won't you come in," he said sarcastically.

She stepped into the private library that adjoined the main suite. Wondrous in its masculine appeal, the room boasted shelf after shelf of colorful, leather-bound books while exotic masks and intriguing artifacts Draven had collected from all over the world hung on the walls. And the space smelled entirely of him.

Draven leaned back in his chair at a desk that was situated before a blazing fireplace. Between the desk and the hearth lay a remarkable tiger skin, complete with bulging eyes and sharp yellow fangs. Isabella closed her eyes for a brief moment, envisioning the werewolf's dripping incisors.

She gulped the image away and squared her shoulders. "I've sought you out because you broke your promise. You didn't send word that you would miss breakfast."

Draven's nostrils flared. "I told my mother in passing this morning."

"Well, she didn't tell me." Secretly annoyed at his brooding manner, she clenched the fabric of her skirt.

"All alone with my mother at the breakfast table, eh?" he said. "I'd rather be trapped inside a mortuary."

"It wasn't as bad as that," Isabella said.

She struggled to study Draven's face at this distance. In the morning light, he appeared a bit more tired than usual, but his features still riveted her. She watched as he took in deep breaths through his arrow-straight nose and clenched his hardened jaw. And the intensity with which he stared at his paperwork was admirable.

Her knees began to tremble. She decided to make small talk so that she could muster up the bravery to ask about his curse. "Thank you for staying with me last night. I was truly frightened."

"You're welcome." He continued to stare at the papers that littered his desk.

Isabella took another glance around the room. Her eyes swept over the intriguing souvenirs that donned his mantel. "I see you like to read. And travel."

"Yes," he responded without looking up.

"Where have you been?" she asked.

"New Guinea, Europe, the Orient. I try to leave the confines of this godforsaken house at least twice a year. At the risk of sounding pompous, travel is why I'm drawn to the shipbuilding industry. Someday I would love to have my choice of vessel in which to further explore the world."

"You must go to Egypt," she implored.

"I've already been there." He penned something on the paper before him.

Her cheeks grew hot. Refusing to be dismissed so easily, she strode closer to his desk and peered at the diagram board he was hunched over. "What are you working on?"

He looked up at her. A hint of pleasure at her interest crossed his face. "Sketches of various vessels."

She smiled. "They're lovely, although designing a ship looks very complicated."

"It isn't really." He turned the sketch so she could get a better look at it. "You see, the building of a ship, whether it eventually meets its fate as a barge or a clipper or a fleet, can be divided into seven distinct phases: design, construction and planning, work prior to keel laying, ship erection, launching, final outfitting, and sea trials."

"You seem to know a great deal about the industry. Have you always been fascinated with ships?"

"Yes." Draven's eyes skimmed over her figure, making her pulse race. He put down his plume and continued on in a huskier tone. "And do you know why?"

"No."

"Sea vessels resemble the female sex in many ways, Isabella."

Her throat constricted at his provocative timbre. "H . . . how so?"

"First off," he said, "a ship is traditionally referred to as a 'she.' Secondly, the wave of the future will soon have shipbuilders replacing wooden hulls with stronger, iron ones—much like a woman's steely resolve contrasts with a man's fragile ego."

She felt her insides vibrate at the lovely analogy.

"And lastly—" Draven leaned forward with predatory eyes.

"Lastly?" she whispered as her lungs hitched.

"Never should a sea-worthy vessel be dry docked. Like a beautiful, young female, a ship must be continually submerged in something wet and slick. To ready its legs, so to speak."

She would have fainted on the spot if the sturdiness of the desk hadn't supported her weight. His lustful words trickled over her skin and raised the hair on her arms. She shivered.

"Are you cold?" he asked.

"I feel a draft," she lied.

"Then perhaps you wouldn't mind closing the door on your way out." His glance returned to his paperwork.

Defiance stiffened Isabella's posture. How dare Draven dangle sexual innuendos in front of her only to dismiss her as if she were a servant? Leaning forward, she raised her voice and said, "I'm not leaving until I get some answers about your Gypsy curse."

Chapter Sixteen

Draven's face flushed with anger as he circled the desk. He started across the room and Isabella's stomach roiled.

Is he going to walk out on me?

She watched as he closed the door with a resounding thud then turned to face her with eyes that flashed with defiance.

"I noticed that things had been rearranged in my dressing room," he said. "You were snooping."

Fear erupted inside her. She moved to him and clasped his hands. "I'm sorry for prying, but I want to help you. I . . . I found your journal." She took in a breath. "You must tell me about your curse."

Draven studied her intensely before releasing her hands. "God help me," he whispered. *"And God help you."*

Her heart drummed wildly.

"I would never hurt you, Isabella. If I have any control over the situation, that is."

She lifted her chin. "What if you don't have control?"

He took her by the elbow and urged her toward the flickering hearth. "You must hear me out. You've already discovered the curse's existence. Now you must know its details."

He guided her to the tiger-skin rug where they lowered themselves to the floor. As they sprawled out before the dancing fire, Draven began to speak in a voice deepened by emotion. "What I'm about to tell you is the story my father told Rogers. He, in turn, relayed it to me after my father died."

Continuing seemed extremely difficult for him. He cleared his throat and looked straight ahead.

"A band of Romanian Gypsies passed through this countryside many years ago. These Gypsies were heavy practitioners of black magic. By chance, my father encountered one of these vagabonds—a woman. She was a bewitching beauty, with long, dark curls and a stunning face. One night as my father rode into town on horseback, this beauty happened to run out into his path. So weakened was he by her allure that he began a brief love affair with her. Thus she became pregnant . . . with me."

Isabella's head spun. *Helena was not Draven's birth mother?* Now their icy relationship—and the fact that they looked nothing alike—made sense. She remained silent since he might not continue the story once he was interrupted.

"Days after she gave birth to me," Draven went on, "this Gypsy woman brought me here to Thorncliff Towers. I believe she truly loved my father because she begged him to divorce Helena and marry her instead. My father refused her pleas. However, Father's cold exterior melted when he saw me, a small babe. He agreed to take me in and raise me as a nobleman—with every aristocratic privilege and avenue of education. However, there was one stipulation to all of this: my birth mother needed to disappear from my life forever."

He took in a breath. "My father tried to give her a handsome sum to leave me here and vanish, but my birth mother turned down the bribe. Still, knowing that I would have a superior life here with my father, she left me at Thorncliff Towers. When she returned to her kinfolk dejected and discarded, her mother—my grandmother, as odd as it seems to say—was beyond angry. Perhaps that's why she returned to this countryside with her band sixteen years later. Maybe she wanted to punish me, the catalyst for her daughter's misery."

Draven pushed himself to his feet. He began to pace nervously while Isabella tried to ignore the alarm sweeping her spine. "On his deathbed, my father told me that I had Gypsy blood running through my veins. I rode into the woods in a dismal state and sought out the Gypsy camp I'd spotted the day before. Since Helena had taught me that vagabonds were filthy, low-class beggars, the fact that I was half-Gypsy made me explode with rage. I ordered the trespassing tribe to leave. A girl about my age informed me that two of the tribe's horses were sick and that they could travel no farther that night. My temper mounted. I ordered the Gypsies to go again. A boy asked what made me so much better than them. I saw red. I picked up a large rock and threw it his way. It was only meant to scare him. But"—Draven's voice quivered—"he ducked and the rock struck the girl in the head. She . . . died."

Isabella watched a fountain of tears flow down Draven's cheeks. Her heart ached. Guilt was a horrible thing.

"It wasn't your fault," she said softly. "It was an accident."

His features hardened. "That didn't matter to the girl."

She paused. "What happened next?"

"An old woman emerged from her wagon. To my surprise she knew who I was. She'd heard of my intolerance of her kind and of my continual efforts to run Gypsies off Winthrop property. After telling me that she was my grandmother, she cast a curse of penance upon me. You see, I'm doomed by a spell that can only be broken if I can change my selfish ways and gain compassion." He scowled. "Obviously that has been more difficult than I imagined. Regardless, since the spell was cast during a full moon, it's considered a *rauna* curse."

"What is a *rauna* curse?" she asked.

He hesitated.

"If you're wondering if you can trust me, I promise never to share this information with anyone," she assured him.

"A *rauna* curse is the most powerful black magic spell in existence," he finally said. "My grandmother predicted that one day a beast would surface within me and would continue to surface during every full moon thereafter. When it did, she prophesied, the beast would match the foul, inner nature I possess."

"You mean you become a monster in the metaphoric sense? An ill-tempered madman?" she asked.

"Y . . . yes." He looked dejected. "That's it."

Isabella squeezed Draven's hand. *This explains his violent streak and his irrational behavior.*

He squeezed her hand back. "The Gypsy also predicted that my curse will translate to any male heirs I might produce."

"So that is why you refuse to have children," she murmured softly.

"It's also the reason I was incensed at the idea of raising a bastard. I know the pain of being one all too well."

Isabella could swear she saw shame creep into his eyes. She shook her head. "My God, how could that woman cast a spell on her own grandson? It's so hard to believe."

"It's true nonetheless." He sat down, his shoulders forming a wall of tension. "My hex was realized on our wedding night."

Isabella's stomach contracted. "I didn't know—"

"I was a damned fool and married you in full denial of my curse."

"You were probably relieved when I left Thorncliff Towers," Isabella said.

"I was relieved, but I missed you terribly. That is why I sent someone after you."

"That hooligan scared me, I'll admit."

"I'm sorry, Isabella."

She began to pace. "There must be some way to reverse the spell."

"Only a member of the Gypsy tribe knows if there is a way," Draven said, his eyes full of tentative love.

"I'm so sorry for what you've been through in the past and for what you're going through now," she said. Moved by the torment she saw in his face, she put a hand to his cheek. "I'm glad you revealed all of this to me."

He caressed her hand. "Isabella, I wouldn't blame you if you were frightened away forever."

"I'm working on not being frightened so easily." She offered him a tremulous smile.

"You've been very brave. Brave enough to come back here. And brave enough to confront me."

She supposed she had been courageous after all.

"I'm glad you sought me out today," Draven said. "I was desperate to tell you but wise enough not to. You now have ammunition to divorce me."

"But what evidence is there of your illegal birthright?"

"None, I suppose."

"No one else knows but Rogers and Helena?" Isabella asked.

He stared into the fire. "No."

"That explains Helena's disdain for you."

"Helena knows I killed someone in the Gypsy camp that night. But she is unaware of my curse."

"There, you see," she said with certainty. "Your birthright will remain our secret."

He fixed his pain-laced eyes on her. Before he spoke again, he took her hand. "Isabella, I have another confession to make. Your beautiful spirit seized me when we met, as did your loyalty to your father. Those admirable qualities inspired me to propose to you and I've come to care about you very much. But I had another reason to pursue you."

"What reason was that?" she asked.

Draven broke eye contact. "I knew about the curse that haunts your amulet. I read about it in the newspaper during a trip to London. Beneath that curse, you are destined to kill the man you love. So that is my hope."

"Your hope?"

"I want you to kill me."

Under normal circumstances, Isabella would have been outraged at the admission of Draven's ulterior motive. He had deceived her. But what mattered in the moment was that he was confessing everything to her. He was also baring his soul and she knew he wouldn't be allowing her in unless he loved her.

She drew back. "I've told you: I don't believe in the curse surrounding my amulet."

"You should." He scowled. "Look at me, a testament to the powers of black magic."

"There must be something else I can do," she said.

His face twisted with intensity as he took her by the shoulders. "You can do nothing but stop this madness."

Isabella recoiled. "I could never kill you!"

"But you are the one I've come to count upon."

"Why haven't you asked Rogers—or Helena for that matter?"

A lock of hair spilled over Draven's winged brow. "Rogers is a loyal servant 'til the end. But this he would never do. And Helena . . . if she knew about my curse, she'd only have me suffer more by returning me to the asylum."

"Draven, you are married to me now. Helena no longer has a say in such decisions."

He paused and stared into the fire. "While we are on the subject of my demise, I want you to know that I tried to end my own life. Bloody knife went in and out of my heart, but my skin healed instantaneously."

The torment her husband continued to suffer constricted Isabella's lungs. He wasn't a fearsome, loathsome creature after all and the thought filled her with emotion as she tipped her forehead into the warm fabric of his waistcoat. In return, he wrapped his arms around her.

"We mustn't think of ourselves," he said. "We cannot chance that I might murder again. I couldn't bear it. Remorse over what happened in the woods put me in that blasted asylum. I sunk into a black hole of melancholia for months. The worst part was I couldn't tell anyone about the guilt that maddened me. You see, Helena saw to it that no one ever learned what happened in the Gypsy camp."

"You let her sweep things under the rug?" Isabella asked.

"It was the only way for me to step into my father's shoes. Taking over the earldom was something he expected. I wanted to honor my father's memory. I was young and I thought it was the right thing to do."

She remained silent.

He took her hands. "I need you to end this nightmare for me, Isabella. It's your destiny."

"Stop saying that." She shook her head vehemently. "Besides, the attempt you made on your life didn't work."

"I will have you use something more effective than a knife."

"No. There must be another way out of this. We need to find your grandmother and convince her to rectify the curse. She simply must undo it!"

"How will we track down a band of Gypsies . . . people who are, by nature, nomads?" Draven dropped her hands in frustration. "God only knows if the old woman is still alive."

"Is there any way to find this Gypsy tribe?"

Isabella could see Draven's veins pump with aggravation.

"Perhaps someone in the village knows of their location," she suggested.

"I doubt it."

"Then perhaps some sort of physician or specialist can be of help."

Again, Draven thrust an agonized look her way. "I told you. I've consulted specialists from the Americas to Salzburg to Paris. There is no magic potion or tonic."

She took his face in her hands. "If there exists a way to reverse this horrible situation, I promise we'll find it. Together."

Torment deepened the lines around his mouth. "If we are going to do that we'd better hurry. Your presence here is fueling my madness."

"What do you mean?"

"All I can tell you is that something about you affects my demeanor. And I might lose complete control of myself very soon."

She released his face and gripped his arm.

"You realize you have every right to seek an annulment considering that I wed you under false grounds," he said in a solemn timbre.

"I don't want to seek an annulment. I want to help you."

He touched a curl that dangled over her ear. "But this overshadows our marriage with humiliation. While I am my father's biological son, my blood is not purely noble. I was born a shameful, half-Gypsy bastard. And according to canon and common law, bastards receive no inheritance because they can never be heir unto any man. If my illegitimate beginnings were ever exposed, I'd be stripped of my title and you would have nothing."

"Your well-being is more important."

"It is?" Hope crested in his eyes.

"Draven, I may have been in dire straits when I married you, but something besides that drew me to you from the very start. Why do you think I was so devastated when you refused to start a family with me?"

"I'm sorry I hurt you, Isabella. Your trust means everything to me."

"You *can* trust me. I will never give away your secret," she whispered.

Draven sat transfixed, as if he were pondering something. Then, very slowly, he ran his thumb across her mouth.

Chapter Seventeen

Draven's touch caused a yielding sensation at the apex of Isabella's legs. She closed her eyes, inhaling the delicate contact. To her, he was like an oasis in the middle of a parched desert—a cavern of delight that contained all of her extreme desires. Since the moment she met him, she had been trapped in a place that ached and pined for his affection. And now she was willing to fight for his devotion. Perhaps even his love.

Would Draven ever show her his feelings through intimacy? He'd written in his journal that he planned to make love to her. Would he right now?

Isabella's breath caught. She flicked her eyes open only to be hypnotized by the orange flames reflected in the black gloss of his eyes. He lowered his mouth to hers, covering it completely. When she rose up to meet his kiss, the feel of his soft lips caused her body to convulse with excitement. Now that their history had been rectified and their passion had exploded into the open, being this close to him felt magical. For the first time since they married, she felt like Draven's wife.

He slipped his tongue into her mouth with a gentle ease and Isabella let her head arch back in surrender. She sucked in a breath while he unclasped the front of her dress and stole a hand beneath the silk of her bodice. He stroked her breast languidly, like one would stroke a luxurious cat, and a low moan escaped Isabella's lips. As his half-hidden hand squeezed and teased the tip of her nipple to an erect charge, she heaved against it to magnify the contact.

Draven urged her to the ground and rolled on top of her. "My Bella. You are the only good thing in my life. I want to make love to you."

Her heart caught. *Could this be happening?*

Draven feathered his tongue over her ear and plucked her stays open with deftness. "I want to see your shining hair and your bare breasts. I want to see all of you."

If only for a moment, Draven's mind-altering touch erased the threat of his instability. He nuzzled the sensitive skin between Isabella's neck and shoulder and she nearly cried out at the wetness the sensation fueled between her legs. Never before had a man caused such a reaction in her. Draven made all of her senses collide into a maelstrom of desire and she refused to repress her attraction to him anymore.

His fingertips searched beneath the hem of her dress until they found the juncture between her thighs. He massaged the soft petals of her core while delight danced through her body. And when he yanked away her dress, bodice, pantalets, and chemise, Isabella felt drunk, completely seduced by his sexuality—as if she had no control over her actions. Before she knew it, she was lying nude and vulnerable before him.

She had planned on seducing him, but this was much better.

Draven's eyes rolled over her body with admiration. "Holy Christ, you're beautiful." When he noticed she was shivering he said, "Allow my body to keep you warm."

He stood and peeled his clothes away one button at a time. At first, it seemed like an erotic dance Isabella was too embarrassed to witness. Then she became captivated by each body part that became enticingly revealed.

Draven flung his shirt to the floor. Her eyes widened at the sight of his muscular chest and his solid, taut arms. His undergarments floated away next, exposing a chiseled torso and sinewy legs. And when his cock stood out from a patch of coarse, black hair, Isabella couldn't help but gasp at its size.

In a fluid motion, Draven swooped down and lay beside her. He covered her with his body and her heart pumped as she struggled for air under his weight.

Will we finally consummate our marriage?

She quivered with excitement as his hand closed over her breast. He kissed her again and she slithered her fingers into the waves of his dark hair. As Draven's tongue found the hardened pebble of her nipple, he tasted it, nearly devoured it—and she couldn't have been happier. She could feel his manhood standing erect against her, its veins bulging and engorged. He kissed her face in a round of tiny pecks while she shifted her breasts closer so that he could tweak her other nipple. When he was done inciting the peach nub into a dark hill, he took her hand and guided it to his shaft. She heard Draven's breathing grow guttural in her ear and felt his body harden like wood as he lay on top of her. She stole a look in his eyes. They were glowing a mysterious shade of red. Alarmed, she gulped against the words that raced through her head.

Her panic was interrupted by a sudden rapping at the door. Draven jerked his head up.

"Who is it?" he thundered.

"It's Rogers, sir. I'm sorry to interrupt yer work, but it's yer mother."

"My mother?"

"Yes, sir. Her ladyship has been taken very ill. She's in her bedchamber and is askin' for ye."

"Yes . . . yes, of course. I'll be right there."

Isabella's heart plummeted. If she didn't know better, she would have thought Helena had planned the interruption.

Draven gave her a quick, but gentle kiss and rose to his feet. He offered her his hand. "We shall go together."

Gathering her discarded clothing, she shook her head. "Hurry and attend to Helena. I shall be along shortly."

He dressed quickly, without making a sound. "We shall continue this later, my beauty."

She shot him a sheepish look before he planted another kiss on her lips. As Draven rushed out the door, Isabella's cheeks flamed.

They'd shared a pivotal moment to be sure. A few minutes more and she would have gotten Draven to shatter the vow he'd made to deny her intimacy, bringing her one step closer to getting pregnant.

Was she crazy to think this progress outweighed the discovery that her husband became violent beneath every full moon?

Chapter Eighteen

Isabella made her way to Helena's bedchamber. Muffled voices filtered through the door, but she couldn't make out what was being said. She rapped lightly and waited. It was the countess's lady maid, Alice, who let her in.

Isabella nodded her appreciation to the young girl then neared Helena's bed. Her mother-in-law lay amid a sea of pillows, pale and still while the physician who'd been summoned spoke with Draven in the corner of the room. Isabella studied the two men as they talked. She found the doctor's serious expression daunting and wondered if Draven felt the same. He spotted her and motioned for her to join them.

"I believe your mother will be fine, Lord Winthrop," Dr. Lamstein said after sketching a respectful bow in Isabella's direction. "What she needs now is plenty of rest. Whatever it was that caused her sudden illness has taken a tremendous toll on her body. Hence, she'll be very weak for a few days. Please keep her in bed and give her plenty of tea and salts."

Draven dragged his fingers through his hair. "What could have made my mother so sick? Something she ate?"

Dr. Lamstein's gray eyes flickered with doubt. "It's difficult to say, but in my professional opinion it was something more than spoiled food. Her ill state evolved much too quickly and violently and the pallor of her skin is suspect. My assumption is that someone tried to poison your mother, my lord."

The color drained from Draven's face. "She was . . . poisoned?"

"As unlikely as it may seem, yes," the doctor replied as he packed his equipment into a black, leather bag. "Does this house have a still room?"

"Yes," Draven said. "In the cellar."

"Then strychnine is my guess. It's a poison distilled from plants. And it is quite easy to make this compound in one's home."

Isabella knew that Draven hated his stepmother with a passion, but did he despise her enough to want her dead? She dug her nails into his arm.

"The countess is lucky to be alive," Lamstein informed them. "If she continues to reject all the food you try to give her, we may have to leech her to release all the poison from her bloodstream."

Draven escorted the doctor out while Isabella's nerves sped. When he reappeared, he instructed Mrs. Eaton, who had entered the room, to stay with his mother. Then he took Isabella by the hand and led her into the hallway where he drew her close.

Heaving out a breath, she stepped away from him with a frown. "Who could be responsible for this and why?"

"The love loss between my mother and me is no secret. But if I wanted her dead, I would have done away with her long ago."

"That's a terrible thing to say!"

"Come now, Isabella. From the look on your face, you are wondering if I'm responsible."

Confused, she said nothing. He hovered over her, such an enormous man and so utterly complex.

"I need to know that you believe me," he said. "I have no other allies in this place."

Leaning her face close to his crisp white shirt, she inhaled his scent for strength. He had placed his trust in her moments ago and now she must try and do the same. "I do."

"Good." His voice was firm. "I plan to investigate my stepmother's poisoning and leave no stone unturned."

"I can't imagine any member of the household staff having any real motive to poison Helena." Isabella bit her bottom lip. "Besides, she and I ate the same things for breakfast this morning."

"Thank God you aren't sick," Draven said. He glanced about to make certain they were alone. "I'll say it once more. I despise Helena, it's true. But I would never try to murder her."

She nodded slowly. Murder was such a heinous act. The thought glazed over her, numbing her like a layer of ice. She raised her tear-rimmed eyes to his.

"Why aren't you showing more signs that you believe me?" he asked with a scowl.

Her dry throat blocked any reassuring words she should have said. All she could think of was that there had been a full moon last night. . . .

"You're known as the Earl of Madness," she finally said. "A man who committed murder in the past."

"And you believe the pathetic gossip that claims I am mad?"

"No. I—"

Draven's hands clenched at his sides. He pressed his lips together until the color drained from them. He stalked away and Isabella's heart dropped. Had they just severed the only signs of closeness they'd ever shared?

Chapter Nineteen

The afternoon hours stretched into evening, with the majority of the servants splitting their time between chores and sitting with Helena. Isabella offered to watch over Draven's mother for a few hours so Mrs. Eaton could prepare some meals. When the housekeeper returned, Isabella decided to confine herself to her room.

A knock sounded on the door as she dined in front of the fireplace. She secured a wrapper and when she discovered it was her father, she let him in. He wrapped his arms around her and the feel of his cold cheek stirred memories of her childhood.

"Mrs. Eaton told me what happened to Helena," he said. "Why on earth would anyone want to poison her?"

She motioned him toward the fire. "I've been pondering it for most of the day. Helena can be disagreeable, but I can't imagine someone hating her enough to want her dead."

Her father shook his head as he sat down. "Poison! Such a ghastly, coldhearted act."

Isabella knelt beside him. She longed to tell him everything yet she couldn't. If she revealed the countess as Draven's stepmother she was sure her father would seek legal recourse to end her marriage on the charge that Draven was born a bastard. "I feel it's my duty to help solve this mystery," she finally said.

Her father paused. "Isa, I didn't believe in the rumors of your husband's madness before you two married. But now I'm reconsidering. Maybe coming back here was a grave mistake."

She twisted her hands together in her lap. She made a promise to stand beside Draven and she wouldn't abandon him again. "What are you saying?"

He leaned forward with a frown. "I'm saying Draven may be dangerous. If he ever harmed you—"

She drew back.

Harris stared into the fire with the strangest of looks. "There is something decidedly malicious about your husband. Maybe he's the one who tried to poison Helena."

Isabella gasped. *He's not evil. He's under a curse.*

Her father rose and cupped his hand to her face. He studied the look on her face before he spoke again. "I'm sorry, my dear. I can see that you truly have feelings for your husband. Of course I want you to be happy together. I just wish you didn't have to rely on Draven for money."

The thought made her feel dirty. She winced. "We both know that working is impossible for you until your memory is restored."

Harris nodded. "And we both know that you returned to Draven in order to help me, and for that I can never thank you enough. But you deserve to be happy, Isabella. We will clear your husband of this poisoning business, don't you worry."

"I know he didn't do it."

"If Draven isn't behind all this, we'll prove it." He pressed a hand against his forehead and slumped to the side.

Alarm swept through Isabella. "Are you all right?"

"Damn these headaches!"

"Maybe you should go lie down," she said.

He said he would. "You look tired as well. Will you go to bed soon?"

She told him she would but she doubted she'd be able to sleep.

The afternoon air felt crisp on Draven's face as he trudged into the woods. He needed to escape the stuffy atmosphere—and the suspecting glances—darting around Thorncliff Towers.

He released his queue and slipped off his silk cravat. More and more, he had the urge to roam free in the outdoors. The fresh air cleared his mind and heightened his senses. He could hear the caws of remote birds and spot the needles of tree branches in the distance. *And the scent of blood.* He smelled it everywhere. In every nearby creature and in every person who crossed his path.

But in no one did he smell it more than in Isabella. Her metallic scent tempted him like a starving boy in a sweet shop. She made his pulse quicken and his loins react. But the way he responded to her was dangerous and the worst part was, she had no idea of the effect she had over him.

Glowering, Draven made his way through a maze of trees. Isabella assumed his curse turned him into a monster in the allegorical sense. And maintaining that assumption, he thought, was best. He had been a fool during the last full moon when he'd watched her through the window. She had realized the beast's eyes were human.

Thank God she hadn't deemed them more familiar than that.

Brushing aside a tree branch, Draven stepped into the clearing in the woods where the Szgamy Gypsies had made their camp all those years ago. His stomach surged and he closed his eyes as the night he killed that innocent girl replayed in his head. He heard the crack of the rock as it hit her head and he saw her dark hair fall over her face as she crashed to the ground. Bile rose in his throat at the memory.

Now Isabella knew he was a murderer. Had he been wise in telling her everything? He wanted to believe that she would never use the information against him. What's more, he desperately needed an ally, someone to support him in light of Helena's poisoning incident. He was innocent, but it was obvious that Isabella doubted him.

He turned away from the conjured scene. Breaking into a sprint, he raced through the forest, desperate to be free of his past, yearning to escape the guilt and the torment it brought. Perspiration beaded his forehead. As he pounded over twisted vines and clusters of foxglove, he realized he was running faster than he'd ever moved before.

The idea of Isabella's creamy neck pounded his thoughts.

Tonight there would be no full moon. Should he seek her out?

Isabella couldn't sleep. The clock struck midnight and she rolled over with a groan. Disturbed by her last conversation with Draven, she crawled out of bed and paced the length of her room. She hadn't meant to belie her suspicions that he'd poisoned Helena, but she had always been a poor liar.

Deciding that she needed some fresh air, she resolved to go for a walk. She layered a shawl under her wool overcoat and scurried into the damp, cold night. To her surprise, she encountered Draven sitting in the garden. His slick hair glistened in rich, black waves and brushed the top of his collar. The sight of him sped Isabella's heart.

She debated returning to the house before he saw her. But he turned in her direction and his mouth broadened into a charming smile. She sucked in a breath.

"Isabella," he said, standing.

She came closer. He reached out and grasped her hands.

"I couldn't sleep," he whispered.

"Neither could I." She cast her eyes downward. "Draven, I'm sorry I suspected you. I thought about it and you couldn't have slipped poison into Helena's food or drink. You were in your suites all morning."

He smiled ruefully. "If I were you, I would have suspected me too."

Relief washed over her. She sat beside him on the stone bench.

"How is Helena doing?" he asked.

"She was sleeping soundly when I left her. The herbal elixir is bringing back the color in her face."

"Is she keeping her food down?"

"Yes."

"That's good news." He exhaled deeply and gazed up at the night sky. "It seems likely that she will recover."

Isabella faced him. "Draven, I spoke to my father this afternoon."

"Does he know about my mother being poisoned?"

"Yes." She paused. "He thought you may be responsible for the attempt on Helena's life."

Draven showed no signs of surprise or anger. "I know my name will remain on the top of the suspect list until the real perpetrator is caught."

Isabella's shoulders sagged.

They sat in silence. The moon peeked out on occasion from behind a shroud of billowing clouds. Draven looked up at the stars and Isabella followed his gaze.

"I've always had a fascination with the moon," he said as his breath lingered in the air. "Scholars claim that we never see more than one side of it."

Intrigued, Isabella tilted her head. "Is that true?"

"We're able to see only the side of the moon upon which the sun shines."

She made an ominous face. "And what do you suppose lurks on the dark side?"

Draven's brows gathered together. "Something dangerous. Perhaps something evil."

Isabella shuddered. She didn't want to think that something as beautiful as a full moon could turn a man into a monster. Especially not the man she was falling in love with.

He rubbed her icy hand with his surprisingly warm one.

"Please," she said as tears sprang to her eyes, "let's not speak of anything sinister."

Draven wiped away her tears with the pad of his thumb. His touch shot excitement to every inch of her body. She was still frightened of him, but not frightened enough to resist her gravitation toward him. He looked so handsome bathed in the glow of the moon. The ivory light exaggerated his dark eyes and complemented the olive tone of his skin.

She, in return, actually felt beautiful under the sincerity of his gaze. Ignoring the caution that coiled in her chest, she decided to let emotions drive her actions.

Would Draven continue what they'd started in his bedchamber?

To her delight, he leaned in for a kiss. She moved against him. As he slid his hand up the length of her arm, her senses began to whirl. And when he reached inside her heavy coat and deepened the kiss, she moaned. Gently, his fingers traced the straps of her nightgown beneath the heavy material. Then they dropped to the lace trim of her bodice to pull her breasts free of the material. Isabella sucked in a breath. Draven drew away with a dark stare to watch her alabaster mounds swell in the pale moonlight. As he fondled them hungrily, his passion for her became apparent. Shifting forward, he dipped a hand beneath her nightgown and inched his fingers inside her pantalets.

While he flicked her clitoris, he ran the tip of his tongue along her neck. Hot moisture surged between Isabella's legs. When he claimed her mouth again, she groaned deep and low.

"You will be mine tonight," he murmured against her lips.

Isabella's blood heated as Draven pulled her to her feet. The feel of his brandy-scented breath floating across her face made her heart pump as fast as a hummingbird's wings.

They stood face-to-face, a mere centimeter of air separating their lips. She felt like screaming aloud for she hungered for the feel of his mouth on hers again. As if he, too, could no longer stand the restraint, Draven burst forward for a kiss more passionate, more deliberate, and more flamingly tender than any he had bestowed on her.

"I have a confession to make," he said, breaking contact. "From the minute I laid eyes on you, I've been waiting to make love to you."

"Then make love to me now," she said breathlessly.

Draven replaced her coat and led her into the house. When they reached the door of his suite, he carried her across the threshold. But this time he didn't drop her to her feet right away—as he had on their wedding night. This time he cradled her in his arms and lavished her with scalding kisses. When he set her down, Draven began to take away her clothing in quick motions. Once Isabella was stripped of every item, firelight flicked her curved shadow against the wall.

Gasping at the sight of her nude before him, Draven scooped her into his arms again and marched through his private library to the bedchamber. When he reached the bed, he kissed her deeply then spread her over the sheets as if she were the silkiest of ribbons. He kept eye contact with her as he disrobed, his stare caressing her body.

When he joined Isabella on the bed, the feel of his nakedness shot a thrill through her.

"Let me do everything to you, my beauty," Draven said. Rolling toward her, he stroked the line of her jaw. "I'll start by tasting your breasts."

Deciding to trust his lead, Isabella demurred and nestled her head against the pillow. Draven's full lips dipped across her mouth and chest, causing her legs to tremble. After flashing a devilish grin, he shifted his lips to her erect nipples. His tongue lapped the pearly buds and sounds of her pleasure bounced between a groan and a pathetic whimper. He seemed to enjoy sucking her breasts into hard points because he drew back every once in a while to admire them.

While Draven feasted, his hand drifted across her stomach to the curve of her hip. He traced its hollow shape before caressing lower to the titian hair between her thighs. His sex bobbed in hot beats against her as his fingers petted her silky mound. Another passionate kiss released more of the fire they had both repressed. And when his fingers found their way inside the folds of Isabella's core, desire exploded through her like a leaping flame.

"Your skin feels like velvet," he rasped.

Isabella clenched the sheets as his experienced fingers explored her sweet, slick sheath. It was uncanny how he knew precisely where to touch her. Tease her. Arouse her—until her wetness flowed like warm honey. Writhing under his hand, her hips danced to the constant rhythm he'd built up by massaging her raised nub. Isabella's eyes fluttered shut as he brought her to a climax.

"My God," she moaned. She never knew that physical intimacy could be so magical, and so incredibly fulfilling.

"Now I can take you," he said. "Open your beautiful eyes, my sweet. They make me hard."

Lust heated her again as Draven reached for her hand and directed it to his erection. His shaft was smooth and thick and moist all at the same time. Her eyes widened at the foreign feel of it in her hand.

"Stroke me," he murmured into her hair.

"Like this?" she asked.

"Oh, yes," Draven groaned.

His cock grew to a new length. Draven's obsidian eyes simmered with readiness as he removed her hand from it and replaced it with his own. Raising himself up on his elbows, he used his knees to spread Isabella's thighs wider. Then, driving the tip of his penis forward with his hand, he rubbed it against the damp folds of her core. He remained outside of her for a moment, taunting and caressing and stroking her until moisture trickled down her legs in urgent streams.

She buried her fingernails into his back. When she could stand it no longer she cried, "Please, Draven. Make love to me!"

He shifted his massive body on top of hers again. Isabella's pulse skittered as he supported his weight by one hand and parted her center with his manhood. She snaked her hands around his neck. Pinching her eyes shut, she knew this was the moment of no return.

Will I get what I want . . . a precious baby?

The tip of his bare shaft began to penetrate her but Draven's body began to tremor and he stopped in midmotion. Isabella glanced up. She thought she saw his dark eyes flash an unearthly shade of red, but she couldn't be sure. As he avoided her stare, she knew what he must be thinking. He couldn't risk impregnating her.

"You drive me to lose my senses. But I must stop," he breathed. "I cannot fill you with my tainted seed."

Her cry of disappointment was muffled against his chest. She was aching with desire, inflamed with the knowledge that he was inches away from showing her how much he wanted her.

"I am being a selfish cad, putting you in this situation," Draven said in a rough voice. "It isn't fair to you."

As she listened to his heart beating wildly, Isabella began to cry. That's where he was wrong. He was being unfair by denying her.

Finding it impossible to dispel the emotion that stirred her soul, she lifted her lips to his ear. "If it makes any difference, I care for you deeply."

Draven reared up like a horse who'd been cruelly provoked. To Isabella's horror, his face convulsed with anger. "You can't fathom the torture I've been through—and I don't deserve your affections!" he thundered.

He whipped a hand into the air. Slashing downward, his fingernails missed her face and arm by inches. She screeched.

When he realized what he'd done, he drew back. "My God, Isabella. I didn't mean to frighten you!"

She didn't want to hear it. *What had come over him?*

Pushing him away, she gathered her clothing and escaped from the room.

Draven flew to the doorway behind her. "Isabella!"

Damn it to hell!

The beast lurking within him was starting to emerge without a full moon—and that beast was far from a metaphoric monster.

He'd been smart enough to stop before he made love to Isabella. But the scent of her blood had been too much for him to bear. He was losing control. Her smell was as sweet and as addicting as a fine wine and it had triggered a hellish wrath.

Soon there would be no difference between Draven the man and Draven the animal.

His Gypsy hex was punishment for the arrogant behavior he had displayed in his youth. And though he was trying to better himself from the egotistical boy he had been, his actions tonight proved he couldn't.

The only pure thing in his life was Isabella. Had he pushed her away forever? He hoped not. He would rather die than be without her.

He stumbled to the mirror where his disdainful reflection stared back. His hair, matted and damp, and his expression, gnarled and ugly, lent him an alarming look. Loathing the person he saw, he drove his fist through the framed looking-glass. Shivers of broken glass rippled outward while he let out a primal scream.

The chilling bay belonged to the beast within him and he didn't give a damn who in the house heard it.

Chapter Twenty

An animal's howl pierced the air as Isabella groped her way back to her suites. It sounded as if it came from inside the house, but how was that possible?

Blinded by her tears, she managed to enter her bedchamber and press her back against the door. Draven's hatred-filled face flashed in her mind. Why had her profession of love spawned such anger?

His disposition was either gentle or violent and there seemed to be no gray space in between.

Heartbroken that Draven had refused her so violently, Isabella thrust herself on the bed. She buried her face in the pillow and sobbed until she fell asleep.

When she awoke the next morning, her face was puffy and tender. Weakened by the horror of the previous evening, she decided that she wouldn't get out of bed today. There was nothing left for her in this horrible place. No husband in the traditional sense. No affection from her mother-in-law. And no freedom to leave it.

Frowning, she tucked the edge of her pillow beneath her elbow and reached idly for the amulet around her neck. It was gone!

Flying upright, she searched the bed-sheets to no avail. Panic replaced Isabella's lethargy and she bolted out of bed. Could Draven have swatted it off with his frenzied swing? She scoured the hallways and every inch of her room, but the amulet was nowhere to be found.

Despair seized her. Either someone had picked up the necklace—or it was in Draven's bedchamber.

A knock at the door broke her train of thought.

"Isabella, please open the door. It's me."

Draven. Her heart pounded painfully against her ribs. "Go away!"

"Hear me out."

"I don't want to see you."

"Please, Isabella. Open the door."

The sound of his voice churned resentment inside of her like acid. "Why? So you can attack me the way you did last night?"

"No. Please listen. What I did last night is deplorable. Inexcusable! But you must understand it was something I had no control over. That is why you must let me in. I need you to do something for me."

"You want to ask *me* for a favor? This is preposterous. For all I know you ripped my amulet off my neck last night just before you slashed the bed-sheets."

"But you had the amulet on when you ran from my room, Isabella," he protested through the door.

If Draven was telling the truth, it would mean that either it fell off in the hallway or somebody came into her chambers and stole the amulet while she had slept. But who would do such a thing? Could it be the same person who wanted Helena dead?

"Isabella, please. I have to talk to you."

She remained motionless, unsure what to do. Could she trust Draven? Did she want to?

"Very well," Draven continued. "I'll discuss this through the door if I must. I'll admit that I'm unpredictable and marred."

"You're worse than that. You're a monster."

"Isabella, you must understand how powerful this curse is. I'm beginning to lose control of my reasonable self. Believe me when I say you are the last person I want to hurt."

Tears blurred Isabella's eyes despite her efforts to fight them back. Her heart was battling her common sense. The war brought her to the conclusion that it was a curse in and of itself to be afraid of the person one cared about.

Yet she had promised Draven that she would help him . . .

Against her better judgment, she stepped to the door. "Why should I believe anything you say?"

"Because remorse is eating away at me."

"Last night's episode did irreversible damage, Draven," she said softly. "You managed to avoid breaking open my skin, but you broke my heart."

He began to pound on the door. "I beg you! Let me in, Isabella. I have to see you."

Her hands trembled. As if she were being willed by an unknown force, she flipped over the latch. Draven entered the room. His eyes were wildly dark, as if he hadn't slept at all.

He raised his hand and waved it in her direction. "After you fled my quarters last night, I put my fist through the mirror in agony. But now the injury has completely healed. Isabella, mysterious—even dangerous—forces are at work here."

Struggling to keep her emotions in check, Isabella closed the door behind him. She walked briskly to the other side of the room and sat in front of the fire. Draven followed. He bent down on one, quaking knee and took her hand.

"I'll understand if you never want to see me again. And the fact that you're frightened of me sickens me to the bone. But I need you by my side more than ever. I need you to help me."

There was that plea for help again!

Isabella snatched her hand from his hold. "Draven," she said, "I came back to this dreary place in good faith. I was hopeful that we could come to at least respect one another in this marriage and start a family. But I'm not sure I can go on anymore—"

Draven reached for her hand again. He flattened her open palm against his unshaven cheek. "God knows how much it would kill me to be without you," he admitted. "But it seems that an inexplicable force keeps drawing us together under a cloud of doom. It's your amulet, Isabella. Listen to me. My curse prevents us from ever being together in any normal sense of the word. And your curse dooms you to destroy me. Our paths are condemned."

Nausea clenched her stomach.

"Don't you see," he said. "What I face upon the rising of every full moon is unbearable. Even if it was an accident, I've killed before. If I commit murder again, I will go mad again with guilt. You must put an end to my agony, my Bella. You must put an end to *me*."

She jerked her hand away and rose to pace in front of the hearth. "I told you I can't help you."

Draven stood and withdrew a tiny pistol with an intricate, mother-of-pearl handle from the pocket of his dressing robe. He placed the pistol in her hand.

Looking at him with a mixture of pity and terror, she shook her head.

"This pistol contains one silver bullet," he informed her. "Silver contains lunar properties that can stop the monster I become. Do it, Isabella. Do it right this instant. Put me out of my misery. Stop me from hurting you or another human being ever again. *It is your destiny!*"

Isabella's fingers shook beneath the pistol's cold metal. She threaded her index finger through the trigger hole and held the weapon out in front of her. Not only did she want to kill him after how he had acted last night, perhaps that was the only answer. If what Draven said were true, it was the only viable way to prevent a killing spree. Isabella knew all too well that he was mentally unstable and violent.

But there must be an alternate way. Like Draven, she could never live with herself knowing she had committed murder.

She flung the gun across the room and collapsed to the floor. "Take your pistol and get out!"

Draven retrieved the pistol from its spot on the rug. He turned to face her with a grave expression while she buried her face in her hands.

She heard him move to the doorway, but he paused before he exited the room. "Isabella, if you won't put a stop to the hell-bent monster I become every full moon, then may God help us both. The blood of all future victims will be on your hands as well as mine."

"Just go," she screamed.

After he left, she slumped into a chair by the rain-streaked window. Minutes stretched into miserable hours as Draven's ominous words hung in the air. They convinced her that if she could turn back the hands of time, she would never have come again to this terrible place.

Chapter Twenty-One

Still nestled in the armchair, Isabella developed a pounding headache. She rose and ate all the scones from the tray Gwyneth had brought her, but her hunger pangs—and her colossal headache—told her that she needed to eat more. After she had supper, she would search for her amulet then prepare to leave Thorncliff Towers for good.

The Elgin clock on her bedside table read six o'clock. She could have Gwyneth bring her supper on a tray, but she decided against it. If she spent another minute alone in her suites she would surely go mad. She padded to the dry sink and filled the basin's saucer from its pitcher. After splashing a handful of water over her face, she rang for Gwyneth's assistance in getting dressed.

The girl arrived in no time and helped Isabella into a dress of primrose yellow embroidered with braids of garnet-colored silk. It was one of the many stunning dresses Draven had given her. Her heart dropped.

As she made her way to the dining hall, a sense of nervousness spiraled up her spine. She wondered what she'd actually say to her husband when she saw him.

Entering the room, Isabella was relieved that there was no sign of her husband. Would her father appear? She wanted to tell him that her amulet was missing. While he helped her find it, she would also let him know that she was going to take his advice and leave Thorncliff Towers for good. But it seemed that their conversation would have to wait.

Nerves humming, she sat down at the table. Rogers appeared carrying a glass of merlot. She had planned on eating downstairs, but now she was in no mood to do so without her father. She asked the manservant to send a tray to her room.

Leaving the dining hall, she crossed the foyer. To Isabella's surprise and relief, her father came hobbling toward her on his cane. He planted a kiss on the top of her head.

"Good evening, darling."

"Papa, I hoped you'd be downstairs."

Harris frowned. "Where have you been all day?"

"In my room."

"You look tired. Don't you feel well, Isabella?"

"I'm fine," she lied.

"Have you been crying?"

She looked away. She couldn't tell her father about the violent episode in Draven's bed last night. Nor could she tell him of his insane pleas to end his life. But she was going to tell him about her missing amulet.

"Papa?"

"Hmm?" He seemed distracted, just as he'd been in her room yesterday.

"You're right. I *have* been crying because the amulet you gave me is missing."

"Missing?" her father said.

"I've looked all over for it, but it's gone."

"What happened?" Alarm rose in his voice.

"I know it sounds extraordinary—and I would never accuse the staff openly—but I presume someone stole into my bedroom while I was sleeping and took it."

"What would provoke someone to do that?" he asked. "We both know the amulet isn't of immense value since I never unearthed the bracelet of Amenhotep."

A blush heated Isabella's cheeks. "Few people in this region know of the necklace's history."

"True." Harris paused. "Are you absolutely sure you had it on when you went to bed?"

Visions of Draven's violent swing made her shudder. "I'm not sure."

"Did you search your bedroom?"

"Yes, but there's no sign of it."

Agitation heated Harris's face. "Well, it has to be here somewhere. I'll arrange for a thorough investigation this minute. We won't stop searching until we find it." He took her hand and squeezed it gently. "Satisfied, darling?"

She wrapped her arms around him. "Yes."

"Not to worry," he said.

Isabella bit her lip before saying, "Papa, after we find my amulet, I want to leave this place."

"That's a very wise decision, my dear."

Isabella gave her father a parting hug and she made her way up the grand staircase. She wanted to tell Helena face-to-face about her plans to leave. Their conversation would stop the noblewoman from criticizing Isabella once she was gone.

When she reached her mother-in-law's suite, Isabella tapped lightly on the door. Alice, a girl with a long, thin face and fly-away hair, opened it and let her in.

"I'm so glad to see ye, m'lady." The young girl wrung her hands nervously. "I'm happy to sit with my mistress, but I feel as if my work is pilin' up somethin' fierce."

"Please go and attend to what's necessary, Alice. I'll stay with her ladyship for a while."

Alice dropped a curtsy before motioning to her mistress's bed. "Lady Winthrop is awake but I'm afraid she's not in good spirits," the girl whispered.

Isabella expressed her thanks. Once the maid had exited the room, she strode to Helena's bedstead. The two women locked eyes.

Helena's body appeared dwarfed in the sea of plush linens and pillows that surrounded her. However, her face displayed a healthier color than it had yesterday and the ornery blaze in her eyes had returned.

"Good evening." Isabella sat in a chair near the bed.

"Isabella, how good of you to check in on me."

"How are you feeling?"

"Much better," Helena answered before taking a sip of her steaming tea.

Isabella took in the décor of the room. Surprisingly, it was precisely how she would have arranged the furniture and the color scheme, if given the chance.

"You look uneasy, my dear."

"There is no easy way to say this, so I'll just come out with it. You do know you were poisoned, don't you?"

Helena's expression remained icy. "Yes, I'm aware of the attempt on my life."

A brief silence passed between them. Helena sipped more of her tea.

"Well," Isabella continued, "I wanted to tell you that, in case you hadn't been informed. I also wanted to tell you that I am leaving this place."

"Again?" the elder woman said callously.

"It's much too complicated to explain everything. Suffice it to say that I feel my life is in danger."

"Danger?"

"Yes."

"Before my poisoning, I would have disputed that fact." The dowager smoothed the counterpane covering her torso. "But it's obvious that a lunatic is running loose in this house. However, I would be more inclined to believe that you were leaving because you realized that you and Draven aren't meant to be in love."

Isabella squared her shoulders. "What are you talking about?"

"You may think that I wanted Draven to find someone to marry," Helena said.

"Didn't you?" Isabella asked sharply.

Helena waved her hand in the air. "One can never wish things for Draven. He can be so volatile and moody. I believe his mind is permanently marred."

Isabella placed a hand over her lower, right arm—the arm Draven had nearly sliced open last night. She cringed.

"Draven is a very handsome young man, an expert charmer in fact. Just as his father was. But you are right to leave him. He is evil and selfish." Helena's eyes formed two, catlike slits.

Isabella raised her chin. "Have you never wanted Draven to be happy?"

"It's not that. He has the capacity for violence. Just who do you think is responsible for my heinous poisoning episode? Hmm?"

Isabella sprang to her feet. "Certainly not Draven!"

"How can you be so sure?" Helena clenched and unclenched the damask coverlet. "I have startling news for you, Isabella. Draven is a man with Gypsy blood in his veins. Despite my best efforts to raise him as a gentleman, he was born a bastard. You see, he is the product of his father's affair with a Romanian tart."

Isabella remained silent.

"Why aren't you surprised to learn that your husband is not my blood kin?"

"Draven told me as much."

The countess sank back against the pillows. "And I thought he preferred to keep secrets."

Isabella clasped the pillars of the bedstead until her knuckles turned white. "I don't think you know him at all."

"You're wrong. As a result of his tainted blood, Draven harbors a raw, uncontrollable side. He is full of hatred and has been ever since he was a child. He used to taunt the Gypsy children who trespassed on our property. He would throw rocks. He even lit one of their caravans on fire. He's never had empathy for others."

"And what did you do about it?" Isabella's temper flared.

"I tried to make him a gentleman, but I couldn't change his inherent wickedness."

"If he's wicked, I suspect you are the reason for it."

Her words seemed to stab Helena like a knife. The dowager's face twisted and Isabella could have sworn she saw remorse shadow her face.

"Perhaps you are . . ." Helena said.

"I am what?"

"Perhaps you are *right*."

Isabella hadn't expected the words.

"I should have pitied Draven for being born a bastard. I should have loved him more. . . ." The noblewoman's voice trailed off.

Isabella was speechless.

But the countess's sentimental moment didn't last long. Her eyes flattened into cold stones. "It would be in your best interest to keep your distance from my stepson. His behavior becomes more erratic every day. You will be free of him when you return to London and that is best."

Isabella knew firsthand that Draven was capable of violence but she didn't want to hear it from her mother-in-law. In fact, Helena's words provoked her to defend Draven to the ends of the earth. "Although Draven has many character flaws, I don't believe he has it in him to poison anyone."

"I hope you are right." The dowager sighed. Closing her eyes as a signal of dismissal, she murmured, "If you're not, that means we are all in grave danger."

Chapter Twenty-Two

Isabella returned to her suites and pulled the bell cord for Gwyneth.

Irritated when the girl didn't appear to help her pack, she went downstairs to find her. As she made her way down the grand staircase, she was surprised to see that her father and eight members of the household staff were gathered at its base.

"What's going on?" she asked.

A proud grin spread across Harris Farrington's face. "I've called all the servants together to search for your amulet."

Isabella took the remaining steps in a shuffling run. When she reached her father, she gave him an enthusiastic hug.

Harris beamed. "Come with me, darling. Rogers will help us search the apartments on the second and third levels while the other servants scour the main floor."

Rogers flung her one of his crooked, but endearing smiles.

Harris placed his hand on the small of Isabella's back and gripped his cane with the other. "After you, my dear."

The trio searched nine rooms in succession but found nothing. Outside Draven's suites, Isabella's stomach tightened. Her father rapped loudly on the door while she exchanged fretful glances with

Rogers. When there was no answer, Harris instructed Rogers to open the door with the master key.

Fear glazed Rogers's expression. "But sir, 'is lordship dislikes being disturbed while 'e's workin'."

"Yes, Papa," Isabella chimed in. "We knocked and there was no answer. Draven must be extremely busy. Or he is elsewhere."

Harris shook his head. "All of this talk is wasting our time. Rogers, we're going in whether his lordship is busy or not. Finding my daughter's amulet is of the utmost importance and, to be perfectly honest, I suspect we'll find it inside your master's room."

Anticipation welled in Isabella's throat. She would forfeit her last breath not to see Draven.

Harris asked Rogers to open the door with his key again. When the manservant continued to hem and haw, Harris snatched the key ring from his hand. Fidgeting with it, he said, "Don't fret, old boy. I'll take full responsibility for this."

Rogers neither spoke nor moved.

"That will be all." Harris dismissed him.

Turning red, the valet cast a sympathetic glance at Isabella before he disappeared around the corner.

"You were rather harsh on him," she said.

Harris singled out a key on the ring. "If one wants something done correctly, one must do it oneself."

"Rogers hesitated because Draven gave him direct orders never to disturb him while he's working."

Her father ignored the comment as he fit the key in the lock and turned it. He swept a lock of auburn hair from Isabella's forehead before they entered. "When it comes to my daughter's happiness, no lock is an obstacle."

Isabella followed him into the chamber and her pulse raced. Although she resisted it at first, she eyed the empty tiger-skin rug. The vision of Draven lying beside her yesterday flooded her memory and warmed her skin. And when her glance rested on the door of the bedchamber, she could feel his solid body on top of hers. . . .

But shouldn't she be surveying the bedchamber for signs of the amulet?

As she started across the room, she spotted her husband leaning against the doorway. His angry stare pierced right through her.

"What the hell are you two doing?" Draven thundered.

Harris straightened from searching the lowest shelf of a bookcase. He came to stand in front of his son-in-law with defiance in his eyes. "In case you haven't heard, someone stole Isabella's amulet. It's very precious to her since it's something I sent her from one of my digs."

Draven brushed past Harris. "I didn't take it, if that's your assumption."

"As a matter of fact, that's exactly what I assumed," Harris challenged him.

Draven whirled in his tracks. "I beg your pardon?"

"You heard me. For reasons I can't yet explain, I believe you stole the amulet right off my daughter's neck while she slept. Furthermore, I suspect you're responsible for Helena's poisoning episode."

Shock rifled through Isabella's body. Her father appeared frail, but his words cut like a knife. "Papa! You don't know what you're saying."

"Think about it, my dear." Harris shot a dark glance her way. "Who else hates his mother enough to kill her?"

Draven's stare flashed to Isabella before it shifted back to Harris. "Think what you will, sir."

Harris continued his challenge. "I vow to get to the bottom of this, after which I'm taking my daughter away from here."

"You seem to forget that your daughter is now my wife." Draven puffed his chest forward.

"Beg off!" Harris bellowed.

"I'm master of this house, not you."

"Stop it." Isabella pried the two men apart.

Harris glowered. "I can see this conversation is getting us nowhere. I just hope to hell you don't have that amulet. I'll find out for certain . . . one way or another."

Draven's face flushed. "You and your accusations are no longer welcome in my house."

Ignoring the comment, Harris turned to Isabella. "We aren't leaving this place until we find that necklace."

"I don't care about finding it anymore." She was unable to keep the alarm out of her voice.

Harris pointed a finger at Draven. "If you hurt my daughter in the meantime, I promise it will be the last thing you ever do."

He stormed past Isabella and Draven as fast as his cane could carry him.

Isabella avoided Draven's stare in the awkward silence that lingered. To get her attention, he took hold of her arm and squeezed it. "So your father thinks I'm a thief, does he?"

"He o-only wants to get to the bottom of this," she stammered.

He studied her with blazing eyes. "You're afraid to be alone with me, aren't you?"

"No." She locked eyes with him with equal heat.

"Has your father convinced you to leave?" Draven demanded.

"I want to go."

His voice dropped to a sultry whisper. "You know you are free to do so."

So my prisoner status has been revoked.

"Before you go, tell me this." His black eyes bore into her soul.

She raised an eyebrow.

"For all I know, you prodded your father to come to my rooms to look for the amulet."

"I did nothing of the sort," Isabella said. "My father insisted on searching every room. Including yours, despite my earnest protests."

Draven's mouth curled into a smile. "So you took it upon yourself to defend my privacy, did you?" He gathered her to him. Her legs trembled as he edged his tongue smoothly over his lips. "What am I to do with you, my dear Bella?"

"I really don't know."

"Everyone in this household seems to despise me," he said. "So, the question remains: Do you have it in your generous heart to loathe me?"

"I—"

Draven drew her even closer. His long fingers played along her back. "Come now, my kindhearted wife. You must be honest."

"I don't hate you," she said. And it was true. Being in his arms and listening to his heart beating wildly was melting her resolve. She forced herself to arch away from him. "I think it best if we simply avoided one another until I find my amulet. After that, I don't wish to see you anymore."

He laughed. It was a deep, throaty laugh that amplified his magnetism.

"What could possibly be so humorous?" she asked.

"I find it funny that you're doing exactly what you accused me of when you returned here."

"What do you mean?"

"You've spoken the words, but your eyes are saying something completely different."

She tried to wriggle free of his grasp.

Another laugh escaped his lips. He fell silent while his gaze shadowed her with lust. Before she could protest, Draven's mouth found its way to the curve of her neck. His breath jostled the tendrils of her hair and tickled her skin. And when he spoke naughty words against it, her core dampened. Draven's tongue thrashed along the length of her neck and against her will, her eyes fluttered shut. She leaned into him.

"You don't hate me," he murmured between sweet nibbles. "That's very encouraging."

"Draven, don't." She gathered a breath.

But her husband was too busy to respond. His mouth traveled up and down the column of her neck, depositing kisses wherever it made contact. One of his hands encircled her waist, the other cupped and caressed her chin. She surged against it, causing his embrace to become more firm.

"Now your words are telling me to stop while your *body* is urging me to continue," he murmured.

He was absolutely right. Isabella parted her lips. His mouth came crashing down over hers while he jerked her buttocks forward. She stole a look into his eyes where torment and want lived. She cared for him, was afraid of him, and felt sorry for him all at the same time. But there was no time to weed through that complicated cluster of emotions. She was swooning in his grip and she couldn't stop her tongue from intertwining with Draven's.

Sounds of pleasure escaped her throat and floated toward the rafters.

"You tantalize my every sense," he whispered. "And you know how I react when my senses are stirred."

He pulled her head back by her hair and nearly bruised her mouth with his lips. Fear mounted inside her. Draven's roughness reminded her of how violent he could become.

"No!" She managed to break free and hurry to the door.

Something made her look back. Draven stood motionless in the center of the room, his face buried in his hands. The stance made Isabella wonder if perhaps he had a heart after all.

She was about to exit the room when she heard him murmur, "I can't lose her."

Chapter Twenty-Three

Isabella headed up the stairs. She had wanted to tell Draven so many things a moment ago, but words had seemed powerless instruments. Now it was too late.

Thunder boomed close to the house, surging panic through her. *Another storm is moving in.*

Even if she could convince Papa to leave without the amulet, foul weather could trap them at Thorncliff Towers for at least another day.

She went to her father with raw nerves. They shared a brief conversation before Isabella sought refuge in her bedchamber. She began to undress while the sound of heavy rainfall thrashed her window.

Gwyneth arrived to confirm her suspicions that there would be no leaving the estate until the storm cleared. The girl fussed about for a moment then closed the curtains against the dismal weather. "Master Draven says 'e's afraid yer carriage will be tossed around like a tiny coin if ye get caught in the middle of this storm," she said.

The girl left and Isabella opened the curtains. Peering into the velvety light of dusk, a distressing heaviness hung over her. Black clouds topped the forceful rain that pelted the sea and the landscape was blanketed by a dreary layer of gray. London experienced days like this, but people went on as usual—and its hustle and bustle always neutralized the melancholic weather.

How she wished she was back in her old parlor before a raging fire.

Nestled in the window seat, Isabella went over the conversation she'd had with her father. She had omitted the part about Draven's Gypsy curse, but she did tell him that her husband's barmy state was increasing, without his control. Inspired by a bruised ego, she also informed Papa that Draven had proposed marriage under the guise of an ulterior motive: her Egyptian curse.

Papa's face had grown redder than a beet. "That bastard lied to us from the very beginning," he'd raged.

She had calmed him down by telling him that she planned to use the information to request a divorcement from Parliament.

A soft knock jolted her out of her thoughts. "Yes?"

Rogers entered, cradling several logs. "I've brought more kindlin', m'lady."

"One moment, Rogers. I'll put on my dressing gown." Once she was properly covered, she let the elderly man in.

"The fire must be dyin' out by now and this room tends to be a bit drafty." He dipped his narrow chin in her direction as he passed her. In the brevity of the moment, she swore she had seen a hint of fatherly affection in his eyes, although it lay below a trained expression.

Rogers made his way across the room to the marble-framed hearth. While he tended to its dying embers, Isabella moved closer to him.

"You're right," she said. "The fire is about to die out. However did you know?"

"I suppose ye could say it's me job to know, m'lady. I can never trust a flighty girl like Gwyneth to check on ye properly."

"It seems you're very valuable to this household, Rogers."

The manservant shrugged as he replaced the extinguished logs with new ones. After he lit them, they filled the room with the scent of the forest.

"Storm's a comin'," he said with a quick glance out the window. "We've buckled the 'ouse down, as usual."

"Yes, I know." Isabella sighed. "I suppose my journey will just have to wait."

"I'm sorry to hear yer leavin', m'lady."

"Thank you," she said. She crossed her arms and rubbed them for warmth. Then she bent down and smiled. Was he willing to tell her more about Draven?

"Rogers?" she asked. "Will you sit with me for a moment?"

He nodded but looked uncomfortable as he slid into a winged-back chair by the fire.

"How long have you been in Winthrop employment?"

"Since before ye were a thought in yer mother's mind, m'lady. I was hired by Master Cyril, Master Draven's father."

"I had no idea. So you were here when my husband was born?"

Rogers stood and churned the flaming logs absentmindedly with the tip of a poker. "Aye. 'Twas a terrible stretch o' time." His face lengthened as he stared at the hearth.

By now, dusk had dimmed to a rich darkness. Beyond the glass-paned window, another crack of thunder split the air. Isabella suppressed a shudder as she tried to focus on the conversation. "Why was it so terrible?"

"Master Draven 'as informed me that ye know about 'is mother so I can speak freely. That Gypsy woman brought him, a babe in arms, to Thorncliff Towers on a night much like this one. She sent the entire household into an uproar, she did."

"Tell me, what was this mysterious lady like?"

"She was beautiful in a way all other women are jealous of. Big dark eyes, long, flowin' 'air. And though she looked every inch the wild Gypsy, she seemed to genuinely care about 'er baby." He set the poker in its wrought-iron stand.

Isabella stood as well. The manservant turned to face her, as if he were searching for her trust. He placed a shaking hand over his heart. "I'm tellin' ye in the strictest confidence that her ladyship was there that night, aware of who this Gypsy woman was."

"Lady Winthrop was there?"

Rogers nodded his answer.

Hiding her shock, Isabella's lips curved into a smile. "You can trust me, Rogers. I'm just as good at keeping secrets as your master."

"And a great many secrets he keeps hidden," the manservant said.

"Why is that?"

Rogers spread his hands apart "I'm afraid secrets are all his lordship 'as."

Truer words had never been spoken. "My husband would be lost without you."

He blushed. "I'm only a servant, but I worry about Master Draven as if 'e were my own child. I wish I could 'ave prevented what he endured in his youth. In those days, I just shook me head with pity."

"Why?"

"Her ladyship was colder to Master Draven than a frozen iceberg."

"I have heard that the countess was cruel to my husband even when he was a baby."

"Aye. And though she'd have my head fer sayin' this, things got worse after Master Cyril passed on from a sudden illness. Tragedy grabbed hold 'a this place and it hasn't let go."

Isabella gave a little shudder. "I feel the black cloud that hangs over this house as well."

Will Rogers tell me all he knows of Draven's curse?

A brief silence passed between them. "For what it's worth, m'lady, his lordship seems distraught that yer leavin' this place."

"Draven has left me no other choice."

Rogers nodded as if he understood.

"I'm afraid of him," she said softly.

"The master has a temper the likes of I've never seen before."

Isabella cocked her head to one side. "Tell me more about his childhood, Rogers."

"His lordship was a mischievous child. Always angry and always gettin' into trouble." He glanced around. "But 'e was a beautiful baby. Decades ago, this room was the nursery. Master Cyril had it painted a pretty shade of yellow."

"Did her ladyship spend much time with my husband in here?"

Rogers frowned. "No. As charmin' as this room was, I don't think 'er ladyship ever set foot in 'ere when Master Draven was growin' up."

"How about the earl? Did he give my husband much attention as a child?"

"He managed to, even though her ladyship tried to forbid it."

She was fascinated. "So, despite Lady Winthrop's cold heart, you maintain your loyal post for my husband?"

Rogers nodded. "I could never leave 'is lordship to fend for 'imself."

Isabella offered him a smile.

He scrubbed a hand through his thinning hair. "Since I've already spoken out of turn, I have a confession ta make. I do believe in the master's curse. I see Master Draven's good qualities as ye do, but ye mustn't be near 'im when his temper flares."

"That's very good advice," she said.

The old man seemed reluctant to leave. He glanced around him. "I told ye this room was the former nursery, but what I didn't tell ye was that a secret passageway runs inside the house."

Isabella's eyes widened.

"It was built by the late earl to connect his rooms with Master Draven's. He used it to make visits to his son, unknown to her ladyship."

Rogers proceeded to warn her how dangerous the hidden corridor could be by telling her a story of someone who'd gotten trapped inside its walls.

"Where exactly is this passageway?" she asked.

The valet hesitated.

"Can you show me?"

"I . . . I shouldn't."

"I must be able to access it from here."

He hastened away without saying another word. Isabella's shoulders rolled forward. By not answering, had Rogers meant to help her—or help Draven?

It was no matter. She began to search for an entryway into the tunnel.

Was it behind the main wall?

Isabella ran her fingertips along the wallpaper that lined the chair rail. Nothing. Reaching up, she removed a candle from its resting place inside the wall sconce. Still nothing.

She spent the next several minutes exploring the room. Then she returned to the brass sconce and pulled it down with a quick tug. The action caused an entire section of the wall to spring toward her!

She lit a candle branch. After swallowing her nervousness, she stepped into the inky blackness of the corridor beyond. Staying within the realm of the light, she tried to block out the pungent smell of mildew. When that didn't work, she covered her mouth with her dress sleeve. She meandered along the stone-lined corridor that paralleled the seaside. A quarter of an hour later, she wound her way into another wing of the house—the wing beneath the turret that housed Draven's suites.

As she treaded along the dark corridor, Isabella could hear nothing of the heavy rain or the crashing waves outside. The only sound that filled the darkness was the clicking of her heels and her wheezy breathing. She was grateful when she saw a set of steps that sloped upward and curved out of sight.

The story Rogers told her came back to mind while she climbed the winding staircase. "Legend has it that the sounds of a servant cryin' inside these stone walls can be heard at night. That woman was panicked at being lost and trapped inside. I like to think she was the only victim o' these black hallways, but I doubt it."

Isabella grimaced at the morbid thought.

She continued on, swearing that she felt rats scurrying over her silk slippers. Too horrified to look down, she hastened to what she figured was the entrance of Draven's room.

Isabella's heart thrummed. Her black-hearted husband sat just behind the wall, no doubt working on his sketches.

Before she could look for a secret latch or a retracting stone, she panicked. She reversed her direction and scampered down the stone steps. As she rushed back to her suites, she knew what her next move would be. Tonight, when everyone in the house was asleep, she would use the passageway to gain access into Draven's bedchamber . . . to search for her amulet while her husband slept.

Chapter Twenty-Four

The wind howled that evening like an angry animal. Isabella twisted her wedding band around her finger, fighting off fatigue until the bedside clock signaled two o'clock.

She rose, lit a candle branch, then moved toward the wall sconce located to the left of her four-poster. Full of trepidation, she opened the panel and inched into the shadowed corridor.

Isabella knew she wasn't doing the wisest thing, but she was beyond caring. She simply wanted her amulet back. After securing the necklace, she would leave this place and never come back.

She hurried beneath the glow of the fresh candles and when she reached the stone steps, she climbed them at a fast pace. Shuddering from the fierce draft that whipped along the stairwell, she stood in front of the stone wall that led to Draven's bedchamber. She assumed that one of the stones would depress and allow her entry. After she pressed on five or six of them, an oversized stone made a latching noise. The entire wall swung away from her. When Isabella followed behind it, she realized she'd entered the room through the wall to the left of Draven's bedchamber hearth.

Her nerves prickled. *What if Draven awakens, angry as the devil that I don't trust him?*

Chiding herself for being so frightened, she crept toward the gigantic sleigh bed. Draven was asleep on his back, snoring softly. Shadows of light and dark spilled over his face and he looked unbearably handsome. He also seemed uncharacteristically peaceful— as if he were free of his usual torment for once.

Resisting the urge to sweep a strand of his black hair from his forehead, she moved to his dressing room where she extinguished the candles and deposited the candle branch. The last thing she needed was its light waking Draven.

Returning to the sleigh bed, she scanned his bedside table for the amulet then dropped to her knees in order to search under the bed. Isabella's judgment became convoluted in the dark and she let out a cry as she banged her head on the bottom of the bed frame.

Draven groaned and rolled over. Heart hammering, she remained still. Stifling the pain, she watched her husband fidget in his sleep before he settled down. Convinced he had slipped back into a deep slumber, Isabella continued her search under the bed only to turn up nothing.

She was just about to stand when Draven yanked her to her feet. He was holding a sheet around his waist and his eyes were flashing madly.

"How did you get in here?" He clutched her shoulder tighter. "I'm in the habit of locking my door at night."

She cleared her throat. "I discovered the secret passageway—"

"You found it on your own?"

She remained silent.

"Ah, looking for your amulet, are you?" he asked. "I thought you and your father were finished searching my private quarters."

Flushed with embarrassment, she tried to escape his grasp.

His black eyes narrowed. "You, my dear, are as cunning as a thief. How do I know you aren't here to *plant* that amulet in my room? Perhaps you and your father have conspired together."

"How dare you insinuate such a thing?" she fumed. "Do you see that I've brought my amulet with me? Well, do you?"

Draven eyed her with uncertainty and released her shoulder.

"My necklace is still missing," she retorted. "And furthermore, you were a *cunning thief* when you robbed me of the prospect of motherhood. I suppose we are even."

Wearing an amused expression, he made no effort to reply.

She put her hands on her hips. "What do you have to say to that?"

His lips curled at the corners and his tone dropped several octaves. "I say, 'Let the passageway be our little secret.' "

She squirmed at the suggestion. Standing this close to him in the moonlight, she became aware of the broadness of his chest and of the cut of his torso muscles. Although he radiated charm from beneath his bed-mussed hair, she pretended not to notice. "Another secret to add to your list, Draven?"

"Secrets are the ammunition of life," he said. "I would be naïve to think you have no secrets to share."

"I don't."

He breathed heavily. "No? But I can think of one. The secret of Joseph Gossington."

Her face burned hotter. "I . . . I know no such man."

"Come now." He tsked. "You shouldn't lie."

"He is an acquaintance of mine. That's all." She wanted to race from the room.

Draven fingered one of her curls. "Don't worry, Isabella. I am well aware that you committed no impropriety with that vulture."

"I-I didn't," she stammered. "But how do you know about him?"

He stepped closer still. "That's another secret I can add to my 'list,' as you called it." He loosened his grip on the bedsheet. It fell to the ground like a drifting feather, revealing his arousal. Isabella gulped.

"Seeing you in your nightgown reminds me of the night you came back to me," he whispered as he reached forward to stroke her cheek. "Your breasts were wet from the rain and asking for a man's touch."

He lowered his hand to the ridge of Isabella's shift. After playing his fingers along its trim, he slid his touch to the outline of her right breast and traced it in erotic circles. A decadent smile spread across his lips while he teased her nipple to full erection. "Did you dream of me as I dreamt of you during our time apart?" He paused. "Do you dare share my bed once more before you leave?"

She batted his hand down and said nothing, though a fiery chemistry blazed between them.

"Well?"

She arched away from him. "You know part of me hates you."

"Yes, but it's the other part of you that interests me."

Draven grasped the nape of her neck and edged her closer. His lips collided with hers and his tongue forced its way inside her mouth. Isabella's head spun. Lifting her nightgown out of the way, he slid his hand inside her underclothes. He caressed her skin with a touch that was nearly too hot to bear. With three stiff fingers pressed together, he lowered his hand and sunk it into her moisture.

Once he'd claimed her mouth with another kiss, he pulled away to gaze into her eyes. "I can't seem to resist you," he murmured with smoldering want. "Give me the chance to convince you to stay—"

Clamping both hands around her waist, Draven lifted her onto the bed. Isabella's hair fanned away as she dropped like an apple from a tree onto the bed-sheets. He hung over her appraisingly then dove in for a kiss. She, in return, wrapped her arms around him with a desperation that surprised even her. Ensnaring her fingers in his hair, she closed her eyes as he devoured her with abandon.

Breathless with desire, Draven opened the drawstrings of her nightshift and tugged the garment off her body. He pressed her bare breasts together and lifted them up, suckling them hungrily, while his gleaming hair draped over her chest. Sitting back on his haunches, he tugged off her pantalets in quick yanks. Stifling a cry, Isabella did nothing to stop him. He pried her legs apart with his bulging arms and slipped his torso between them. Rising up on one arm, he grabbed his hard shaft and rubbed her slick folds with it.

"By God you're wet enough," he rasped. "But I won't take you just yet."

His eyes blazing and his cock as stiff as steel, he put his swirling tongue to the tender spot beneath her chin. Streaming it down her neck and chest, it reached her dark nipples in a trail of excitement. Taking her nubs in his mouth, Draven pulled them into hard points.

An impatient whimper escaped Isabella's throat. She wanted him more than she'd ever wanted anything. Would he enter her?

Draven drank in the sight of Isabella under him, flushed and breathless, and he wanted to scream out. She looked like a radiant angel, innocent and pure—yet evocative enough to make any man go mad. Her hair, the color of rich cinnamon, draped across the pillow like a silken sash, and her lips, as glossy as a still lake, hardened him like a rock.

Draven's mind whirled. Should he reach for a sheath? That he would leave her with child was a slim possibility. From that slim chance there was a fifty-fifty probability he would plant a male seed.

He made no move for the sheath. After all, having a child is what Isabella wanted.

If I make love to her without protection maybe she won't leave.

Meeting her eyes with a deep-seated passion, Draven tested her readiness again. She was as moist as dew. He found her budding center and eased his sex inside of her. Isabella sucked in a sharp breath. His shaft fit like a key's perfect entry into a lock.

She was tight at first. He didn't want to hurt her, but he had to break the barrier he felt deep inside her. He pushed. She winced then groaned. His throbbing charge filled her while blood rushed through his veins like a mighty river. Cries of their pleasure mingled together. The moonlight streaming through the window made her body shine like marble. Now that he was inside Isabella, he wanted to ride her until night brightened to day.

Draven grabbed her hips and fisted the flesh around it. Pulling her buttocks off the bed, he dove into her at a steeper angle. With her pelvis lifted toward him, her stomach became hollow and her breasts stood at attention. He gazed into her almond-shaped eyes and rocked his hips forward fast and hard, making his cock throb hotly inside her. Isabella's center pulsated around him, further intensifying his thrusts. Sweat beaded on her breasts and she clung to the sheets as if her life depended on it. Draven crushed his chest against her mouth and she tasted the salt of his flowing perspiration.

Isabella had given him a reason to live and he was about to make her his. Nothing on God's green earth could possibly make him more aroused. A spark-flying friction brought him incredibly close to glory as he pumped his way in and out of her. And when Isabella's squeaks of delight heightened to cries of ecstasy, he couldn't withhold his seed any longer. Emitting a protracted grunt, he shattered a long and satisfying climax. She responded by flooding his erection with her own rush of warm liquid. As he slumped forward, the rise and fall of his breathing vibrated against her breasts. He gasped for air while her tears dampened his skin—and he wondered if he'd hurt her.

"My Bella," Draven whispered against her neck. "I've waited so long to show you my passion."

* * *

A myriad of emotions rushed at Isabella. Her heart raced and her face whitened. Had she lost her mind? She was leaving Draven. Why hadn't she urged him to use protection during their lovemaking?

Could I have been impregnated? If so, let it be a girl.

Draven had bedded her, which meant she'd just gotten her wish. Why then did she feel so confused?

A chill raked through her but before she could speak, a series of primal howls rang out in the night.

Chapter Twenty-Five

Draven rolled off the bed and sprinted to the window. Isabella followed close behind. Through the steamed glass, she saw a dozen wolves lined up within the courtyard.

"What on earth—?"

"Don't be frightened," he said.

She covered her ears against the deafening howls. "I don't see the black wolf among them."

"No." Draven's voice was odd.

Isabella frowned. "Where did they come from?"

He turned to her. "I don't know."

"How will you get rid of them?" she asked as her mouth grew dry.

Someone knocked on the door. "Master Draven!" Rogers cried. "There is a pack of wolves in the courtyard. One o' them crashed through a window and is wanderin' through the house!"

"Keep everyone in their bedchamber!" Draven cried. He turned to Isabella and urged her to dress and go back to her room via the secret passageway. "You'll be safe there. When you reach your suites, lock yourself in."

The thought of the rat-infested labyrinth made her stomach plummet. She shook her head. "I'll come with you."

"No!" he shot back. "The last thing you want to encounter is a wild wolf."

"Then I'll stay in here."

"You can't."

"Why?"

"Do as I say. I must go."

Isabella eyed the candles visible from inside Draven's dressing room. She estimated that, if she hurried, she'd have enough wick to return safely to her room.

"Be careful," she said.

Another howl split the air.

Draven nodded as he pulled on a shirt, trousers, boots, and swirling greatcoat. After he escaped the suite for the courtyard below, Isabella returned to the window and peered out. Both Draven and Rogers emerged into the frosty night. Her husband was wielding a pistol. He raised the firearm to eye level and moved slowly toward the incensed pack of wolves. She could see that he was speaking to the animals that, strangely enough, seemed to obey him. They released their snarled expressions and hung their heads.

As Draven crept closer to the wolves, they padded backward out of the hedge-trimmed courtyard then vanished into the night.

Isabella had never seen anything like it.

A howl resounded from inside the house. Heart hammering, she dressed, retrieved the candle branch, and rushed toward the secret passageway.

Time to head back into the depths of hell.

With quivering hands and unsure feet, she re-entered the open panel just beyond the shifted hearth. After closing the section of wall behind her, she lifted her skirts and descended the moisture-caked steps down to the passageway below.

Suffering through the twists and turns of the hallway, Isabella glanced at her burning branch. Its four candles had melted at a simultaneous rate, mere centimeters from being extinguished. She quickened her pace. If she became imprisoned in the dark, the rats would have a field day with her.

As she took another step forward, her shoe caught on a raised stone. She tumbled forward into the blackness and the candle branch flew out of her hand. The flames disappeared seconds before her head hit a section of the cold, stone wall.

When she regained consciousness, the blinding darkness felt like the controlling cloak of the devil. Groggy and disoriented, she had no idea how long she had been lying on the bumpy stone floor.

Was it still dark? Or had daylight peaked?

A gush of liquid flowed over her forehead. Isabella could only assume it was blood. With a great deal of effort, she struggled to her feet and stretched out her hands. She felt the barriers of the wall, but she had no idea in which direction she faced. She shuffled slowly along the corridor, using her hands as a guide.

Whimpering from the pain that gripped her head, she called out for help. She pounded her fists on the walls that held her captive, but there was no answer, only silence. Inching her way without the light of the candles, she resisted hysteria. She forced herself to continue but stopped when her foot struck something. She bent down and swept her hands over the ground until she felt the candle branch lying on its side. Relief rang inside her. Perhaps she could strike the stones with it to attract attention. If anything, it meant she was going in the right direction.

More time passed as she searched.

Where was the panel?

She journeyed along, exhaling with frustration. When she turned to assure herself that the wall behind her hadn't led off in some obscure direction, the candle branch knocked against a jutting stone and flew out of her hands again. She jerked in the direction of its clatter. But in which direction was she facing now? Sinking to the floor, she buried her head in her hands and began to sob.

"Isabella!" a voice called.

Draven?

She wiped away her tears and pulled herself to a standing position. Something clamped its teeth into her foot and pain radiated up her leg. Screaming, she kicked the rat away and stumbled along in the direction of her husband's voice.

"I'm here, Draven!" Her hoarse throat muffled the words.

A glow of light stretched around a corner of the passageway. The vision was followed by Draven grasping a candle branch.

"My God, Isabella!"

Her vision spun in vicious circles as she crumbled to the floor.

Chapter Twenty-Six

Isabella awoke to find Draven grasping her hand with a fierce protectiveness. His eyes were bloodshot and rimmed with shadows. She assumed he had been awake all night.

He touched her hair with his free hand. "You gave me quite a scare."

"I . . . fell and dropped my candle branch."

Draven hushed her as he smoothed the bed-sheet and tucked it beneath her arm. "Rest now," he said. "Dr. Lamstein has attended to your rodent bite and to the nasty bump on your forehead."

"Thank you for saving me," she whispered, blinking against her tears.

Lines of concern creased his forehead. "I don't know what I would do if I ever lost you, Isabella. This has made me more determined than ever to convince you to stay."

His dark eyes moved in and out of focus, thanks to the painkiller Dr. Lamstein had administered. "Did you capture the wolf that got inside the house?" she said in a weak voice.

"Yes," he said.

As Isabella drifted off to sleep, her mind flashed on the vision of

Draven talking to the wolves in the courtyard. *How strange that he seemed to communicate with them.*

After watching a pale and shaken Isabella succumb to sleep, Draven stood and paced the room with a deep scowl. Regret raged through his veins. He had practically raped his own wife before insisting she take the passageway back to her room. He, for one, didn't have to imagine the degree of terror she had experienced in the pitch black. As a boy, he'd been imprisoned by the very same walls. Full of impertinence as a lad, he thought to worry everyone by hiding in the passageway. He'd waited for at least three hours before he was discovered. By the time Rogers rescued Draven from the darkness, he had used up all of his youthful tears and could barely breathe.

The memory reminded him that any barrier separating a person from their freedom is a powerful thing. It made him regret that he had insisted Isabella stay at Thorncliff Towers forever.

He had saved her and made love to her, but did she hate him regardless?

Assured by the doctor that his wife would sleep for several hours, Draven took the stairs back to his suite. He thrust the door open and plowed through his private library to the sitting room. That is where he came upon Rogers, who was drawing him a bath.

The elderly man smiled. "I thought ye could use a warm bath and yer concoction after the scare with her ladyship."

"You're a godsend, old boy." Draven rubbed the back of his neck. He paced while the valet tended to the setup. "I was the one who suggested Isabella use the passageway back to her suite. She was frightened out of her mind—and who could blame her?"

Rogers nodded as he hung Draven's blue silk dressing gown on the edge of the wardrobe door.

After the two men discussed Draven's own boyhood peril, the valet helped his master undress and slip into the frothy suds. "I was scared for ye as a lad, but ye were nine years old. Her ladyship is a grown woman who can survive the worst o' challenges."

Draven raised an eyebrow. "Challenges like me?"

The skin around the manservant's eyes crinkled. "Aye."

"Isabella is rather like a tigress," Draven murmured more to himself than to Rogers. "Quite remarkable, really."

"She has impressive qualities, indeed. And I suspect she'd make a poised countess, if she weren't leavin' this place." Rogers handed him a glass. "Yer nostrum, m'lord."

Draven made a face as he accepted it. "She can't leave, damn it!"

"Calm down, m'lord. Now remember. Yer to sip the drink as ye sit in the warm water."

Several years ago, a fortune-teller in a traveling circus had suggested this combination of herbs when Draven had approached her about cures for lycanthropy. The nostrum consisted of echinacea to purify one's blood, arnica for its healing properties, and butternut to expel impurities via one's digestive tract.

It did seem to calm Draven's nerves, as the fortune-teller had promised. The only problem was its wickedly foul taste.

Rogers laughed and placed his hand over his spindly knees. "Ye seem like a child when ye make those faces."

Draven cocked his head back, finished the nostrum, then wiped his mouth. "I'd like to see you drink it, old boy."

"No, thank ye," the valet said before he took the glass.

Draven grunted.

The valet handed him a washcloth. "We must do all we can to stop these transformations."

"Let's not speak of them. They are a sore subject," Draven said as he washed his body. After he was done, he dropped the cloth into the water and gripped the sides of the tub. Taking a deep breath, he plunged his head underwater then popped out, shaking his hair to and fro.

Silence filled the room as Rogers shaved Draven's face. When the manservant was finished, he wiped away the excessive lather with a towel and handed over a mirror.

"I like it," Draven said. He stroked the tiny slip of a goatee Rogers had left beneath his bottom lip.

Rogers emitted a heavy sigh. Draven turned to look at him. "What's wrong?"

"What are ye to do durin' the next full moon, m'lord?" The valet's eyes glowed with concern.

Draven emerged from the water and whipped the towel around his waist. "I don't have the foggiest. Right now my goal is to convince Isabella to stay. She doesn't know that I literally transform into the black wolf. I hope to find the Gypsy woman responsible for the spell before she learns the truth."

Rogers smiled. "I suppose the warm baths and concoctions don't do a damned thing to help ye."

"Somehow they make me feel better." Draven smiled. "As do you, old boy."

A soft pink color rose in the valet's cheeks. He lifted the dressing gown to shoulder height. After slipping the gown on, Draven went to comb his hair. Rogers followed. "Yer lordship, perhaps ye can woo her ladyship anew by showin' her the heartfelt letters ye wrote her in her absence. As for liftin' yer curse, I went ta town yesterday fer supplies and the villagers were dronin' on about Gypsies makin' camp along the pond."

"I encountered a family of three who got separated from their band. But who gave them permission to stay on my property?"

"I did. And if ye don't run them off, it will be a step to showin' some kindness and redemption," Rogers said firmly.

Draven slapped the man on the back with affection. "All right, old boy."

"Nothin' but good will come of it, I assure ye."

"I hope you're right. Now where are those letters?" Draven asked distractedly.

Chapter Twenty-Seven

By week's end, the bite on Isabella's foot had nearly healed and the gash on her forehead had begun to do the same. The search for her amulet had led nowhere, yet her father remained at the house—determined to find the necklace before he went back to London.

Draven sat by her side all the while, reading her love sonnets, poems, and chapters from novels. She'd had no idea that he liked to read as much as she did. She loved to watch his full lips form the words, and the way his strong hands clasped the books warmed her heart.

Quotes from Lord Byron were lovely and a relatively new novel called *Mansfield Park* was intriguing, but what moved Isabella most were the letters Draven had written to her during their separation but had kept to himself. She could hardly believe the man who'd shown her such cruelty on their wedding night was capable of this kind of unhindered romance and tenderness.

On a cold Saturday morning, Isabella begged Draven to read her favorite letter again.

He gave her a sheepish look but acquiesced nevertheless.

My dearest Isabella,

How can I ever say I am sorry enough times? How can I convince you of my remorse for treating you with hostility instead of temperance? While I cannot explain my actions on our wedding night, I can apologize for them—and hopefully reduce their drama by this letter. You have captivated my every sense, my every need to share myself with someone. You have spurred my every passion and I suspect that, if you ever grace my life with your presence again, you will make me a better man.

If ever I have the courage to give you this letter, you will know how my heart aches in your absence and how my arms long to embrace you. You will know that my soul has pounded with a sadness I have never known. If you return to me, you will show more courage than I, apparently, can muster to contact you.

I hope you are well. For the possibility that you, an angel sent from heaven, are suffering in the slightest of ways, is something I cannot bear.

> *Your ever-faithful husband,*
> *Draven*

"That is the most beautiful thing I've ever heard," Isabella admitted.

Just as Draven rose out of his seat to kiss her, Gwyneth bounced into the room holding a tray of tea and confectionaries.

"Perhaps you can knock next time, Gwyneth." He frowned.

"Yes, m'lord."

After setting the tray on the writing desk, the abigail flittered to the bed in order to smooth Isabella's sheets. "How are ye feelin', yer ladyship?" she asked. " 'Tis a good sign that ye have some color in yer face."

"I'm feeling better every day, Gwyneth. Thank you." She smiled. "I really don't know why everyone is making such a fuss."

The girl threw her hands in the air. "Ye had the staff scared out of our minds, m'lady!"

Draven turned Isabella's face toward him. "You had me scared as well."

"I'm just glad I survived the ordeal," she said, touching the heavy wrapping that encircled her head. "When can I take this bandage off?"

Gwyneth tsked. "Doctor says ye might have a concussion. So, ye must leave it on for another week, yer ladyship. Now, is there anythin' ye need?"

"No. Thank you, Gwyneth."

The young maid nodded and left the room. Draven helped Isabella wrap a dressing robe around her shoulders. He supported her as they made their way to a window seat padded with silk.

"Are you really feeling better today?" His eyes looked tender in the morning light.

She nodded distractedly.

He followed her gaze to the steely haze that blanketed the waves below the house. "If the weather wasn't so dismal and you weren't recovering from that horrific ordeal, I'd take you to the fields behind St. John's Abbey. They offer a spectacular view of the North Sea.

"That sounds lovely." She put a hand to her head, which felt heavy from being out of bed. It took a moment for her to stabilize herself. "I wouldn't wish the terror of being trapped on my worst enemy."

He took her hand. "An enemy like me?"

"You aren't my worst enemy."

"That's right," he said puffing out his chest proudly. "I'm your husband . . . a husband who was delighted to make love to his wife for the first time a few days ago."

She blushed as she took a sip of tea. "It was wonderful, if not worrisome."

"Isn't a baby what you desire?" he asked.

"It is. But—"

Draven looked her straight in the eye. "If you're carrying our child, God would not be so cruel as to give you a marred son."

She tore her eyes away. She could hardly wait three weeks—when her courses either came or did not. But there was no use in discussing it until then. "I survived that trauma in the passageway but I haven't found my amulet."

"I suspect you'll come upon it soon," he said sincerely. "And I hope you decide to stay after you do."

The cool light of sunrise spilled into the room as Isabella pondered his plea.

When she said nothing, Draven pushed his shoulders back. "Right. We shall take this one day at a time. The doctor said you shouldn't travel for a few more weeks . . . just enough time to persuade you that living here at Thorncliff Towers doesn't have to be so gloomy."

"Persuading me of that shall take a miracle, I'm afraid."

He gave her a charming smile. "In case you haven't noticed, I'm adept at persuasion."

"You're off to a very good start," she said as visions of their wild lovemaking rose to mind.

He stood. "Tomorrow we shall get you out of bed and outdoors. Fresh air will do you a world of good."

The next morning, a dapper-looking Draven came to escort Isabella to breakfast in a dark blue waistcoat and breeches that fit him like a second skin. She could tell that he'd just come from his ride because he smelled of pine and salt air. After they ate a hearty meal of potatoes, eggs, and porridge, he convinced her to take a walk with him around the estate's grounds. Striding hand in hand, they made their way from the back of the house, past the garden slope, to Thorncliff Towers' stone façade. Isabella wasn't thrilled about her head injury, but it had prevented Draven from suggesting she join him on his horse ride today.

The wind felt cold and refreshing. Draven provided a sturdy anchor as she strolled. When she noticed how the wind blew his coattails askew and flushed his cheeks, her pulse leapt. She forced her stare away as they meandered beneath a giant elm that must have been a sapling centuries ago.

Draven took a turn sliding a glance her way. His expression turned thoughtful while he gave her a long history lesson on Thorncliff Towers. Patience was a side to him Isabella hadn't seen before and she didn't know how to interpret his newfound kindness.

They had nearly completed a circle around the house when Isabella noticed a barn house at the edge of the headland. While she and Draven chattered on, Mrs. Eaton came streaming out of the structure carrying the hem of her skirt.

"Lady Winthrop! Come quick!"

There was no time to ask questions. Isabella lifted her own skirts and followed the housekeeper inside the barn. Draven was right behind her. He clutched her shoulder as they came to stand in front of a rabbit yard. Alice was there, leaning over the side of the low fence wearing a genuine look of concern. She pointed to a female rabbit, a doe, lying within the pen that was writhing in pain.

"We came to check on the animals and discovered that this poor rabbit is the only one left," she said. "The door to the barn was left open last night. The other rabbits have mysteriously disappeared."

The wolves, Isabella thought. "Thankfully this doe survived," she said. "She looks pregnant."

"She is," Mrs. Eaton replied. "But she's havin' a hard time givin' birth. She's ill. Maybe losin' the others made her sick."

"We've tried everythin' to help her," Alice interjected. "But we don't know what to do. Since ye were a governess, m'lady . . ."

"I don't know if that experience will help, but I did have a dog growing up," Isabella informed them. Miss Blue had been the Farringtons' English Springer Spaniel. A magnificent canine with shining fur, Miss Blue had been loyal and playful. Sadly, she died shortly after Isabella's mother passed away. "I assisted when my spaniel birthed four puppies," she offered.

Draven had been standing silently by as the women conversed, his arms crossed. But the more he looked at the pathetic rabbit curled up in a ball, he became more sympathetic and he released his arms and sat on his haunches. "Is it the end for the doe?"

"I don't think so," Isabella said.

From the look of the hole dug within the yard, the animal had made a typical birth-giving nest. Shallow and cup-shaped, the hole was inches away from the weak rabbit. Isabella, who was still weak herself, climbed over the low fence and stepped inside the yard. She peered into the nest and saw that it was coated with tufts of the doe's fur. She didn't know much about rabbits, but she did know that bunnies were born without fur. Her heart tugged. The pregnant animal had plucked its own fur in anticipation of caring for her babies.

"She needs to squat over the nest," Isabella said quietly.

Picking up the limp rabbit, she stroked its back and talked to it gently. Mrs. Eaton and Alice were watching her with empathetic eyes while Draven's expression held a cool disdain.

"What if it has a disease?" he asked.

"You don't ask that when you eat Mrs. Tidwell's stew," Isabella replied sternly.

Draven made no comment as she tried to coax the doe to stand erect enough so that it could start pushing. Under normal circumstances, the rabbit would have bit her. Now it looked at Isabella with gratitude in its vulnerable state.

Making a mewing sound, the female began the birthing process. Isabella started to sweat as she knelt before the nest. After twenty minutes, her arms grew weary. Her head ached and her vision grew distorted enough to make the landscape tilt to one side.

"She's nearly there," she said. "But I can't hold her anymore. Will you take over for me?" She shot a look at Draven who had distanced himself from the scene.

He put a hand to his chest. "Me?"

"Yes. This will take a while and you have strong hands."

"I don't know—" he sputtered.

"Go on, Master Draven," Alice encouraged him with a smile. "The poor rabbit is too weak to do ye any harm."

Exhaling, he took off his jacket and rolled his shirtsleeves up. He stepped intrepidly inside the yard and took the doe from Isabella. At first, he held it at arm's length like it was something contagious. Isabella had to smile at how awkward he was with the quivering animal, but he managed to show a degree of tenderness at the same time.

After thirty minutes, the doe gave birth to seven adorable, closed-eyed bunnies.

"You did a first-rate job, yer lordship!" Mrs. Eaton cried.

Draven smiled as he let the housekeeper and Alice step in and take over the care of the exhausted female and her offspring.

"Wasn't that amazing?" Isabella asked.

"It was bloody fantastic." His face lit up while he put his jacket back on. "I've never been a part of something like that before. However, I'll never eat rabbit stew again."

She laughed. Then her smile faded. "I hope the doe will survive for her babies now."

"I hope so too. The ability to give birth is truly a miracle." He took her hand and squeezed it.

They walked away from the house and came to sit on a knoll that overlooked the bay. Isabella plucked at an arched vine while Draven's broad shoulders bunched as his arms dangled over his drawn-up knees.

"It was a good thing you knew what to do with the doe, Isabella. You have kind instincts."

"Thank you." She looked beyond the bluff to the encroaching tide.

Does Draven think I'd be a good mother? Am I pregnant right now?

She put a hand to her belly as she studied her husband's symmetrical profile. From this angle, his features were more exotically handsome than classically so. She gave a little smile as his charcoal lashes curled lushly against his eyelids and his dark, shimmering hair flapped enticingly in the breeze.

Instead of fighting the impulse to touch the fluttering strands, she reached over and threaded her fingers through them. He locked eyes with her and smiled.

"You impressed me with that rabbit today," she said. "Did you ever have a pet growing up?"

"Never," said Draven, taking her hand. "The closest thing I had to a pet was a bird I caught by the beach. It was a young seagull, but it managed to burst out of the lame cage I made for it. I suppose it wasn't right for me to imprison it in the first place." His palm grew moist despite the chilly air. "Just as I was wrong to insist that you stay here forever."

"Caring for someone means giving them the freedom to make their own choices."

"Said like a true governess." He chuckled to lighten the mood.

She put her hands on her hips and feigned offense. "I should put you over my knee for that."

He slid closer and kissed her seductively. "You can put me over your knee anytime."

She blushed. "There you go persuading me again."

He held her close as the salty sea air swept over them. "I just had a brilliant idea."

"What is that?"

"We should throw a party to celebrate you being alive and well."

Isabella drew away. Draven made her heart speed, but she still felt inclined to protest. "Joyous celebrations hardly fall under the Winthrop style."

"Poppycock," he said. "I can throw one hell of a fête as well as the next aristocrat."

"It doesn't seem like something you'd enjoy."

"You mean: why would I want to throw a party when I loathe people?"

She didn't reply.

"I'll do it for you. A ball will show all of London Society that I've received you with open arms—to dispel your current reputation. It will also be a send-off to my mother. An announcement as it were, telling the world that soon she will be living in London."

Isabella took in a breath. "Helena agreed to leave here?"

"Not yet. But she will when I discuss it with her." He continued to hold her hand and a thrill raced along her skin.

"I've heard that Helena is uneasy in the presence of a large group," Isabella said, putting a hand to the bandage on her forehead.

Draven gave her a mischievous wink. "All the more reason to throw a party."

"I don't think I'm ready for something like that."

"Come now. Aren't we supposed to be curing you of your serious ways? Besides, a party shall be an excuse to spoil you. You deserve a dress made from the finest material in England. I am picturing you in gold."

She finally smiled.

"I think a gathering is just what we need in this house—to take our minds off the recent chain of events," Draven went on.

"And the details of this celebration . . . ?" she asked, giving in.

"It will be a ball grander than any before it. With mountains of flowers, oceans of candles, and rivers of champagne. It will be the reception we never had the chance to indulge in."

"Our wedding celebration *was* rather pathetic."

"Thanks to me." Draven smiled sheepishly.

"We've been married for over two years," Isabella said. "Is it proper to throw a party like this?"

" 'Proper' is a notion I threw out the window long ago."

Isabella let out a laugh. "Said like a nobleman with the means to scoff at convention." She paused. "Very well. Have your party. I would protest more, but I suspect you'll do what you want anyhow."

"You know me too well."

"Shall we tell Helena?"

"Let's get you inside so you can rest some more," Draven instructed. "I will inform her about the ball, among other things."

* * *

Draven pulled a chair up beside his stepmother while she was eating her nuncheon. When he told her of his plan, Helena met the news with an open mouth.

"After this celebration," he explained further, "I'll have Alice accompany you to the Mayfair house. Once you've established yourself, you must hire a new staff."

"Why are you asking me to leave now, Draven?" she said.

"If I have any chance of keeping Isabella as a wife, I must do all I can to convince her to stay. That includes allowing her the privacy she deserves in her own household."

"Just say the words." Helena scowled. "You'd be happy if you never saw me again."

Draven answered her by crossing his arms defiantly.

"Very well. I'm not an invalid," she retorted. "I'll be perfectly capable of taking care of myself in London. Furthermore, I do not wish to remain where I am not wanted. As for this frivolous celebration, you must keep the guest list to those I insist on inviting."

"You are agreeing?"

She offered him her most ruthless smile. "I would have left long ago. But you never asked."

Draven's face turned as red as a ripe cherry.

After his stepmother took a sip of her Earl Grey tea, she stood and placed her napkin on her chair. "If you'll excuse me, I have correspondence to read. I'll be in my room."

Draven stayed in his seat after Helena left, pondering his next move. He had one more thing to do in his attempt to permanently capture Isabella's heart. And it meant searching the entire house on his own.

Chapter Twenty-Eight

Isabella climbed the main staircase to the second floor.

Nine days had passed since her ordeal in the secret passageway. Though it had been a horrendous affair, something positive had come from it: she'd gotten a glimpse of Draven's attentive side.

He had spent nearly every hour of the day with her lately. Fussing over her. Entertaining her. And he'd been nothing but kind and docile.

With her head buried in a book, Isabella continued along the corridor. She felt a hand on her shoulder. Wheeling around, she stared into Draven's face. Bright-eyed and unusually enthusiastic, he had his black hair tucked back at the nape while his freshly shaved face gleamed like a swatch of silk.

As dashing as he appeared, Isabella was mostly struck by the clarity he emanated—as if any signs of his madness had completely vanished.

He took her hand and led her into her chambers without saying a word. After he directed her to the upholstered window bench, they sat. She breathed in whiffs of his toilette water and leaned against him, as excited as a schoolgirl.

Draven said nothing as he caressed her hand. When Isabella

opened her mouth to speak, he stopped her by placing a single finger to her lips.

She studied the expression in his ebony eyes. There was something decidedly different about him today. It was a keen sense of purpose she had never seen in him before.

"What is it?" she asked.

"I found your amulet."

Her shoulders rose. "What did you say?"

"Your amulet. I've found it. And you'll never guess where it was."

"Where?"

Unclenching his strong jaw, Draven plunged into his story. "First let me say that I was more than a little upset when your father accused me of stealing your necklace. Besides the fact that you claimed it has no real monetary value, I would never take something from you that holds a sentimental place in your heart."

Isabella eyed him skeptically, yet nothing but genuine concern stared back at her.

"I was determined to locate it for you," he said. "I searched this household from top to bottom by taking out drawers, moving furniture. I even checked inside pockets of clothing that didn't belong to me."

"And?" An anxious lump blocked Isabella's throat.

He looked at her from the corner of his eye, as if it would soften his next words. "I found it in your father's room."

She sat in silence for a moment, completely stunned. "What?"

"I know it sounds preposterous, but it was there, in his bedside table drawer, plain as day. And now," he said as if he were at odds, "I'm returning it to you."

Flabbergasted, Isabella watched as he withdrew the amulet from his waistcoat pocket. For a moment, the necklace's stone glimmered in the air before he draped it across her bosom and clasped it behind her neck.

She touched the lapis. Its surface felt familiar and comforting. "When did you search my father's suite?"

"When he went into town early this morning." He paused. "Isabella, I'm very sorry to be the bearer of this sort of news."

"But there must be some sort of logical explanation for the amulet being there! Maybe my father found it earlier but hadn't gotten around to telling me yet."

"Perhaps," Draven said. He took her hand and traced the fine veins on its surface.

She leaned against him. "Do you think I should confront my father?"

He shook his head. "Let's allow him the benefit of the doubt. If he gives up his search of the amulet, we'll know he's hiding something."

"I don't understand why he'd steal it in the first place."

"Has your father ever asked you to return the amulet to him?"

Isabella thought for a moment. "Just after he arrived here, he offered to take it and have it cleaned and restored."

"What was your answer?"

"I told him I preferred it exactly how it was."

"Well, I suppose it's anyone's guess as to why he confiscated it." Draven paused. "Bella, I know you love your father. And I know how relieved you were when you brought him back home after his accident. But I suspect he may be suffering from dementia based on amnesia. I've read a great deal about it in a medical journal written by a doctor in London."

"Amnesia?" She squeezed his hand for stability.

"Yes. The physician's name is Nicholas Van Sant. After conducting a barrage of interviews and countless exams, this doctor concluded that a severe blow to the head can erase one's memory and alter one's personality drastically."

"Papa has seemed quite different to me," she admitted. "He's lost sections of his memory and I never remember him being so stern. On the other hand, there are times when he is exactly as I recall."

"It's not your father's fault," Draven said. "I hope you don't mind, but I've secured an appointment for you with Dr. Van Sant. During your meeting, you may ask any question you like. Perhaps you'll learn how to help your father. However, keeping your appointment will mean traveling to London for a day or two."

Isabella smiled and overlapped his hand with her free one. "Thank you so much."

He frowned. "Just promise me you shall return."

She smiled. "I shall return to tell you what Dr. Van Sant said."

"This must be very difficult for you."

Draven had no idea just how hard it was for Isabella. But a bright spot shone this day. The fact that he had hunted for something so precious to her while showing real concern for her father was exhilarating. "You searched this entire house for my amulet?" she asked. "You did that for me?"

His hot stare met hers and the fortress she'd constructed around her emotions began to crumble one brick at a time.

"I'd do anything for you, Isabella," he whispered.

She snuggled into the curve of her chest and sighed. "Draven?"

"Hmm?"

"May I ask you something?"

"Of course."

She sat up and looked at him. "I'm learning to trust you again, so there is something I must know. Promise not to get angry?"

He reached up and stroked her cheek with the back of his hand. "Ask me anything."

"Was it you spying on me during my bath? When I first arrived?"

"No." He smiled forlornly. "I told you, it was probably a pubescent hall boy."

Strangely, she believed him. "I want to ask you something else."

"Of course."

"The first night I was in your bed, when I said I cared for you deeply. Why did that statement provoke such violence?"

Draven's expression dimmed. "All my life, I've never considered the feelings of others. Therefore, I feel as though I don't deserve to be cared about."

"Everyone deserves to be loved," she said. "But you haven't felt that in your life, have you?"

To Isabella's surprise, he knelt before her. She traced the outline of his diamond-shaped face with her fingertips.

"Only two people have ever shown me love," he said. "And to them I am forever grateful."

"Who are they?"

"My father and . . . you."

Her eyes misted over at his admission. "I showed you love, but then I refused to help you, didn't I?"

Draven dropped his stare from hers and hung his head. "You're not to blame. I asked more of you than most people would ever agree to."

"It's odd," she murmured. "I feel as if something led me here—to be with you and help you. I'm afraid I can't resist you."

Concern lit his dark eyes. "Maybe the power of the amulet is the force behind that attraction."

"No. What I feel is real." She paused. "Draven, we will find a way out of this. We have to."

"Thank God I found you, Isabella." He rose up and caught her mouth with a scorching kiss. His touch warmed her like a blanket on a frigid night and she felt as if she were truly home. A surge of joy shot through her. At that moment, nothing else seemed to matter. Not the attack on Helena. Not her father's mysterious behavior. Not even Draven's violent personality. As she melted against him, all that was important was her vow to stand by him—despite the consequences.

Draven wrapped her in his protective embrace and murmured to her between tender kisses, "My God, how I've longed to touch you while you recuperated. I adore everything about you, Isabella. Let me pleasure you."

Before she could respond, his mouth was on hers and his hand was drawing up her skirt. His fingers teased the curve of her ankle bone beneath her petticoat. He removed her shoe and stroked his fingers along the delicate bones of her foot. His hand made its way up her thigh and the lightness of his touch made her entire body quake. Gently, slowly, Draven untied the lace fastening of her pantalets and peeled away her stockings, leaving nothing but cool, bare skin beneath her dress.

Wearing the sultriest of expressions, he urged her back against the windowpanes and lifted her hem to one side. Draven brushed her mouth with a kiss before he disappeared to work his magic between her parted legs.

At first, his tongue felt like an airy feather against her anxious core. To her delight, he teased and licked the outer folds of her womanhood with quick, naughty flicks. Despite her best efforts to stay still, Isabella wiggled and shifted against the slickness that escaped. Surprised at her own aggressiveness, she fisted his hair and encouraged him to her pulsating center. With just the right pressure, Draven tugged and lapped and sucked at her sensitive nub. After moments of insane anticipation, he brought her to the top of a pulsating crest.

Purring like a spoiled cat, she raised her hand against the steamed windowpane. They hadn't made love, but Draven didn't seem to mind. Rather, he appeared content with her satisfaction. In a gallant motion, he brought her up to a sitting position.

"You, sir, are very talented at that," she said.

He grinned as he sat down beside her and nuzzled her neck. "And you, my fair lady, are a most attractive subject on which to perfect my talent."

They sat side by side for a while, listening to the rain fall. "If we are ever parted, no other man could ever measure up to you." Isabella sighed.

Draven encouraged her chin upward so that she could lock eyes with him. "No man shall *ever* touch you, my Bella. And you shall never be rid of me unless it is over my dead body." He studied her with those intense, obsidian eyes. "I love you."

Her heart kicked inside her chest. She had longed to hear those words since the day she had agreed to marry Draven. What started off as a marriage of convenience had finally richened into a union of true feeling. For her, the words he had just spoken completed an essential circle.

Happy and content, Isabella curled against his muscular body. "I love you too."

He drew her closer. "I will be a proud husband tomorrow night at the ball."

She smiled as they sat in a comfortable silence. Gradually, her eyes dropped to the soft lull of the rain and her mind started to drift along a wave of contentment. That is, until a horrible thought struck her. According to the Egyptian prophecy, she was doomed to kill the man she loved—once they became lovers.

Chapter Twenty-Nine

The elegant strains of a string quartet drifted up to Isabella's bed-chamber.

Standing before a full-length mirror, she eyed herself with admiration. The gold beaded evening gown Draven had commissioned for her on London's fashionable east side accentuated the color of her hair to perfection. With its cap sleeves, flowing train scalloped in a brilliant bullion, and snug-fitting bodice that nested her impressive cleavage, she knew she would impress Draven at the party.

Gwyneth had fastened Isabella's dense mane into a soft chignon while allowing small curls to canopy her oval face. It was a popular look worn by the finest of Europe's noblewomen and she felt very daring when she looked at the finished result in the mirror.

After applying a dash of red-rose lip-stain and a rare spot of perfume, she stepped into the hallway. Making her way down the curved staircase to the heavily populated ground level, she took in a surprising sight.

The ambience of the house was astounding. Never before had Thorncliff Towers looked so grand. Mrs. Eaton deserved praise for arranging for the ball so quickly and so thoroughly. Iron candelabras glowed with the light of a hundred candles while butlers in formal dress served guests from silver platters in subdued tones. And the music emanating from the ballroom was simply intoxicating. It had been much too long since Isabella enjoyed a dance but, considering her mood, it was going to be difficult for her to laugh and enjoy herself.

Her eyes darted about the crowded room for any signs of her dark prince. She spotted him standing before a wall of draped windows. With one hand pressed to the small of his back, he was engaged in conversation with an elderly couple. The woman was fluttering a fan nervously beneath her sagging chin while her husband had his head thrown back in hysterical laughter. It appeared Draven was at his most charming this evening.

He spun slowly around and when he locked eyes with Isabella, his dashing image stole her breath away. Dressed in a finely cut waistcoat of pale yellow silk that turned back into tails, he ignited that familiar spark within her. His debonair ensemble was completed by a pair of black britches worn over silver ribbed stockings and an outsize cravat that encircled his neckline. From beneath longish hair that waved about his ears, Draven flashed a devilish grin as his skin bronzed against the citrine color of his coat.

Abandoning the elderly couple, he sauntered toward her like a graceful panther. Once he reached her, he sketched a charismatic bow. "You look positively beguiling tonight, Lady Winthrop."

"Thank you." Isabella forced herself to echo his light tone.

"May I have the honor of this dance?" he asked.

"Certainly."

He waited patiently as she scooped her train off the floor and flung it over one wrist. Then, with a firm hand on the small of her back, Draven drew her close and twirled her onto the dance floor in time to a melodious quadrille. As Isabella promenaded with her hand planted in the center of Draven's palm, she watched his powerful jaw clench and unclench as he spoke. He bent his head forward in an intimate gesture as he led her with confidence. She gave a pleasurable shudder as his hot breath jiggled her ear baubles. And when he cradled her so, she never wanted him to let go.

Could they ever become a force powerful enough to conquer his Gypsy spell—or her Egyptian prophecy?

Last night they had made love, though it was a protected union since Isabella had insisted. Afterward, he had persuaded her to go to Romania with him. There, they planned to search for anyone who knew the Gypsy woman. Draven told her they would leave very soon and because she knew that the full moon, which was drawing dangerously near, might further corrupt his mental state, she decided to revel in this dance while it lasted.

"You truly look stunning this evening," she heard him repeat in a whisper.

"Thank you." She paused. "Do you remember the night we met?"

"How could I forget? You were the only thing that sparkled at that dull party."

"It was the one and only time we danced together."

Draven grinned. "That's when I suspected you were beautiful beneath that frumpy gown."

Her dark mood was finally lifting. She smiled. "Frumpy gown, was it?"

"I believe every guest in this ballroom would agree that you've blossomed into the brilliant beauty I saw in you that day."

Isabella turned to see if Draven was right. But the smiles that greeted her told her that they were being stared at as a couple. She had melted disarmingly into the curve of his chest and it was obvious that people found them a well-suited pair. In fact, a crowd had formed in a semicircle around them since they were the only remaining couple on the dance floor.

"Lord Winthrop is the black wolf!"

Isabella halted at the words. She whirled around to see a withered Gypsy woman and an old man who appeared to be her husband standing by an open window. Behind them were at least five villagers grasping pitchforks and sickles.

"You Gypsies have no place here!" Draven thundered.

The woman stepped forward. Her boldness made several guests gasp.

"I know you are the black wolf," she cried.

Draven's face flushed. "How dare you come here and cast accusations. I was kind enough to give you a place to stay."

"You banished us from your property after we got settled," the Gypsy man chimed in. "You're heartless!"

"I didn't banish you," Draven said from beneath a deep scowl.

The woman clutched her scarf tightly beneath her chin. "Your messenger told us to pack up and abandon our camp. He said you wanted nothing to do with our filthy kind."

"Messenger? What are you talking about?"

"The *rauna* curse," the Gypsy cried. "I've seen the vision. You, Lord Winthrop, are nothing but a bloodthirsty werewolf!"

Werewolf? Sickness inched its way up Isabella's throat. Her balance began to slip away. Could Draven be the beast she'd seen outside her window? *Could the baby I may be carrying be such a creature?*

She clutched his arm with ferocity. "Is it true?"

Ever so slightly, Draven hesitated. "Of course it's not true. They have no proof. No one saw me transform—"

What? Isabella stepped back.

Draven gasped. "I didn't mean to say—"

The villagers began to rush at him. He called for his male servants to form a barrier in front of the intruders. Some of the male guests did the same and no one was able to get through.

"I am still magistrate of this region and I command you to leave," he raged.

"We'll leave, ye black-hearted cad," a villager threatened. "But ye never spent a shillin' of yer precious money to help Dunwich. It's washin' out to sea and we hate ye for it. We'll be back, before ye kill any more of our livestock or pets. Before ye kill one of us!"

The room began to swirl around Isabella. *I've been so stupid.* Her psychological fear of werewolves had prevented her from seeing straight. From putting it all together. But now she knew: the beast outside her window had Draven's eyes. And the wolf that had burst into Thorncliff Towers the other night was searching for its alpha male.

Draven's curse made him no "metaphoric" monster beneath a full moon—*it made him a werewolf.*

Floundering for something to hold on to, Isabella's legs gave way and she lost consciousness.

Chapter Thirty

When Isabella awoke she found herself staring at the ceiling of her bedchamber. No doubt Draven had deposited her on the bed and left her before she could demand an explanation.

Her stomach wrenched as the sickening horror over his deception gripped her anew.

How long was he going to let me go on believing he was a madman instead of a vicious wolf?

She hastened off the bed and knocked something to the ground in the process. Peering down, Isabella saw Draven's journal lying on the rug. She picked up the book and opened it to a passage marked with a ribbon.

June 12, 1807
Tonight Father died. Tonight I have been cursed.
Killing that girl was a god-damned accident. I don't know if that woman's spell will come true. Time will tell, but her words shall haunt me forever:

"On your twenty-seventh birthday, Draven, you shall see— the horror of the spell I cast upon thee. It is the night you are doomed to become—a bloodlusting wolf with a dark kingdom.

Your outer self will match the selfish beast you truly are—have
no doubt your sons will also be marred!"
    The rauna *curse . . .*

Isabella's heart thundered and her lungs constricted.

Draven had been doomed to become a bloodlusting wolf. *It was*
all true.

She thrust the book down and opened the door. Hurrying to the
balustrade, she leaned over but she saw no one amid the hushed silence. Apparently all the guests had fled after the Gypsy cast her ac-
cusation.

Where was Draven?

Rushing to the foyer, Isabella found Rogers and asked after her
husband's whereabouts.

"His lordship is in the cellar."

"The cellar?" she repeated.

"Yes, m'lady. But his lordship is in no shape for a lady's eyes."

Isabella swept past him and made her way to the kitchen. After
asking Mrs. Eaton for some direction, she followed the housekeeper
to a narrow doorway that topped a stairwell. The woman handed her
a candle branch before returning to Mrs. Tidwell's complaints about
the mess the servants had left in the kitchen.

Without wasting another minute, she gathered her train in her free
hand. Raising the flickering branch to eye level, she inhaled a deep
breath and descended the cramped stairwell toward the cellar.

The bowels of Thorncliff Towers smelled dank as Isabella touched
her foot off the last step. Along the dim corridor she saw no signs of
life but released a shudder at the sound of rats scurrying about in the
darkness. Much to her relief, she noticed a light coming from a storage room in the western half of the cellar.

When she neared the lantern-lit room, laughter echoed in her ears
and the aroma of expensive-smelling cigars and aged brandy filled
her nostrils. She hesitated for a moment in the doorway. A swatch of
dark green clothing had caught on the sharp, wooden doorframe. Removing the piece, she realized it was fabric from a male waistcoat.

Could it be Draven's?

She doubted that he'd been down here recently, but then she remembered what Dr. Lamstein has said following Helena's exposure
to poison.

If you have a still room, the poison could have been made in this very house.

There was a still room in the cellar. Gwyneth had told Isabella so. If Draven was a werewolf he was certainly capable of poisoning someone.

She marched into the storage room. Her husband was the first to see her. With his arms crossed over his chest and his solid form tilted away from the table in a grandiose manner, Draven appeared every inch the thick-skinned rogue he'd been when Isabella married him. Next to the nobleman sat a larger gentleman who was downing a swig of brandy. Beside him, a third participant twittered as he scooped a disassembled deck of cards together.

"Ah, Bella," Draven said between puffs on a fat cigar, "I had no doubt you'd come looking for me."

She stood her ground.

He took a sip of brandy then pounded the glass on the table. The ruby liquid swirled in violent circles. "While this may look like an ill-reputed game of chance," he said in a drunken sputter, "it's actually a high-stakes round of Shuttlecock. Do you care to join us?"

"Lord Winthrop," the larger of his two companions thundered, "a gentleman never asks a lady such things." Then the man burst into laughter, nearly choking on his liquor.

Draven met the jest with his own throaty laughter. Once his humor subsided, he took another gulp of brandy. "You're absolutely right, my lord. I do owe the countess an explanation for my appalling behavior. But first, Lord Taverly and Sir Bartholomew, I must introduce you to this beautiful woman who is my wife." Slurring his syllables he turned to face Isabella. "Did you know these good fellows came all the way from Warburton in Greater Manchester for this grand gala? Funny—they've been down here all night playing cards. Missed all the drama in the ballroom. Lucky bastards . . ."

The beefier of the two men exploded with laughter again then wiped the perspiration from his brow. He acknowledged Isabella's presence with a less-than-graceful rise.

"This place smells to high heaven." She directed the stench away with a wave of her hand.

"It smells like a gentleman's heaven and, in my opinion, the stench is far better down here than it is upstairs," Draven muttered.

"The sweet cologne worn by those old fatwits makes my stomach churn."

His face grew solemn as he held up his hand of cards.

Anger still rippled inside of Isabella and she wasn't backing down until they could speak. "My lord, how can you sit there and act like nothing has happened? I want a word with you alone."

"In a moment," he replied without looking up. "There is the matter of one hundred guineas I must attend to first."

The remark sent the three men into hysterics.

"You're all foxed!" she cried. She refused to be a part of this madness any longer. "I'd like a word, *now!*" When she reached Draven's chair, she yanked the cards from his hands and threw them vehemently on the table.

"I think your wife means business," squealed the third player who hadn't spoken until now.

"You're right, Sir Bartholomew. Very well." Draven removed the cigar from his mouth and extinguished it. He carried his off-balance frame into the corridor where Isabella followed him. With every step they took, the echo of laughter faded behind them.

Isabella stopped in the dim shadows and turned. "Do you take nothing seriously?"

Draven dropped his head. She waited as he swayed on his feet. But instead of raising his voice in defensive anger, he slurred his next remark. "My whole world has just been dashed to hell. I didn't think there was anything left to do but have a drink."

"You mean: have a dozen drinks."

Draven took her by the arm. "I'm sorry the people of Dunwich feel the way they do. The money I used to start my shipbuilding business is money I should have used to help them."

"That's not why I'm angry," she blazed back.

Draven remained silent as he teetered back on his heels.

"Your lack of help is bad enough, Draven," Isabella continued. "But you have deceived your own wife. Now I know that the man I'm chained to becomes a blood-driven beast when the full moon shines—"

He rocked closer to her, reeking of brandy. "If I had told you the truth I would have lost you."

"At least I would have learned it with dignity, instead of during a public display." Isabella's eyes narrowed. "Do you know what kind of man makes the most frightening werewolf of all?"

He looked humbled, defeated. "No."

She couldn't lie. "A madman like you. You have two sides to your personality even without the provocation of the moon. A manipulative, charming side and a dirty, lying side."

She began to storm away but Draven's words stopped her. "The citizens of Dunwich plan to rally together with villagers from neighboring towns. With every available resource they're determined to fight this vicious black wolf . . . this *werewolf*."

It seemed strange to hear him say the word.

"My God," she said under her breath.

"Isabella, it was just a matter of time before someone discovered me. It's my guess that no matter the arsenal of weapons they bring forth—stones, wolf bane, torches, pitchforks, or perhaps a silver bullet—it will ultimately result in my demise."

He came to stand by her. Before she could move away, he took her by the shoulders and pinned her against the cold wall. "Don't you see? We can never be together. As I told you before: our love is doomed. I didn't need the power of your curse to make that happen. I am truly sorry."

Isabella fought for a breath. The happiness they'd shared yesterday had been snatched out from under them. *And so quickly.*

"This is about murderous evil of which you have no idea," Draven said. "Why do you think I begged you not to come back here after our wedding night? Why do you think I pleaded with you to end my life? When I become this monster, it takes every fiber of my being not to hurt anyone."

Tears pooled in her eyes as he continued.

"You hardly knew me before my curse was actualized so you may find this hard to believe. But a change in me has occurred. I was selfish, spoiled, and unloving before you came into my life. But you've helped me transform. I feel now. I want to shower you with love and I want to be loved. You are the only good thing in my life. And I refused to let anything push you away. But now my alter ego is consuming me. It's possessive and taunting and it's ruining all that I feel and all that I do. Maybe it's best that you left—"

He pitched forward. Isabella steadied him. In this state, he seemed so pitiful and vulnerable. Draven looked at her tenderly for a long while, his defenses all but gone. How many times had she considered coming back to him after their wedding night, to see him gaze at her just this way? She had replayed the moment he held her for the first time over and over again. She felt as safe in his arms as a bride at the altar—as if she finally belonged to someone who could take care of her, as she'd always cared for others. To someone else those feelings might seem pathetic, but the way she'd grown to care for Draven was what it was.

Now everything was spiraling downward.

They embraced for a long while. Isabella drew away and Draven brushed the tears from her cheeks.

"I understand you need time to think," he whispered.

She nodded. Her common sense was having a horrendous battle with her overwhelming empathy for Draven.

"Leave this place for a while," he said. "Take your father back to London and see to his health."

"Perhaps you should go somewhere as well," she said. "Someplace far beyond the long hand of the lynch mob."

"Where shall I go? To Scotland? To the Americas? No. The risk of a killing spree will follow me."

She tore her gaze from the pitiful look in his eyes.

"What I am telling you is that you are free to choose your fate," Draven said in a voice coated with emotion. "But promise me that you will return to tell me if you wish to remain my wife."

She made no reply in her confused state.

Before he slipped into the shadows, he feathered a soft kiss across her lips. "Always remember: I will love you until the last moon rises."

Chapter Thirty-One

Isabella informed her father straightaway that they would be leaving Thorncliff Towers. As he prepared to go with her, Harris hadn't yet revealed his possession of her amulet, but that was the least of her worries.

She suspected that while she was in London, Draven would shut himself away from the world again. Would the walls of Thorncliff Towers protect him against the murderous mob?

Isabella felt a familiar rush of nerves as she encountered him in the dining hall the next afternoon. He was sitting in front of an untouched plate of roasted beef, distress deepening the lines of his forehead.

The heaviness in her heart had stolen away her appetite, so she stood rigidly beside the table. She cleared her throat in order to get his attention.

Draven remained silent as repressed emotion surfaced in his bloodshot eyes.

She laced her hands together. "I'm leaving in an hour. I will return before the next full moon—to tell you of the direction I shall take."

Draven, hunched in an anguished pose, ran his fingers through his hair. "I'm sorry, Isabella." He paused. "So this is good-bye for now?"

She nodded.

He reached for her hand but she refused to unbraid them from her firm clasp. The action seemed to claw at him like a sharp dagger.

"You have no idea how my feelings for you govern my every thought and action," he said. "Bella, you are everything I've ever wanted in a woman, from your honesty and intelligence to your extraordinary spirit."

"Why didn't you say these wonderful things long ago? And why didn't you tell me the truth?" Her heart accelerated. "I shall return before the next full moon." She spun on her heel in an attempt to hide her tears. As she left to attend to her packing, a single thought plagued her mind: *Will learning I'm pregnant make me return permanently?*

The ride into Dunwich seemed to take forever. Isabella, seated across from her father, tried to engage him in trivial conversation, but he seemed preoccupied all the while, as if his thoughts were adrift on a distant sea.

"Papa," she said in a loud voice, "since we're alone, I must tell you that an enormous lynch mob is gathering. You heard the Gypsies who appeared at the ball, didn't you? The mob intends to capture Draven."

Harris broke his eyes from the landscape and met her gaze. "If your husband isn't the black wolf, he will have nothing to fear."

"That is hardly what I expected you to say." She stiffened in her seat.

After a moment, his eyes turned soulful. "I'm sorry that you ever married that madman, Isa. If I'd only listened to those rumors of Draven's insanity—"

"Draven suffers under a terrifying curse, but he is not insane," Isabella said, her heart aching.

"Then may heaven help him."

She heaved a sigh of frustration. She could only hope the doctor in London could help Papa. He neither acted nor spoke as she remembered. After a brief silence, she decided to broach the subject of her amulet. She inhaled for courage. "There is something else I have been meaning to talk to you about."

"Oh?" Harris said distractedly. He stroked his chin and continued to glance out the window at the rural scenery.

"Yes. It's about my necklace."

That seemed to capture his attention. He leaned forward on his cane and looked her directly in the eye. "What about your amulet, my dear? Have you found it?"

"No, but apparently *you* have." She wrung the thick cord of her reticule nervously around her fingertips.

Confusion shadowed his face. "I don't understand."

"I was beside myself when it went missing. Draven took it upon himself to search for it. That is why he went into your room. No doubt you found it in disarray."

"I did," he said slowly. "And?"

"And . . . Draven told me he found the amulet in your bedside table drawer."

Her father remained silent beneath a dubious expression.

"Naturally, Draven was excited," she continued, "so he kindly returned it to me."

Harris crossed his arms. "And you believed him? That I took it, I mean?"

"What reason would he have for lying?"

"I can't say for certain, but let's suppose he lied to cover up the fact that *he* stole the amulet from you while you slept."

"Are you insinuating that he stole it with the intention of returning it to me later?" she asked.

"Considering the problems you've been having, it makes perfect sense. Ultimately, he wishes to appear the hero."

Isabella shot a look out the window as yet another small village rolled by. She hadn't anticipated this suggestion. Who would she believe now? On the one hand, Draven did have a great deal of ground to make up after he practically clawed her in his own bed. However, if Papa was guilty of taking her amulet, maybe he intended to sell it for a much-needed profit. It was likely that he would go to any length to protect the act.

Her expression turned solemn. "I'm sorry, Papa, but I believe Draven. If you wanted the amulet back, you should have simply asked me. So, no more lies. We're going to London to see a doctor who specializes in amnesia."

"Your loyalty lies with your husband now," he said softly. "I understand."

She reached for his hand. "You haven't acted like yourself since the accident. Maybe this doctor can help you. Promise me you'll consent to an examination."

"Is my behavior that strange?" he asked.

"Yes."

Harris put his hand to his forehead and grimaced.

Another headache, Isabella presumed.

"Very well." He gave her a weary smile. "I give you my word."

Chapter Thirty-Two

Draven was struck by how quiet the house seemed after Isabella departed.

He wandered into the library to read, but found no joy in it. He took Lucifer for a ride, but even the stallion seemed despondent in Isabella's absence.

A bundle of nerves, he finally retired to his private chambers where he took a light supper in solitude. He was about to ready himself for bed when there was a knock at the door.

"Yes?" he called out while he wound his pocket watch.

"It's Rogers, sir."

"What is it?"

"Ye 'ave a visitor, sir."

At this hour? Draven moved closer. "Who is it?"

"I don't know 'ow to put this, m'lord—"

"For God's sake, old boy!"

Rogers lowered his voice. "She's a Gypsy who says 'er name is Marga Yavidovich. Sir, she claims she is the grandmother of the girl ye killed when you were sixteen."

"What?" Draven released the pocket watch and it slipped to the floor.

"She arrived moments ago by neither horseback nor carriage." Rogers's voice cracked. "Sir, she must 'ave walked all the way up the steep cliff to Thorncliff Towers . . . on foot."

It took a moment for Draven to realize that this was a very good turn of events. Perhaps the woman could tell him how to find the witch who thrust the curse on him. "Show her into the drawing room, Rogers. I'll be there momentarily."

Draven donned his silver waistcoat in haste and as he descended the staircase, he struggled for composure. Entering the drawing room, he clasped his hands behind his back to hide the fact that he was shaking like a leaf. His visitor sat dwarfed in an oversized armchair. Yet the resolve in Marga Yavidovich's expression told Draven she was a strong, determined woman. Her hands were calmly intertwined and her dark brown eyes studied him intently.

When Draven came to stand before her, she neither stood nor smiled. Instead, she cocked her head to one side. He guessed her to be upwards of sixty years of age. As he studied her lined face, it seemed truly ironic that she was born of the same blood as he, for she seemed overcome with poverty and persecution. Perhaps the only similarity between them was the same dark defiance in her eyes that always seemed to cause a commotion in his.

His shame over what he'd done to her granddaughter grew as he stared into that dark insurgency.

Draven asked the woman if she cared for something warm to drink. She refused so he waved Rogers out of the room. He sat on an ottoman and he and the Gypsy proceeded to stare at one another for what felt like an eternity. Assuming he would have to initiate the conversation, he finally spoke.

"I must ask you why you've come here this evening, Marga. May I call you that?"

Nodding, the woman leaned forward. She encouraged him to do the same with a crook of her forefinger.

"I've come to see if Ekaterina Stella's curse has come true. The curse of a Romanian *vârcolac*. A werewolf."

Draven could restrain himself no longer. "It bloody well has!"

"And what has that been like for you?"

"*Like?* That damned spell has forced me to live on a nightmarish carousel. It's impossible for me to get off, no matter how I try. I assure you that during the next full moon, the transformation will happen again."

Apparently satisfied with the answer, the woman sat back in her chair. "I see that over the years, you've become a true *romero*. You appear to be a noble and elegant gentleman."

"My manservant informed me that you are the grandmother of the young girl I accidentally . . . killed." He forced gentleness into his voice. "If this is true, I do not expect compliments."

"Are you aware that your birth mother, though she was younger than I, was my best friend?" she asked in a thin voice.

"No."

"Do you have any idea what happened to your mother?"

"No," he said.

"She drowned herself in the pond at the edge of Dunwich." The pain in the woman's eyes was obvious. "You see, when Miranda came to this house with you, a babe in arms, your father offered her money to disappear forever."

Emotion tugged at Draven. "Miranda? Was that my mother's name?"

She nodded. "Miranda refused the money but she agreed to leave you here. She left this place without you and without any sign of love from your father. For her—and for your grandmother who watched her suffer—it was devastating."

He folded his arms across his chest. "So the story goes."

"And you have no feeling for their pain?"

"I never knew my real mother. Besides, the harsh reality is, she gave me away instead of caring for me."

"No, no," the woman said as she wagged her finger in distress. "She relinquished you out of love. She came to this house hoping to form a family—Miranda, you, and your father. When the earl insulted her by offering her 80,000 pounds to go away, she was heartbroken. But she could also see that your father carried a soft spot for you in his heart. When Miranda set foot in this grand house and saw how opulently the Winthrops lived, she realized that if you were raised at Thorncliff Towers you, too, would have the finest things money could buy. She told me that she didn't want the disoriented and nomadic Gypsy life for you. So she left you here. Afterward, she told everyone that saying good-bye to you was the hardest thing she'd ever done."

A ping of sadness vibrated inside him. "That is why she killed herself?"

"Yes," Marga said solemnly.

"I didn't know my mother committed suicide."

"Because we were as close as sisters, a part of me died the night Miranda took her life." Tears welled in her eyes. "The rage I felt was so severe, it ate away at me for many years. Adding to that rage was the contempt I felt toward you. *You took away my only grandchild.*"

Draven leapt up and began to pace. "I regret my actions. I didn't intend to kill your granddaughter. You see, I lost my father moments before I came to the camp. He told me on his deathbed that I have Gypsy blood in my veins. I didn't take the news well, to say the least."

Marga nodded. "Turning your back on your own people propelled the *rauna* curse. You did a terrible thing by killing an innocent girl from your clan."

He nodded solemnly.

"But," she added, "you have suffered because of it. My visions have verified this. The torment you endured in the asylum and the guilt you still carry proves that you have gained compassion, despite your innately selfish nature."

Hope stirred inside him. "Will this sever my curse?"

"It is not enough," she replied.

"Please"—he dropped to one knee before her—"where is my grandmother now? She must undo this hideous spell!"

"I'm sorry to tell you that your grandmother is dead. I, however, have become the matriarch of the tribe. I have directed my people back to this countryside in order to seek you out."

"So you can revoke the spell?"

"No. Only the Gypsy who laid the curse in the first place can undo it."

Draven rose, a scowl contorting his face. "If my grandmother is dead, why did you come here? To torture me with your presence and to inform me that I will suffer as a werewolf forever—unless I am shot with a silver bullet?"

Her sharp nose twitched. "You know you may will your own death."

Draven's heart plunged. "I have already tried to kill myself. It didn't work. My immortality prevailed."

"That is because Gypsies consider suicide a selfish act. It creates too much pain for those who are left behind. Thus, your mother's death was not only tragic, but shameful. That fact enraged your grandmother even more."

"Gypsies are a complicated lot," Draven said sourly.

"Fortunately, willing your death is different than committing suicide to a Gypsy," Marga said. "Someone must end your life out of an agreement you make with them. To me, you have proved that you have gained compassion and humility, but it is the forces of black magic that must be convinced."

"How do I do that?"

"You must command someone to shoot you with a silver bullet. If the dark forces believe you have shown enough change, you will resume your human identity as a result. If you have not changed enough in the eyes of the underworld spirits, you will stay a beast forever—with no morphing back and forth into your human form."

Draven's gut wrenched. "I cannot live as the beast any longer. This bloodlust is beginning to destroy me."

"Until you feel you have gained enough compassion, *te na khut-shos perdal tsho ushalin.* Try not to jump over your own shadow. The werewolf that lurks inside you makes you one entity."

"I beg of you!" Draven cried. "The evil this spell produces is overwhelming. *It must be stopped!*"

"It is not up to me to stop it," she said. "You have the purest, and the darkest, Gypsy blood running through your veins. The Szgamy tribe can trace its roots to the Carpathian Mountains in Romania—the very center of all black magic."

Draven looked crazed. "That heritage is poisoning everything about me. My sexual appetite . . . everything. I fear I will destroy my wife."

"Szgamys are undeniably passionate. And you, Draven, were a man who always loved with your body and never your heart."

"All that has changed. I love Isabella with every ounce of my being. And this blasted curse is standing in our way."

The woman's tone quieted. "Are you forgetting about Isabella's curse? Perhaps it is *her* spell that is standing in your way."

Draven's eyes narrowed. "What are you talking about?"

Marga shrugged. "You have chosen her and you love her. But the amulet made Isabella choose *you*. She is destined to destroy you, unless you can find the bracelet of Amenhotep. Because the Egyptians were the first practitioners of black magic, their spells are even greater than ours."

"I don't believe it," he said.

The woman pulled herself to her feet. She placed a weathered hand on Draven's arm. "I only came here to tell you about your mother and to let you know that I forgive you for my granddaughter's death. *Akana mukav tut le Devlesa.* Now I leave you to God."

"God? How can you speak of God? He cannot help me now, but you can. You must revoke the curse."

She looked as if she were pondering something. Then she shook her head.

"Wait." He took hold of her bony shoulders. "You said I can die if I will the action. If I can convince someone besides Isabella to shoot me with a silver bullet then my wife will never have to bear the burden of ending my life."

The idea was a good one, but its outcome gripped Draven with sorrow since it meant being without Isabella.

Marga's expression grew grave. "A *rauna* spell is extremely powerful. It is a curse of penance. A person under its spell is transformed into an unfeeling, murderous creature on their twenty-seventh birthday. It is up to them to prove that they regret the disloyalty they've shown their people. If you are going to command your own death, Lord Winthrop, you can only do so during a full moon. It will honor your connection to the Gypsy culture and to the Dark Arts. It will also show that you know you have changed but that you are giving up your life selflessly regardless." She paused. "The moment the silver bullet pierces your heart, you'll know whether you will continue to live in your human form—or in your wolf form."

Draven sucked in a breath. He was willing to take the chance that he would be a beast forever if it meant sparing Isabella from killing him. "Tell me exactly what to do."

The Gypsy woman rolled her shoulders forward in an act of surrender. "You will not like it."

"Nothing can shock me now."

She looked up at him. Fear replaced the defiance in her black eyes. "After someone shoots you with a silver bullet, they must place you in a freshly dug grave that lies next to your mother's resting place. This will make Miranda's spirit happy for she will know that she is finally with you. Hopefully it will also end your identity as a werewolf forever. Do you think you can do this?"

Draven paced back and forth by the roaring fire. He stopped in front of her. "Of course I can. Where is my mother buried?"

"She rests by the pond where she drowned. Her grave is marked by a small, wooden cross. As it is too painful for me to go there, I can only hope the cross remains as a marker."

His eyes narrowed. "But how will I choose who will shoot me?"

The woman reached up and took his hands in hers. It seemed imperative that she have his full attention before she spoke again. "The one who shoots you can be no ordinary person. They must be someone who loves you."

Horror swelled in Draven's eyes. "But . . . but there is only one person who loves me and Isabella refuses to pull the trigger."

Marga wrapped a dark shawl over her cape for added warmth as she prepared to take her leave. "It is the only way to reverse a *rauna* spell."

"You don't understand. She won't do it!"

"It is you who doesn't understand, Draven. She will do it because it is her destiny. After she kills you, she will kill herself. I have seen the vision of her pulling the trigger of a gun."

"You have been no help at all. I wish you'd never come here," he shouted as she moved toward the door.

She didn't react. "I will be staying at the Gypsy camp on the edge of town. Come to me and I will give you a special silver bullet that I shall pray over."

Before Draven knew it, the woman had slipped out of the room and left him inert in its center. His mind whirled. The woman hadn't come to offer him forgiveness. She had come to torment him back to the brink of madness.

There was no way out and the possibility churned his stomach like a foul disease.

Chapter Thirty-Three

Isabella had promised Draven that she would return before the next full moon—to tell him whether she would resume living with him or not. In the interim, she would learn if she was with child.

Waiting those three, long weeks was agony for Draven. He passed the time as impatiently as a child forced to attend the symphony. And he had tortured himself with various scenarios.

Should he tell Isabella everything? Or should he remain silent about what he had learned from the Gypsy woman?

If only he could get his hands on that god-damned, Egyptian bracelet. But that was impossible. The bloody piece of jewelry was probably sitting in the vast Egyptian desert, buried beneath the shifting sands.

Knowing that the next full moon was drawing near, Draven neither slept nor ate. Rather, he constantly thought of the knowledge Marga Yavidovich had given him. And that evilness wasn't something he could dispel unless he agreed to make the ultimate sacrifice. Isabella would be repulsed to know that the Gypsy woman believed it was she who would end his life before turning the gun on herself.

No, Draven decided. Isabella must never know these things.

It is up to me to find an alternate way out of my curse.

* * *

Almost three weeks after Marga Yavidovich's appearance, Rogers announced another visitor at Thorncliff Towers. Draven, annoyed that his morning sleep had been interrupted, responded to the valet in a groggy voice. "Whoever this unexpected visitor is, he or she must wait for me to dress. I shall receive them in the music room."

"The music room, sir?" Rogers asked.

"That's what I said, damn it!" Although he wouldn't admit it, Draven didn't wish to relive his encounter with Marga in the drawing room. He proceeded to pry himself out of bed and a quarter of an hour later, he greeted a kindly faced man sitting on the pianoforte bench.

"I'm sorry to have you wait," Draven mumbled as he covered the length of the room. "I am afraid I was awake all night."

"It's quite all right." The stranger spoke amiably, but irritation shone in his gray eyes.

"You are . . . ?" Draven asked.

"Benjamin Rayburn." The gentleman stood and the two men exchanged handshakes.

"Please be seated," Draven offered.

While Rayburn resumed his place on the bench, his tufted eyebrows and bushy mustache twitched. After he cleared his throat, he went on to explain that he was a friend of the Farrington family. He also claimed that he'd sent Harris Farrington correspondence ten days ago to arrange a visit.

"I had hoped to see both Sir Harris and your wife." Agitation surfaced in Rayburn's tone.

Draven strode to the picture window and threw back the curtains. He stared at the mist that rolled along the ground toward the gazebo. "I'm afraid that your timing leaves much to be desired, Mr. Rayburn. Lady Winthrop and her father are in London. She intended to seek medical help for Sir Harris."

"I don't understand. Is Harris sick?"

"Let's just say that he has not been himself lately. Perhaps that is why he forgot about his appointment with you."

"I see." Rayburn tugged on the points of his vest. "And when will Lady Winthrop be returning?"

"Tomorrow," Draven said, pivoting to face his visitor. "If you wish, you may stay the night as my guest."

"No, thank you. I must return to London."

"Shall I give my wife a message from you?"

"Yes," Rayburn replied. "The most important thing I wish to relay to Lady Winthrop is that her uncle, Morton Farrington, has never been condemned to Fleet's debtors' prison."

With that, Rayburn rose and handed Draven a business card. "Please have your wife contact me at her earliest convenience."

Claiming that he preferred to show himself out, Draven's visitor disappeared from the room with a quick gait.

Never been condemned to Fleet's? Draven mulled the words over in his mind. Now his curiosity was completely aroused. And though he dreaded telling Isabella, he decided she must know the discrepancy in her father's story.

Relief rippled through Draven as Tuesday arrived. He picked at his nuncheon then stepped outside to meet his wife's coach. Standing by the enormous front doors with his hands clasped behind his back, he realized that staying in that spot wouldn't make her coach appear any earlier. He decided to pay a visit to his father's gravesite.

Encased by a low, wrought-iron fence, the family cemetery was located to the east of the house over a small knoll. Draven tugged his frockcoat lapels up against the sharp autumn breeze. He took the five-minute walk to the small graveyard under dreary, overcast weather that provided a perfect atmosphere for his visit.

The yard contained only eight honorary plots because it was reserved for blue-blooded Winthrops—the first of which found their resting place here as early as 1596. Draven knew that if his illegitimate birthright were discovered, he would never be buried here.

The familiar bitterness over his Gypsy heritage resurfaced. He stepped lightly among the headstones, and when he reached his father's plot, he read the inscription he'd seen a thousand times before.

HEREIN LIES CYRIL OCTAVIAN WINTHROP

EARL OF DUNWICH

1757–1807

DEVOTED HUSBAND AND FATHER

" 'Devoted,' my foot," Draven murmured under his breath.

Helena would have placed any words on the headstone if those words portrayed her marriage in a good light. But he faced a problem graver than Helena's insecurities. Could he prevent the woman he loved beyond all reason from being responsible for his death? If he succeeded in that, he would remain a wolf, forced to snatch away innocent lives while driving Isabella away in the process.

Either resolution seemed heartbreakingly final.

Draven raised his head at the sound of wheels crunching over gravel. Marching to the other side of the grounds, he watched the estate's post chaise rock to a stop in the courtyard. Rogers clattered down from the bench and approached him with a troubled look.

"Yer lordship, Lady Winthrop did not arrive on the carriage from London. Apparently she has decided to stay in London."

"God's balls!" Draven began to rage.

Rogers laughed, his eyes twinkling.

He shook his head. "Not funny, you old coot."

The valet hastened back to the post chaise and opened the door. Draven drew in a breath as Isabella alighted. His wife's pretty face appeared from beneath a fashionable, lavender bonnet. He had missed everything about her including the charming way her auburn hair framed her luminescent skin and how finely etched her small nose was. She was his whole world and his heart pounded.

When their eyes connected for the first time in three weeks, he smiled. "My Bella."

Isabella cast her eyes downward.

Draven's nerves skittered. *What is her decision?*

"How was your journey?" he asked as lightly as he could.

She frowned. "Bumpy and uncomfortable, as always. But it's no matter."

"Where is your father?"

"He informed me that he won't be returning here since my amulet has been found." Isabella took his outstretched hand. "Our conversation was horrible."

He wanted to console her but he didn't know how. "Shall we take a stroll?"

She nodded stiffly. "I need some fresh air."

"What exactly did your father say?" he asked as she walked beside him, clutching her fur-trimmed muffler.

"He denied taking the amulet. He suggested that you had it all along—so that you might return it and appear a hero. I rebuked your involvement and there was a tension between us one could cut with a knife."

Draven scowled. "Harris can create a million, strange explanations to cover up what he did, but I know what I saw, Isabella. I'm convinced he's playing mind games with you, but I'm not sure why. Where is your amulet now?"

"Safely concealed in the lining of my portmanteau."

"Excellent," he said.

Isabella's eyes remained glued to the ground. "I arranged for him to stay with my cousin again." She paused. "I'm just grateful to see you."

Draven's insides flamed.

They strolled as Isabella chattered on about her appointment with Dr. Van Sant. She told him that the doctor described amnesia as a very difficult condition to treat. Besides the fact that its victims don't realize there are gaps in their memory, the ability to recall things needed to be restored on its own.

The garden's dry leaves snapped beneath their feet. Barren and brown, the desolate space seemed to want for a ray of sunshine—just like Isabella. Draven sat beside her on the stone bench amid an awkward silence.

"No doubt your father hates me," he said.

"He doesn't trust you."

He gave her hand a squeeze. "Do you trust me?"

"I've been doing nothing but thinking. As much as I wanted to, I couldn't bring myself to stay in London." Torment swept over her face. "I grew incredibly hot, as if I had a fever, yet I didn't. The doctors said it wasn't illness, but it felt like a crippling disease. My bones ached. My mouth went dry. I lay in bed for days."

"Are you . . . with child?" Draven struggled to get the words out.

"No." Her face betrayed a host of emotions. "Pregnancy wasn't making me sick, but I felt deathly ill. Strangely enough, I started to feel better as I prepared to return here," Isabella said.

It's the power of the Egyptian amulet at work.

She gazed at him with the innocence of a child. "I must tell you where I stand."

He held his breath.

"People may think me mad, Draven, but I want to be with you."

Tears glazed her golden eyes. "Monster or not, I know another side of you. I know you are capable of gentleness—and love. And we shall fight this together."

Relief brought Draven's shoulders crashing forward. He drew her to him. His soul sang with unbound happiness as he tried to push aside the fact that she was in danger being here. "I've missed you terribly. I could think of nothing but you."

Isabella sighed into the fabric of his coat. "You look as though you haven't slept at all."

"I haven't," he admitted.

"Is there something else you want to tell me?"

Only the fact that I feel more doomed than ever because of my curse.

"A gentleman by the name of Benjamin Rayburn arrived here at Thorncliff Towers yesterday." He held her at arm's length so he could see her face. "The man was cordial, but he seemed put off that your father wasn't here. He claimed that your father was expecting him."

"That's very odd." Isabella's face twisted up. "My father never said anything about expecting a visitor. Why didn't Uncle Ben stay until we returned?"

"I'm not sure. But he handed me his calling card. I'm to give it to you, not your father."

She took the card from Draven. "I shall contact him immediately. Did he say anything else?"

Draven lowered his voice. "He told me that your uncle Morton is not at Fleet's. In fact, he's never been sentenced to serve time there."

"But that's what Papa told me." Confusion clouded Isabella's eyes.

"Yes, I know."

"I don't understand," she said in a trembling voice. "What does this mean?"

"It means that we must be extremely careful about whom we trust from this point on."

A droplet spilled down her cheeks and Draven caught it with the tip of his finger. He planted a gentle kiss on her cheek in replacement.

When Isabella glanced about the bare garden, he followed her stare. "This is the spot where we met the night my mother was poisoned," he said. "Do you remember that frigid evening?"

Isabella nodded with nostalgia. "We huddled on this bench and stared up at the moon."

He tugged her face toward him. "It was also the night I scared you."

"I remember—all too vividly." She blushed.

"I will never do that again, Bella." He raised a hand to the softness of her cheeks. "Your decision to support me makes me very happy. And I want to show you how much. Will you lie with me again?"

Her expression turned serious. "I'm not afraid of you, if that's what you mean."

"Then come to me after supper. I'll wait up for you, and the door will be unlocked. And wear nothing beneath your nightgown."

She pressed her fingertip to his lips. "Until tonight."

Chapter Thirty-Four

For Isabella, making the decision to return to Draven hadn't been difficult. It was as if she'd had no choice.

She had become devastatingly ill while she was away. She had lain in bed with a raging fever and her thoughts had become hazy, confused. In her weakened state, her courses came and went, confirming that she was not with child.

When she learned the news, she had mixed feelings. It was true that she'd been desperate to create a family with Draven. But now, of course, they had much to sort out. Until they did, she decided that their lovemaking must still take place under the protection of a sheath.

Seeing Draven again made her wonder if having a child was actually in her destiny. *Maybe God has other plans for me, plans that involve helping him.*

Isabella traveled down the darkened hall and up to the fourth floor. When she arrived in front of Draven's bedchamber doors, her stomach tightened. She tried the doorknob. It slipped open in her hands and she stepped into the sitting room.

At first she didn't see Draven. *He must be in bed before a fire.* She followed the flickering shadow of the hearth but found the bed empty.

"Bella."

She wheeled around at the sound of his voice.

"I've been waiting for you." Draven was sitting casually in an overstuffed chair beneath the window. Bare-chested, he sat with one leg dangling freely over the side of the chair, his untied trousers tight against his manhood. As he lounged there in that provocative position, he appeared more sexually potent and delicious-looking than any man she'd ever seen. Isabella's eyes roamed over his chiseled torso and his massive shoulders. He resembled an ancient carved statue, the most perfect specimen of a human male she'd ever seen. Her heart thundered.

He waved her closer. "I left the door unlocked as promised. Did you do as I asked? Did you wear nothing beneath your shift?"

She took a step backward and removed her garment so that he might have his answer.

He sucked in a breath. "Now take down your hair."

In response, she removed a pin from her chignon. In a single tumble, her reddish-brown curls spilled over her shoulders and bounced between her bare breasts.

Draven gasped. "You're stunning."

Isabella started to speak, but he stopped her by putting one finger to his closed lips.

"Join me, my sweet." He extended his arms forward.

She moved to him. As she clasped his hands, her palms became damp against the heat of his body. Inhaling his musky fragrance, she licked her lips and willed herself to shut out the violence he'd shown her the first time she had shared his bed.

"You have blossomed into an amazing woman in your time here, my Bella. A woman strong enough to control her own destiny. I want you to pleasure yourself before I take you," he said hoarsely. "Straddle my thigh and move yourself against it."

Trembling, she separated her legs and mounted him. Draven took one of her hands and cradled the back of her neck with the other. He stared at her with smoldering admiration while her mouth hovered above his. Exhaling, his warm breath rose to greet her face and before she knew it, he was catching her lips with fiery kisses—kisses that made it nearly impossible for her to breathe.

"I dreamt of you every night while you were away," he rasped as an undeniable urgency exploded between them.

His tongue darted in and out of Isabella's mouth, exciting her. Fulfilling her. With his mouth sealed over hers, he traced the outline of her jaw before his touch moved along her bent neck to the shadowed spot between her breasts.

"Move your cunny in small circles against my leg," he urged between kisses.

She had never pleasured herself before and wasn't sure what to do. Draven shifted his sinewy thigh upward so that she could rotate her sensitive core against its solidness. The friction intensified against her depths, tantalizing and dampening them. She gyrated slowly at first, then faster. In the meantime, Draven continued to catch her mouth with hot kisses. He teased her nipples to a high charge, causing low moans to escape from somewhere deep inside her throat. As the sounds filtered into the air, Draven's desire flamed.

"Make yourself come," he coaxed her.

Isabella writhed against the strength of his leg while he kneaded her buttocks. Her body began to tremble and she wanted to scream at the dizzying sensation. When her center stopped pulsating, Draven delved his fingers beneath her to gather her wetness. He smiled.

"Now it's my turn." He guided her hand into his breeches. She released his throbbing shaft and this time she knew what to do. She boldly tightened and released her grasp up and down the length of his sex, making it as solid as iron.

"Are you ready?" he whispered gruffly into her neck.

"Yes." She was literally aching for the feel of him inside of her. She stood briefly so that she could tug off his breeches with two firm jerks. He sat and pulled her to him.

"I want you to use a sheath," she whispered.

Disappointment flickered over his face, but he did as she asked. Once he had secured the pigskin over his penis by tying its ribbons, Draven didn't waste another minute. He grabbed her hips, parted her legs, and urged her body on top of him. While she straddled his shaft slick with want, she gripped the wings of the armchair on either side of his head. Rocking up and down with heightened rapture, her breasts swung before him. Draven gathered them together in one fist. He took them in his mouth and suckled them fiercely until they turned dark.

Empowerment swelled inside Isabella as she realized she liked being above Draven, claiming the husband many said was mad and unfeeling. She knew him in a way no one else did and she wanted to protect him, love him, and cure him as only a wife could do.

Reveling in the titillating pressure she'd built up by being above him, her eyes fluttered shut and another moan of ecstasy filled the air. The pressure was so intense that she bit her lip to prevent herself from screeching.

Draven too, grunted with passion as he buried his face in the crevice between her breasts. He pressed his hands to her hips and kept them captive over his stiffness.

There! The petals of her core began to pulsate again as he rocked his hips upward. The rhythm escalated and the vibration seemed to last forever. Draven came too. His body shuddered before he withdrew from her. But an instant later, his pleasurable expression vanished.

"What's wrong?" she asked.

"Bloody hell," he cried. "The sheath broke!"

Isabella flew into a panic. "My God—"

"I . . . don't know what to say." Draven avoided her gaze.

Putting a trembling hand over her mouth, she broke down.

"Please don't cry." He took her hands in his.

She slumped against him, sobbing uncontrollably.

"Shhh." He tried to comfort her by stroking her hair. "Isabella, please don't despair. Everything will be fine."

"How do you know?"

"I can't tell the future, but I know how I feel at the moment. You are a ray of sunshine that slices through my world of darkness. Not only have you saved me from my solitary existence, but you've shown me that there were things about me—even before I was struck with this curse—that needed changing. And I can never thank you enough. You are an extraordinary person through and through, and when we have a child, that child can be nothing but good as well."

Isabella forced a lump down her throat. "I never believed in curses, until I met you. What if I give birth to a boy, a boy born with your hideous curse?"

Draven looked at Isabella and his heart raced. Her pink cheeks glowed like an enchanting Christmas candle and her auburn hair shone like flowing nectar. She was beyond beautiful, yet her eyes housed a silent torment. He loved her more than anything, but he knew he was putting her through hell.

He'd known about Tousret's curse and had been selfish to marry her in the first place. *But no more.* An epiphany erupted inside him and suddenly he knew what it meant to be compassionate. To be selfless. To love unconditionally. He must love someone else more than he loved himself. And that person was Isabella.

Pulling on his breeches, Draven directed her to sit on the edge of the bed. While she tugged on her nightgown, his stomach clenched. He was going to have to tell her that she was in danger here and he must send her away. "Bella, this is the last time we will be together for a while."

She frowned as his words came out in a rush. "What did you say?"

"My next request may appear to have come out of nowhere, but I hope it's something you'll agree to."

"A request? Agree to?" she echoed. "I don't understand."

"Hear me out," Draven pleaded. "You must leave this place."

"Leave? What are you talking about? We just made love—"

"Try and understand."

"If you are worried about me being pregnant, please don't," she said. "We will deal with it the best way we know how."

"It's not that."

Her eyes widened with confusion.

"It's imperative that we part ways," he repeated.

She crossed her arms over her chest. "You owe me a better explanation than that, Draven."

"This place holds nothing but danger for you," he said. "You must go somewhere and wait for me. Until I can figure things out more clearly."

Little does she know that I'll never come for her because I'll be dead.

"Go without you? You're scaring me."

"I don't mean to scare you." Leaning in, he gently reached for her hand.

"But I just came back. Why did you let me return?"

"I didn't come to the decision until right now. When I realized the hell I was putting you through."

She eyed him suspiciously. "I don't buy that explanation. Did something happen while I was away?"

"No."

She wriggled her hand free from his grasp. "It must have. Tell me what happened."

He shook his head and turned his gaze toward the fire.

"After all we've been through, I deserve to know," Isabella insisted.

She was right. But he must protect her at all costs. "It's nothing I can speak of. Just promise me you'll leave this house at once. Resume your governess position, if that is what makes you happy."

"You expect me to leave you, but you won't tell me why?"

Anger began to pulsate in Draven's veins. "Damn it, woman!" he growled. "What part of this don't you understand? If you stay here at Thorncliff Towers, you'll surely die."

Tears continued to flow over Isabella's cheeks. "You're just saying that to frighten me away."

"It's the truth."

"I won't do it."

His blood boiled and his hands shook. He was losing control. And though he tried to tear himself away from her, his wrath kept him glued to the bed. Isabella's eyes filled with fear as he grabbed her elbows roughly and bit down on one of her shoulders. *Perhaps that will convince her to leave.* She screeched and tried to pull away from him. He hated himself in that moment, just as he hated himself for killing the Gypsy girl.

Isabella screamed again. She tried to slide past him—which made him grab hold of her more tightly. The action smeared her blood on his hand, but as she wriggled free, Isabella swatted it down before the smell could tempt him. Then she ran from the room.

In a mad fury, Draven thrust the window open and heaved himself into the frosty night air. To satiate the urge he had to run, he scaled the outer wall of the house and flew across the headland in his human form. And as his pace increased, his heart thudded with the knowledge that his love for Isabella and her love for him were the cruelest curses of all.

Chapter Thirty-Five

Isabella walked along Dunwich's jagged coastline at the break of dawn.

Last night she had awakened Gwyneth and Rogers so that they could take her to the town inn. Now, as she pushed her feet along the sand, nausea knotted her stomach. She was fixated on the fact that Draven had made passionate love to her before his personality had taken a violent shift.

She strolled along in a daze, a shell of her former self. She felt as if her soul had left her body and she had no more tears left. Two years ago, she had arrived at Thorncliff Towers brimming with every bride's expectations of romance. Later that day, Draven had caused her to flee in terror. It had taken all of Isabella's courage to return to him and when she did, she had discovered all of his darkest secrets.

Despite those secrets and in light of Draven's violence, she'd fallen madly in love with him. Now he was sending her far away—possibly forever. It was enough to drive a woman mad.

Weighted against the forceful wind blowing in her direction, she gathered the lapels of her overcoat to her neck. She had sanitized and bandaged the bite Draven had taken out of her shoulder, but the wound was still incredibly painful.

Glancing over her shoulder at her footsteps in the sand, Isabella knew that none of her husband's actions made sense. She wanted to find out whether Draven meant to protect her—or be rid of her—but she didn't know how.

Wondering about the time, she climbed up the embankment and joined Gwyneth who had been waiting for her. The abigail glanced at the small pin-watch attached to her jacket. "Shall we get a cup a' tea, yer ladyship? We have more than an hour before the next post chaise leaves for London."

"You go ahead, Gwyneth. I think I will lie down."

"Very well, m'lady."

Gwyneth started across the street while Isabella moved in the other direction. A tall, dark-haired gentleman walking ahead of her caught her eye. He was moving at a brisk pace and appeared to be headed toward the edge of town. She strained her eyes to catch a better glimpse of him. With long hair that covered his stand-up collar and broad shoulders that complemented his regal height, he reminded her of Draven. But that was unlikely.

What would Draven be doing here in the village?

To her surprise, the man came to an abrupt halt at the edge of town. Standing in front of the dressmaker's shop, he turned in a circle as if to confirm that no one was watching him.

It was Draven!

An intense curiosity spiked within her. Perhaps if she followed her husband, he would provide her with some long-awaited answers.

Gathering her skirts, she slipped through a gate nestled between rows of cottages behind the dressmaker's shop. The gate led to an open meadow. Dry and brittle, the thirsty winter vegetation crunched beneath Isabella's boots. Elevating her body by the balls of her feet, she tried to catch sight of Draven's hat.

There he is!

Since he was more than a hundred feet in front of her, she was able to follow him unnoticed. As he approached the ridge of the bordering forest, he disappeared into a wall of trees. She entered the forest several moments behind him, careful not to make a sound. The fir trees stood at attention around her, resembling eerie rows of blank-faced soldiers. She gave a shudder.

Forcing herself to press on, she became unnerved by the silence. Every so often a bird flitted noisily from tree to tree and the sound stirred her heartbeat.

Keep Draven in sight. He seemed to know where he was going.

He came to the edge of a small pond and stopped. Crouching down, Draven examined something by the water's embankment. It was difficult for Isabella to make out what it was, but once he moved on, she saw it was a wooden cross marking a grave.

She crept behind him until he reached a clearing in the woods. As soft violin music lofted in and out of ear range, she spied six colorfully painted caravans encircling a roaring fire. Dogs barked while several people dressed in dark clothes and jeweled scarves milled about the area.

Isabella inched closer. She saw Draven remove his hat and climb a ladder into one of the wagons. Convinced she was hidden well enough beneath the ladder itself, she strained to make out an exchange between her husband and a woman.

"Why have you come here?" the woman asked in a thin voice.

"I have come to ask one last time: is there an alternate way of revoking my curse?"

"No, Lord Winthrop. I told you: our spells are much too powerful to be derailed from their path."

Isabella sucked in a breath. *Why didn't Draven say he'd spoken to this Gypsy?*

"You said it is Isabella's destiny to end my life before she takes her own," he said with determination. "But I have sent her away."

"She will return. She loves you too much to be parted from you forever."

Isabella repressed a gasp. *Is it my fate to kill Draven after all?* Her entire body trembled at the thought.

"I refuse to believe that Isabella's destiny is written in stone."

The woman's voice grew firm. "I told you: I have seen a vision of her pulling the trigger of a gun."

Isabella's mouth went dry. So that is why Draven sent her away!

He hesitated. "Are your visions always correct?"

"They are." She paused. "But I must say, in all my years I have never seen anything like the double curse that plagues you and your wife."

"Our love cannot end the way it was predicted," Draven thundered.

"The laws of the universe are greater than us," the woman said. "Now, I will give you the silver bullet Isabella must use."

There was a pause. The floorboards creaked. Then there was the unmistakable scrape of wood as a drawer opened and closed.

"Draven," the woman said, "sending Isabella out of harm's way and putting her life before your own shows you have learned what it means to be a merciful human being. But, as I said before, the dark forces must be convinced."

Draven remained silent.

"Your mother would be proud of you at this very moment."

"I wouldn't have changed without my wife," he answered.

Emotion quaked through Isabella.

"Learning to love selflessly is part of the spirit cycle," the woman said.

"Well, the spirit cycle can go to hell as far as I am concerned," Draven growled. "I just want to be with Isabella."

"Unfortunately you have no choice. The next full moon rises in two days. Isabella will kill you at your mother's gravesite by the pond. Did you pass the spot today?"

"Yes, it is still marked by a cross, but Isabella—"

"She will certainly fight it, but she will kill you then kill herself. At that time, both curses will have come full circle."

The revelation that Draven had begged her to go to avoid fulfilling the amulet's curse, made Isabella love him all over again. Desperation clogged her throat as she heard the woman's voice again.

"Here is the bullet."

"My life is nothing without Isabella by my side. I won't let this happen," Draven vowed. "I will find another way."

Before Draven could leave the wagon, Isabella took flight into the forest. As she retraced her steps through the maze of trees, she could hardly function. The conversation between Draven and the Gypsy woman repeated itself in her mind, pelting her with emotion.

This is utter madness!

She wiped away her tears and tried to think clearly. If only she had the bracelet of Amenhotep. But she wasn't that lucky.

Since nothing dire would happen until the next full moon rose two nights from now, Isabella decided to go to London to speak with

Uncle Benjamin. It was a ten-hour journey each way, but it was plausible. Though she'd lost contact with Benjamin after her father's disappearance, she remembered him as a gentle, honest figure—and she valued his advice a great deal.

Would Uncle Benjamin think her mad? Or would he listen without criticism?

Regardless, she would seek his counsel before coming back to Thorncliff Towers in time to stop the prophesized plan of execution.

Chapter Thirty-Six

When Isabella arrived in London proper, the late-afternoon sun was giving way to the impatience of dusk.

As she and Gwyneth climbed out of the post chaise, they blended into a stream of street vendors peddling their wares. Heavy fog rose from the harbor below London Bridge while scents from the rolling carts wafted beneath Isabella's nose. Hot cross buns, baked apples, even the smell of syllabub enticed her empty stomach. But this was no time to think about food.

While the masses hurried against the cold near the St. James coaching station, Gwyneth dragged Isabella's heavy portmanteau down the street. Isabella tried to flag down a closed carriage without success. To add to her frustration, worry over Draven's fate built inside her.

Gwyneth, who had traded her flimsy cap and maid's costume for a more fashionable bonnet and dress, looked equally frustrated. They had been standing by the roadside for nearly a quarter of an hour. The girl finally stuck two fingers in her mouth and blew an ear-piercing whistle. A closed carriage stopped with a jerk. Isabella and her maid hastened forward and were relieved when the driver handled their baggage.

"Where to, Miss?" the burly man asked politely.

Isabella retrieved the card her uncle had given Draven and recited the address to the driver.

"Inns of Court. Right away, Miss."

The two women settled against the rear bench as the carriage rattled forward. Gwyneth started twisting a handkerchief nervously around her fingers and Isabella shot her a puzzled expression. "Is something wrong, Gwyneth?"

"Oh, I 'ate to be difficult, m'lady, or speak out a' turn, and I'll certainly be happy to attend to ye anywhere—"

"You've seemed uneasy ever since we left Thorncliff Towers. Please speak freely." Isabella realized her tone was impatient, but she couldn't help herself. She had too much on her mind.

"Mrs. Tidwell said this mornin' that I shouldn't jeopardize me post . . ."

Isabella waited for her to go on.

"Well, my fiancé lives in Dunwich and considerin' that we're to marry come November, I was wonderin'—"

"—how long I'll be in London since you don't intend to work for the Winthrop household after your wedding?" Isabella smiled.

The girl's eyes filled with tears. "Oh, thank ye fer understandin', m'lady. Yer as kind as they come."

Isabella patted the girl's hand. "Something tells me I shall be returning to the coast very soon."

Gwyneth wiped the moisture from her enormous blue eyes. "If it isn't too bold, m'lady, can I speak about another matter?"

Isabella frowned. "Yes."

"It's Master Draven. He's the reason I'm leavin' the house. He frightens us all."

No doubt the servants heard the Gypsy's accusations during the ball.

The girl's stare housed genuine terror. "'Aven't ye heard them, m'lady? Bays of a wolf comin' from inside the manor 'ouse? From the master's suites? Do ye really think he's the black wolf?"

Isabella looked away. She wished they had a dog so she could blame the sounds on the animal. But they possessed no pet and there had been no one else in her husband's bedchamber at the time. "I've noticed the howls too, Gwyneth. And I've come to London to help his lordship."

The maid nodded. "I'm glad to hear it. We're forced to lock our doors at night and—"

It is a wonder there are any servants left at Thorncliff Towers, Isabella thought. "Gwyneth," she said gently, "the last thing his lordship and I need is hysteria from the staff."

"Yes, m'lady."

To Isabella's relief, the girl remained silent for the remainder of the ride. In the meantime, she prayed that her uncle was still in his office at Britain's Inns of Court at this late hour.

The carriage finally bustled to a stop before a tree-lined square just south of Strand and Fleet Streets. Isabella looked up at a sign hovering from a gold chain: MR. BENJAMIN RAYBURN, ESQUIRE, ESTABLISHED BARRISTER.

Sucking in a deep breath, she stepped into the haze of twilight. Instructing Gwyneth to wait, she left her valise with the twittering girl. When she pushed the door open, a delicate bell announced her arrival.

"May I help you, Miss?" A young intern glanced up from his paperwork with irritation.

"I'm Lady Draven Winthrop. I'm here to see Mr. Rayburn."

The young man's expression didn't change. He placed his quill on the desk and folded his hands neatly together. "Do you have an appointment, your ladyship?"

"No, I don't. I'm Mr. Rayburn's niece. Well, I'm not actually his niece—"

"Are you or are you not Mr. Rayburn's niece, Lady Winthrop?"

"Excellent tone, Nathaniel! Use it during your next cross-examination."

Isabella glanced over at the sound of the familiar voice. Grinning, Benjamin Rayburn stood up from his desk and circled round a small partition. "I taught that boy everything he knows."

A straight flagpole of a man, Uncle Ben was just as Isabella remembered. His bulbous nose hovered over a bushy mustache and his salt and pepper hair brushed the tops of his substantial ears. She smiled as she realized his witty, gray eyes still studied those around him with humility and grace.

"I apologize, sir," the intern said.

"Quite all right, Nathaniel. But there is no need to interrogate this young woman. She is the closest thing to a niece I'll ever have. Let me look at you, Isabella." Although his words were kind, his expression was grave as he clasped her hands in his. "You've certainly grown into a lady of stature."

"Thank you, Uncle Benjamin. But you haven't changed a bit."

"It's wonderful to see you," he said. Again a worried expression washed over his face.

"Is something wrong?" Isabella asked.

"I shall tell you shortly." The barrister tipped her chin up with two fingers to analyze her countenance. "And you. Do I sense a dark cloud somewhere in your midst?"

She couldn't lie to him nor did she wish to. "Yes."

Benjamin withdrew a gold pocket watch from a tiny slip in his vest and glanced at it. "I think we've been at this long enough, Nathaniel. What do you say we close up shop? If you will lock up, I will escort this elegant lady to supper."

"Yes, sir," the intern replied as his employer tossed him a small ring of keys. "Good night, sir. Good night, your ladyship."

After Isabella had sent Gwyneth ahead to Uncle Benjamin's residence, Rayburn donned a fashionable beaver hat and strolled with her arm in arm until they reached a nearby pub. Benjamin seemed to be a regular patron at the establishment as he was greeted with exuberance. The pair was shown to a secluded booth in the back where they ordered the shepherd's pie.

Isabella settled against the soft leather pads of the booth and let out a sigh of exhaustion.

"My dear," Benjamin began, "you must tell me what is happening at Thorncliff Towers. I came to meet with your father several days ago. Do you have any idea why he wasn't there to receive me?"

"He was with me here in London." She lowered her voice. "He mentioned nothing of your planned visit. Lately, I've been concerned about his behavior, Uncle Benjamin. He hasn't seemed himself since the accident in Egypt. In fact, I've consulted an amnesia specialist about him."

Benjamin looked troubled. "And what did this specialist say?"

"Nicholas Van Sant is a very reputable physician. He said my father's irrational anger is perfectly normal. A great jar to the head can bring suppressed emotions to the surface. It can also stir sides of our personality we weren't in touch with before. The doctor claims Papa's loss of short-term memory is normal as well."

"Very interesting. You assume this is why your father forgot about my scheduled visit?"

"Perhaps. Many things slip his mind lately. As I said, Papa seems to be a different person."

"I'm glad you have noticed," Rayburn said, his gray eyes darkening. "But amnesia is not the reason your father seems so queer to you."

Chapter Thirty-Seven

Isabella's forehead creased. "I don't understand."

The barrister rested his elbows on the chipped table. "I've received some rather startling news, my dear. That is why I came to Thorncliff Towers."

"If you're going to tell me that Uncle Morton isn't in debtors' prison, my husband has already informed me as much."

"I'm glad he relayed the news to you. But that is not what I was going to tell you."

"What then?" Her eyes widened.

Overlapping his hands, he leaned forward on the table. "Isabella, they've unearthed your father's remains in Egypt."

"What are you talking about? My father is alive!" The shrillness of her voice caused the other patrons to glance over.

Benjamin looked sympathetic as he ignored the stares. "I'm afraid he's not. Think about it. Morton is your father's *identical* twin brother."

Isabella's hand flew to her mouth. Benjamin continued as tears spilled down her cheeks in streams. "When your father resurfaced in Society, I expected him to contact me but he didn't. Naturally, I deemed it strange after our long history of friendship and that's when my suspicions began. I wrote to the second in command at Harris's archaeological site. A Mr. Simon Collingsworth. Miraculously, Mr. Collingsworth managed to survive the terrible landslide and vowed at that point not only to repair the damage done to the Valley of the Pharaohs, but to restore it to a level beyond even what your father had managed to do before he disappeared.

"I told him I would pay handsomely if he continued to search for your father's body in the process. You see, something was telling me that your father was not who he seemed to be. After a long, arduous process, Collingsworth discovered your father's remains." He paused and clasped her hands with empathy. "Isabella, Harris's skull was bashed in. The Egyptian authorities have deemed it foul play."

She struggled to make sense of what Benjamin was saying. "Papa was murdered before the landslide took place? I don't believe it."

"It's true," Rayburn conceded. "I told Collingsworth that I suspected Morton was involved. He wrote in his reply letter that Morton had talked your father into some antiquities dealings—to help finance his lengthy dig. Collingsworth discovered that these antiquities dealings were disreputable and unprofitable. I believe that Morton showed up in Egypt and that the two brothers argued. Morton killed Harris, set the landslide into motion, then seized the chance to become his twin. It was very easy for him. After all, he is a man with the coldest of hearts and the blackest of souls."

Isabella's hands began to shake. "But why did Morton kill my father?"

"Hasn't Morton always been envious of Harris?" Rayburn asked.

She nodded.

"Envious to the point of obsession, in fact. Your father had everything Morton desired—fame, notoriety, a beautiful family. I know it is hard to fathom such a jealousy, but I think that overwhelming envy gave Morton reason to dedicate his life to destroying Harris."

Hot tears continued to sting Isabella's face. "I can't believe my father is dead."

"I'm sorry to be the bearer of such terrible news."

She accepted the handkerchief he offered and shook her head. "It's no wonder I thought my father was acting strangely. His sudden outbursts seemed so uncharacteristic. Uncle Morton stole my amulet from me—the one Papa sent me from the Valley of the Pharaohs."

"I know why Morton took your amulet," Rayburn said. "Collingsworth told me that during the conversation he overheard, Harris asked Morton to contact you. Your father wanted you to know that the amulet he sent you is very valuable after all."

"It can't be—not without the bracelet of Amenhotep."

Without saying a word, Benjamin withdrew something from his greatcoat pocket. A circle of pure gold glittered in the light. He handed the infamous bracelet to Isabella with a smile.

"My God," she whispered.

It was a heavy thing, inlaid with sparkling jewels and an intricate border design consisting of polished coral. Thicker than four inches, it opened by way of a hinged clamp. Her fingers trembled around it.

"Be very careful with it, Isabella. Morton might know that Collingsworth discovered it among your father's belongings. Out of respect for your father, he gave it to me to pass on to you. Of course, if Morton doesn't know about the bracelet's discovery, he may be trying to get the amulet from you and return to Egypt in an attempt to unearth it. Together they are worth a fortune."

With her other hand, Isabella touched the coldness of the stone that dangled from her neck. The fact that these two pieces of jewelry were in her possession feathered her spine with a shiver. *If I can get Amenhotep's bracelet on Draven's wrist, I could avoid killing him altogether.*

Rayburn studied her in the dim light. "This is what I think," he said. "Under the guise of Harris, Morton planned to bring you to Thorncliff Towers, confiscate the amulet, and do away with all those involved so that he could profit from Draven's money." He paused. "Morton is a very dangerous man."

"I need to warn Helena and Draven that my father is an imposter," Isabella said.

Benjamin put his hand over hers. "Try and calm yourself, my dear. You shall stay here in London with Willa and me. After a few days, I will accompany you to the Winthrop estate and together we shall tell your husband and his mother. Then we will find and confront Morton."

Isabella's thoughts flew to Draven's daunting time-line. "Thank you, Uncle Benjamin, but there is an urgent reason I must return by tomorrow afternoon, at the very latest."

"What reason is that?"

"I cannot tell you everything except that I've fallen in love with my own husband," she answered in a soft tone.

He smiled forlornly.

"In being cruel earlier in his life, he has isolated himself from everyone. Now I'm all he has," she said.

"Very well then." Rayburn finished the last drop of ale in his glass. "Since the last post chaise to the coast has already departed, you'll stay the night at my home and make the journey back to Dunwich first thing in the morning."

"Thank you so much, Uncle Benjamin."

"Of course, my dear. Before we take leave and get you home to Willa, tell me where Morton is."

"He's here in London. With Fiona. He said he had no desire to return to Thorncliff Towers."

Rayburn seemed relieved. "Good. Since I'll need time in the morning to round up the proper authorities, I will come to Dunwich shortly thereafter."

As they left the pub, they walked in silence for a while. Then Rayburn placed a hand on her arm to stop her. "Remember, if Simon Collingsworth is willing to testify about what he heard, we can have Morton arrested on three legal counts: murder, illegal business dealings, and stealing his brother's identity."

Chapter Thirty-Eight

Draven's head was heavy with confusion as he stormed back to Dunwich. He could swear he had smelled Isabella's blood at the Gypsy camp, but when he'd exited the wagon, he saw no trace of his wife.

Of course, the multitude of scents within the camp had bombarded his senses and he could have been mistaken.

What dominated his thoughts even more were Marga Yavidovich's words. The Gypsy never said that a *woman* must shoot him with a silver bullet. It made Draven wonder: could a man who loved him like a father pull the trigger instead?

A man such as Rogers?

Draven knew this was one request the faithful valet would turn down, but he was determined to persuade the old man otherwise.

Once he retrieved Lucifer in Dunwich, he directed the horse back to Thorncliff Towers. Before he spoke with Rogers, Draven wanted to tie up some loose ends with Helena. They had never had it out with one another and he considered that silence unfinished business.

Since his stepmother felt no maternal affection for him, she would probably be happy that he was going to vanish from her life forever. A long line of nannies and tutors had raised him without any effort or involvement from Helena. During that time, she never bothered to show an interest in him or inquire about his development. Bitterness had always plagued him on that account, but now he must release himself from it. And he wanted Helena to share in the moment.

He yanked Lucifer to a halt in front of the stables. After tossing the horse's reins to Viktor, he entered the house with his riding crop in hand. Striding determinedly throughout the first level, he was called to the parlor by the shadow of the flickering hearth. Entering the room in a rush, he saw Helena reclining on the divan, enjoying a glass of sherry. She didn't seem to notice him standing there.

"For once, Helena," he said, "I'm glad to see you."

Her brows dipped into a frown. She turned to him. "You needn't concern yourself with my presence much longer," she said. "I am leaving for London in the morning."

"Having a sentimental moment, are we?" he asked, eyeing the glass of sherry.

Helena's look went sour. She glared at the riding crop her stepson held in his hands. "Did you torture your horse during your ride, Draven?"

"Of course not." He shunned her sarcastic tone. "And I wasn't riding for pleasure. I had business in town."

"What sort of business?"

Draven squeezed the leather rod until his knuckles turned white. "Business I must discuss with you here and now."

"Certainly," she said vaguely.

Draven sat across from Helena on a low, cushioned stool then leaned forward anxiously.

"What is it you wanted to talk to me about?"

"There is no delicate way to bring this to your attention, Helena, so I will get straight to the point."

Her tone grew impatient. "What *are* you talking about?"

"Did you know that my maternal grandmother placed a curse on me after I killed that Gypsy girl? A curse that would ultimately transform me into a murderous beast?"

She set her sherry on a side table. Crossing her arms, she shifted uncomfortably in her seat. "Yes, I am aware of that."

Draven stared at her in disbelief. "You knew? And you never discussed it with me? You couldn't have thought to prepare me for what would happen on my twenty-seventh birthday?"

"I followed you into the woods that night, Draven," she said. "I saw you kill that girl."

His face flushed.

She put a hand up to calm him. "You told me that it was an accident when you returned to the house, but I knew firsthand that you were telling the truth."

"Still, you buried that secret by having me committed?"

Her stare softened. "To protect you."

He drew back, confused.

"You see," Helena explained as her demeanor completely changed, "I heard that woman cast her curse. And I thought that if you were safely tucked away in an asylum, you couldn't be hurt, or hurt anyone else."

Anger heated his stare as she struggled for composure.

"Though you were not aware of it at the time," she said, "I visited the asylum. I saw how you were being treated by those inexperienced doctors. And when I saw those torturous machines, I ordered you to be released."

"What were you thinking before you had me committed?" Draven scowled. "That time spent in an asylum would equal a stay at a high-class hotel?"

"No one could have guessed how terrible that place was."

He flew to his feet. "I don't believe it. This is a bunch of rubbish. You hate me. You've always hated me."

She drew in a defiant breath. "No. I hated your father for what he did to me. The humiliation was more than I could bear and seeing you every day reminded me of his infidelity."

"So you transferred your hatred of my father to me?"

"I did. I was outraged over his betrayal. So much so that you became a pawn in our relationship. I am certain you've learned this from servant gossip, but I threatened your father with divorce if he ever left me. I had proper grounds to do so."

"And my father refused."

"Yes. He enjoyed being a well-respected earl with an impeccable reputation."

Draven's teeth tingled with hatred. *Why must she tarnish Father's memory?*

Finding her familiar air of superiority, she continued. "Cyril and I were very much in love at one point. Then he had the gall to succumb to that bedeviling woman. Following their tryst, we never placed ourselves in the position to have children of our own. It's something I never forgave him for. Therefore I wasn't about to allow him to disgrace me *publicly*. That explains why, to this day, no one in Society knows that you are illegitimate, Draven."

He wanted to strangle her, but the notion that Helena had gotten her fill of pain over the years would have to do. He took a moment to calm himself. "So you felt that all Father left you with was me?"

"Yes," Helena's face twisted with despair. *"You."*

Before Draven could pose his next question, Helena said something quite unexpected. "I never told you this before, but a part of me regrets not being a proper mother to you. Resentment paralyzed me from being maternal in any way."

The statement caught him completely off guard. What did she expect him to say? That she had always been as cold-hearted as they come and that it was perfectly fine with him?

"I have my own confession," Draven said. "I allowed you to stay here at Thorncliff Towers on the thread of a hope that you would become more affectionate. After all, you were all I had left after Father died."

"Is that true?" Pain laced her indigo eyes.

Draven pushed his fingers through his hair, unraveling his queue. His voice quivered and belied his emotion. "I regret never knowing my birth mother. Did you know that she committed suicide on the very night she came here to Thorncliff Towers to speak with Father?"

"Committed suicide?" Shock rocked Helena's voice.

He nodded. "She drowned herself in the pond just beyond Dunwich. It's safe to say that giving me away broke her heart."

Her face went ashen. "I had no idea. H . . . how did you know?"

"I've had contact with a member of the Gypsy tribe. The grandmother of the girl I killed, in fact."

She leaned forward. "Have you asked her to revoke your curse?"

"Yes. I practically got down on my knees and begged her to lift it. Do you know what solution she presented me with?"

Helena shook her head slowly.

"She said that the woman I love is doomed to end my life whether I like it or not."

"Isabella's Egyptian prophecy—" Helena gasped.

He tossed the pearl-handled pistol into her shaking palm. "This gun contains a silver bullet. Supposedly Isabella will kill me with it tomorrow evening, as the full moon peaks. This will stop my reign of terror as a wolf."

Staring at him in horror, she thrust the gun back at him.

"I can think of no one who despises me more," Draven said, "so I'm sure this is all you ever dreamed of. To be forever rid of me, a scandalous thorn in your side."

Helena tilted her head back in her regal fashion. "I can't deny that I have wished you out of my life many times."

Draven gave her a half-smile. "After tomorrow night, you never have to worry about being publicly disgraced again. I'll be dead. Isabella will be in London. And you can remain here."

"But I thought Isabella would be dead too, according to the prophecy."

"I have another plan."

Perspiration beaded his upper lip while Helena's hatred for him resurfaced.

"This is morbid beyond belief," she said.

As difficult as it was, he had come here to tell Helena that he didn't blame her anymore. Never thinking he'd see the day he would pose the words, he took in a breath. "Since we're speaking so frankly, I'd like to tell you something. I know my father made you suffer greatly. I also know that I shouldn't have been born the bastard son of a Gypsy woman. I should have been *your* son. For that reason, I forgive you for hating me. In fact, I consider you vindicated."

"You are . . . forgiving me?" She seemed flabbergasted.

"Yes. And for what it's worth, I wasn't responsible for poisoning your food. It may not matter to you, but it's my wish to inform you of that before I'm gone."

Draven rose, spun on his heel, and left the room in order to spend his last afternoon elsewhere.

Chapter Thirty-Nine

By late afternoon the following day, the post chaise from London deposited Isabella and Gwyneth in front of Thorncliff Towers' double doors.

Isabella had cried over the news of her father's death during the entire journey. Gwyneth had tried to comfort her, but halfway through the trip, the girl gave up and left her to her sorrow.

Now the abigail lifted the ornate knocker and let it crash forward. As Isabella waited for entry, she practically burst with the knowledge she wanted to relay to Draven.

Mrs. Eaton greeted them with a look of surprise. Isabella, who had no desire to explain why she had come back, rushed across the threshold and glanced around in a sort of frenzy. "Where might I find Draven and Lady Winthrop?"

"Master Draven 'asn't left 'is quarters for hours and 'er ladyship is keepin' to 'er room as well." The housekeeper crooked a finger toward Isabella, drawing her closer. "I'm glad ye're 'ere, m'lady. And if ye ask me, the two o' them seemed unusually distraught today. Between them there's a silence and a tension the likes of I've never seen before."

While Isabella was aware of the reason for that tension, she was not about to discuss it with a servant. "Thank you, Mrs. Eaton. Kindly have Rogers bring my belongings back up to my suite."

The gray-haired woman nodded. "Yes, m'lady."

As Isabella ascended the staircase, dread over her ensuing confrontation with Helena escalated with her every step.

Helena hates me. Why would she believe me over Uncle Morton?

When she reached the second-floor landing, Isabella turned toward Helena's chambers which were located in the farthest wing of the house. After treading over the paisley-patterned carpet, she stood outside the countess's door. She raised her fist to knock. Footsteps sounded behind her. Before she could whirl around, a heavy object struck the back of her neck.

Blinding pain encompassed Isabella's skull and her vision went black.

Isabella awoke slowly, her eyes struggling to focus on her surroundings.

As her grogginess began to lift, she realized she was lying on her stomach with her hands bound tightly behind her back. Her mouth was gagged.

Trying to ignore the throbbing pain at the back of her head, she stared into an unforgiving darkness. Panic gripped her as she forced herself to a sitting position despite the tangle of her skirts.

She could only guess that Morton had come back to Thorncliff Towers and had attacked her. She also assumed that from the familiar smell of mildew that surrounded her, he'd locked her inside the secret passageway.

He learned of the corridor the day I was trapped. Would he be back for me soon? And is the bracelet of Amenhotep still in my pocket?

Grunting, Isabella looked about. There wasn't a source of light anywhere. How could she possibly fumble around in the darkness without hurting herself? And how was she to sever the ropes that incapacitated her hands and mouth?

Because she had no idea what time it was, horror flooded her emotions. She must escape before the full moon reached its nighttime ascension.

Heaving her back against the damp stone wall, Isabella used all of her strength to stand. In an effort to gather her bearings, she ran her fingertips along the stones behind her and shuffled her feet to the right. Perhaps she could recognize some configurations of the passageway from its curves and corners. Following a few, futile attempts however, she stopped. Every inch of the stone passageway felt the same.

Biting her lip, she tried to calm her nerves. It was her best bet if she hoped to get to the grave of Draven's mother. She searched feverishly for something sharp enough to cut through the ropes. But only the dark abyss was there to terrify her out of her mind.

Reversing her direction, she crept along, taking tiny steps, keeping her body close to the cold wall. *I need a candle to illuminate the way.*

That's it! Isabella thought. The day she was trapped in this same corridor, she had dropped her candle branch before Draven rescued her.

Was it still inside the barriers of the passageway?

She could only hope. If she managed to locate the object in the dark, it would give her a point of reference as well as provide her with something to cut the ropes.

She had dropped the branch near the entrance to her bedchamber, but where was she now? With aching arms, she moved in the opposite direction. There were no other passageways, so it shouldn't be difficult to locate the candle branch. Feeling with the tips of her toes, she waved her foot back and forth in front of her, hoping to touch anything hard in the foreboding blackness.

Perspiration dripped from her brow while frustration replaced her panic. She retraced her steps over and over, becoming completely disoriented. Being without sight was horribly debilitating, but blindness did heighten one's other senses. The pungent aroma of mildew swirled heavily in the air. She listened for any sound indicating help was nearby as she searched about for several more minutes. Suddenly, the stillness was interrupted by the high pitch of a voice.

Gwyneth was calling her name. Where was she?

Desperate to notify the abigail of her location, Isabella shuffled around with greater speed. Then her foot tapped something heavy and hard. It was the candle branch!

She lowered herself by sliding her backside down to the ground level. Entirely by feel, she could tell that the large branch, with its ornate iron leaves, rested in a corner of the passageway on its side. Without wasting another minute, she started to rake her wrists back and forth against the leaves. Her pulse quickened as she tried to prevent piercing a vein or an artery. After a few minutes, the sharp ironwork had sliced through the rope.

She was free, but it was too early to celebrate. She was confined inside this passageway and Gwyneth's voice was gradually fading. Isabella dragged the rag away that restrained her mouth and started screaming at the top of her lungs. She hollered again and again. With tears pricking her eyes, she groped in the dark for the handle that would trigger her bedchamber wall to open.

Shoving her hand into the pocket of her dress, she felt for the bracelet of Amenhotep. Despair seized her when she discovered it was gone.

Had Draven been able to convince someone to shoot him with a silver bullet? *Where was he?*

Several minutes passed and Gwyneth's voice disappeared completely. Isabella's fingertips began to bleed from the rough surface of the stone. If no one knew she was in here, what would become of her? And what would become of Draven?

She groped for the panel's handle once more. As if the motion were cast down by God himself, she located it and the wall slid away. Isabella slumped into the fresh air of her bedchamber with a thud. Gwyneth hastened into the room.

"M'lady!"

Isabella's throat was parched. "It was my father," she croaked. "He is not who he says he is."

"He put ye in the passageway?"

She nodded weakly.

"But I never thought—"

"Never mind that, Gwyneth. I must get to Draven. He's in the woods by the pond."

"Yes, yer ladyship." Placing a hand beneath her arm, the abigail helped her stand.

Isabella's breath rasped and her head ached.

The girl frowned. "Do ye want me to go with ye?"

"No. I must do this alone."

In one sweeping motion, Isabella ripped the bottom ruffle from the expensive, silk frock Draven had made for her and threw it aside. She also removed the dress's paneled jacket for the last thing she needed was cumbersome clothing getting in her way. Faster than she'd ever moved before, she streamed down the grand staircase and out the front door.

Chapter Forty

Rushing to saddle a horse and reach the pond before it was too late, Isabella scrambled down the embankment toward the stables.

Ignoring the frigid wind, she ducked inside the structure. It only took a moment for her to see that Draven's stallion, Lucifer, was missing. Thankfully, her old friend, Dante, was lounging against a dark corner.

"Come here, Dante!"

The titanic animal stood and she moved closer to stroke its brow. "This is no time to be difficult. We were beginning to grow fond of one another during our first meeting, right?"

The horse threw its head back in response.

She readied the animal in haste and led it into the crisp, night air. After swinging herself into the saddle, she streamed toward the dim light of dusk.

Straining her memory, Isabella tried to retrace the path she and Draven had taken into the woods. "You may have to remember for me, boy."

In response, the stallion moved like a shooting star through the thick maze of trees. To her relief, the sunset seemed to be holding out. She wouldn't be able to make the same journey in the dark.

Tree branches scratched her chest and legs and her wounded head throbbed heavily. Commanding the horse onward, the thought of what would happen if she was too late to save Draven's life stabbed her heart.

Dante was galloping along at record speed, but it seemed like an eternity until horse and rider reached the edge of Dunwich. Isabella stroked the panting animal in gratitude.

"I know the way from here," she reassured the horse. Slowing its pace to a trot, she led the creature to the open field where she had followed Draven. The murky pond bordering his mother's final resting place wasn't far now.

She decided to walk from this point so she wouldn't be heard. Taking Dante's reins in her hand, she dismounted quietly and hurried toward a clearing at the south end of the pond.

Moving in closer, Isabella heard voices arguing in the otherwise silent forest.

Draven and Rogers are here.

After tying Dante's reins to a tree trunk, she swept a branch aside and peered at the chilling scene.

Draven stood in an empty grave beside a substantial mound of freshly dug earth. Rogers was visible at perhaps ten or eleven feet in front of him. Looking as though he had seen a hundred ghosts, the manservant was pointing a pistol at Draven's heart.

"I cannot believe ye talked me into this, m'lord." Rogers's voice shook. "Tis complete insanity!"

"Nevertheless, we will go through with it," Draven said with authority.

Isabella craned her neck and caught a glimpse of her husband's grim face. She prayed that Rogers would reconsider his participation in this madness at the last minute.

"On the count of three," Draven instructed. "One, two—"

"Wait," Isabella cried from the shadows. "Don't do this!" She bolted from the brush and positioned herself between Draven and his manservant.

"Isabella," Draven growled. "What the hell are you doing here?"

She faced him, wide-eyed. "I followed you to the Gypsy camp yesterday and I listened at the foot of the caravan while you spoke with that woman. That's why I came back."

"You can't be here," he said. "Rogers, quickly take her ladyship back to the house. Then return so we can finish what we started."

"I won't go," she insisted. "Please listen, Draven. I had the bracelet of Amenhotep. But someone attacked me inside the house and took it."

"You had the bracelet?" His tone rang with surprise. "How did you get it?"

"There's no time to explain now, but if you help me find it, it can end all of this madness."

"Who attacked you?"

"I did." Morton Farrington stepped into the triangle that connected the trio. Before anyone could move, he snatched the pistol out of Rogers's hands and turned it on them. Isabella backed away swiftly, into Draven's arms. She could feel his heart beating like a wild animal's.

This may be the end for her and Rogers, but did Morton know he couldn't kill Draven?

"Sir Harris," Draven thundered. "What is the meaning of this?"

"He isn't who he says he is," Isabella cried. "He's Morton Farrington, my father's twin brother!"

"Silence, my prying niece. So you escaped from the passageway, did you?" Morton asked slowly. "I would have thanked Gwyneth for telling me where you'd gone, but sadly I killed her before I could get the words out."

"You're despicable," Isabella said.

"Be quiet, you impertinent brat!"

"Let her go, you bastard," Draven roared. "I knew there was something suspicious about you. You tried to poison my mother."

"You're right." The admission poured from Morton's mouth like a malevolent toxin.

The swatch of fabric I found in the cellar. Isabella's mind raced. *Morton was trying to find the still room.*

"I slipped strychnine into Helena's empty teacup before I left the house. Fortunately for me, it's a clear, powdered poison that went unnoticed."

"It could have killed her," Draven barked.

"That was the idea."

"So it is true," Draven said. "You've been impersonating Harris Farrington."

"At this very moment, my father's remains are being shipped from Egypt to London." Isabella spoke through her tears. "My uncle killed his own twin so that he could assume his brother's identity. What's more, he knocked me unconscious and left me to rot in the hidden passageway. Tell them everything, Uncle Morton. It's time to admit as much."

"Be quiet, you horrid girl."

"Tell them!"

"I *will* since I plan on killing all of you anyhow," Morton said. "Yes, I've been pretending to be my brother. His life was far superior to mine. We looked exactly alike, but Harris was the golden child. He did better in school and when we grew, he achieved notoriety and created a beautiful family. I, on the other hand, became a criminal and sank into despair over my intense jealousy."

Morton's chartreuse eyes formed catlike slits as he continued. "After I did away with my brother, I made that landslide happen in Egypt—to grant myself a new start."

Isabella's knees shook as the last sliver of daylight dropped below the horizon.

"You won't see a penny of Winthrop money!" Draven's warning sliced the tense air.

"Oh, but I will. I'll be the last remaining beneficiary." Greed glazed Morton's voice. "Too bad the villagers of Dunwich didn't destroy you sooner, Draven."

"Did you send the Gypsies off my property, posing as my messenger?" Draven asked sharply.

"Of course I did. It was all part of my plan to make everyone despise you."

Isabella gulped. She looked over her shoulder and saw that Draven's eyes glowed with fury.

Morton didn't seem to notice. His mouth curved into a wicked grin. "I have the bracelet of Amenhotep and now I need that amulet. Where is it, Isabella?"

She searched her pockets for it. "It's gone!"

"You're lying," Morton seethed.

"No. I had it inside a secret pouch of my dress while I was riding through the woods just now. It must have fallen out."

"Don't worry. I'll find it after you're dead."

The glow of dusk deepened into night. Draven reached for Isabella's hand and she could feel the start of a tremor in it. He would be transformed into a savage beast in less than a minute. Was this the last time he would ever be human? Would she end up killing him in self-defense, fulfilling the Egyptian prophecy?

"No more talk," Morton demanded. "Rogers, you stand over there. Isabella and Draven, get into the grave." He held his cane in one hand while he prompted them into the shallow hole with the loaded pistol thrust forward in the other.

"The curse accompanying Tousret's amulet fits into my scheme perfectly," he explained. "Isabella, you will shoot your husband and then turn the gun on yourself. Your fingerprints will be on the pistol. After you and Draven are dead, I'll shoot Rogers, bury him along with the pistol, and return to the house to kill Helena. When her body is found in the woods, it will appear as if she was ravaged by the werewolf that roams this countryside."

Isabella leaned against Draven. She craned her neck back in order to steal a look at the moon. Its eerie light began to glow from behind a veil of clouds. Panic clogged her throat.

"Take this gun, Isabella," Morton said. He tossed the pistol Rogers was about to fire into her hands. At the same time, he extracted another, smaller pistol from his coat pocket and turned it on her to ensure that she would heed his commands. "It contains a round of silver bullets in case your husband is indeed a werewolf. Now shoot him or I will shoot you!"

The metal of the gun felt like ice in her hands. She wanted to fling it to the ground, but Morton left her no choice but to squeeze her hand around it.

"Shoot your husband!" her uncle urged.

Slowly, she turned around and met the pain in Draven's eyes. Her heartbeat drummed at a frenetic pace while Draven inched backward, to the edge of the grave. She did everything she could to resist lifting the pistol in his direction, but the will of the amulet was too strong. It seemed that even though she wasn't wearing the necklace, its otherworldly force was propelling her actions. Raising her hand to eye level, Isabella threaded her finger through the trigger. The way her arm shook made the pistol bounce.

Draven faced her aim with a heart-wrenching sense of loss.

How had it come to this?

As if an invisible hand were commanding her, Isabella targeted

Draven's heart. She managed to drag her eyes to the full moon. It was about to escape the cloud cover. Her arm continued to shake as she held the gun.

"It's all right, Bella," Draven whispered. "I deserve to die."

Hot tears streaked her face. *I refuse to kill the only man I have ever loved.* She shook her head. As she summoned all of her strength, she resisted pulling the trigger.

Draven's stare shifted to Morton. "Burn in hell!" he hissed.

"I'm sure I'll see you there, but not today." Morton closed his eyes and threw his head back in laughter.

Isabella seized her chance. She jumped out of the grave and leapt onto Morton's back. He teetered off balance under her weight and dropped his gun. Still, with a violent spin, he managed to shake her off and she went slamming into a tree without the pistol he'd given her. Draven dove for Morton and they began to struggle. Using his cane as a weapon, Morton struck Draven in the head. Then, wearing a satanic grin, Morton yanked away the cane's handle and out slid a sword attached to it. He was about to stab Draven when Rogers came from behind and brought the shovel he'd used to dig the grave down on the imposter's head. Morton crumpled to the ground, unconscious.

Bright moonlight streamed through the clouds. When it settled on Draven, he sunk to the ground and began to convulse. Isabella wanted to go to him, but she knew she couldn't be of help without the bracelet of Amenhotep.

"Rogers!" She heard Draven screech as she searched Morton's pockets for it. "Shoot me, for God's sake!"

She tried to block out Draven's screams while she continued to look. *Where the devil was it?*

She glanced at Draven again. He was still writhing in pain but he hadn't changed into the wolf yet. Knowing that she had mere seconds to save her husband, Isabella dug her hand into the one place she hadn't checked yet: the left pocket of Morton's trousers. Her heart gave a surge as she located the bracelet and rushed to clamp it over Draven's wrist. A moment later, he stopped convulsing.

Rogers and Isabella helped Draven to his feet. Draven shook away his grogginess as he pulled Isabella into his arms. "Thank God Morton didn't hurt you," he murmured into her hair.

"I'm so glad you're alive." She buried her face in his shoulder.

"Without you, I had nothing to live for," he whispered.

"I couldn't kill you," she said. "I love you too much."

He squeezed her tighter.

Rogers stepped in. "Let's get both of ye back to the house."

"Good idea, old boy."

After Draven clasped the loyal servant's arm, he put his hand out for Isabella to take. She reached for it and felt Morton stir beside her. His snake-green eyes flashed open and he flew to his feet, sword in hand.

"Draven!" Isabella cried.

But it was too late. Morton sliced Draven's arm with the sharp blade. Then, with a vicious stab, he sunk the sword into Draven's shoulder.

Draven clutched his wound while Isabella lunged for one of the discarded guns. She took dead aim at her uncle's heart and fired. Morton shuddered and heaved his last breath as Draven pitched to his knees, bleeding profusely.

Distant voices penetrated the clearing. Isabella whirled around and saw an army of torches bobbing behind the trees.

The lynch mob is coming for Draven.

It was more than she could take. Teetering toward a tree trunk, the forest turned an ominous shade of black and she abruptly lost consciousness.

Chapter Forty-One

Cognizant of daybreak, Isabella opened her eyes and forced them to focus on the unfamiliar environment around her. Dark, velvet curtains framed a pair of tiny windows. A disheveled pile of tarot cards sat next to an ominous crystal ball on a small table. Dangling from the walls were carcasses of miniature animals.

She was lying on a cot inside a Gypsy's wagon.

Isabella raised a hand to her aching forehead and massaged her temples. Still fatigued, she let her head fall back against the pillow.

Was last night a dream?

Her physical state told her otherwise. Her chest stung from the scratches inflicted by the tree branches and Draven's blood had dried in clumps on her dress. Close to tears, she knew the image of Morton dead on the ground would be forever etched in her memory. She had killed her own uncle. Worse yet, what had become of Draven?

A woman's face hovered over her. Deep lines creased comfortably around a pair of black eyes—eyes that matched Draven's in their shape and color. A scarf splattered with every hue of the rainbow encircled the Gypsy's head and when she moved, the coins sewn to her skirt jingled softly.

"You must be exhausted, my dear," the woman said.

It was the voice Isabella had heard the other day—when she stole close to the caravan of wagons. She met the woman's words with a nod.

"Would you care for something to eat, my child?"

"No, thank you. I'm afraid I don't feel very well."

"Do you want to tell me what happened last night?" The woman remained standing. She folded her hands together patiently.

"Well"—Isabella scrambled to gather her thoughts—"it all seems a bit hazy, but I do know that my blackhearted uncle is dead. And my husband—"

"—is right here." A strong hand gripped hers.

She looked up and her heart skipped a beat. "Draven! I thought I'd never see you again. The mob was coming."

"It never found me." His pallor and dark-rimmed eyes told Isabella he'd touched the depths of hell and had barely lived to talk about it. "I wasn't under the power of the curse anymore, which meant the villagers could have killed me. So I ran."

Wearing a sling around his injured arm, he knelt beside the cot. Marga placed a hand on his back and he looked up at her.

"You believed it was Isabella's destiny to shoot you, my lord," the old woman said, "but the vision I saw was that of her pulling the trigger to kill her uncle."

He squeezed Isabella's hand tighter. "Thank God the Egyptian bracelet severed my spell."

Marga shook her head. "That is not what ended your curse. You see, I knew all along that my vision involved Isabella killing her uncle. The moment you realized that you loved Isabella more than you loved yourself, the wolf's spell was severed. And when you planned your own death, you proved that you valued someone else's life more than you valued your own. No one was required to shoot you at all, Lord Winthrop."

His eyes widened. "I wasn't going to change into the black wolf?"

"No," Marga replied. "You finally convinced the dark forces that you've learned the meaning of love."

"I have," he said, turning back to Isabella. "I love *you,* heart and soul."

Isabella's eyes filled with tears.

"I had to protect you when you blacked out, Bella," Draven said. "I carried you here to this camp—as far away from the mob as possible. The villagers think the Gypsies hate me, so they would never have thought to look here."

Isabella felt as if an enormous weight had been lifted. She reached over and traced the curve of her husband's rough cheek. He looked shattered.

"Thank you," she said.

"For what?"

"For excluding me from your curse's revocation."

"I could never harm you." He inhaled a shaky breath. "It is I who should thank you for finding the strength to resist the amulet's prophecy."

She smiled ruefully.

"It's over," said Marga as she made her way out of the wagon. "My lord, your curse has been lifted forever."

Draven sat beside Isabella. He pressed her open palm to his face and closed his eyes. "As it should have, the spell left me a better person. Remorse is a terrible burden to carry, but I know I deserved the punishment I was given."

Isabella shifted against the strength of his chest. "It couldn't have been easy for you all these years."

"It wasn't. But if it hadn't been for you, I would have never changed. You saved me, Bella."

"I think you had the capacity to change all the while," she said softly. "We just helped each other along."

"How have I helped you?" Draven asked.

"You taught me that life is too precious to take so seriously."

He drew her close.

Isabella's next question was a provocative one. "Can you find it in your heart to forgive your grandmother for casting the spell in the first place?"

"I believe I can," he said. "We all have things in our past we regret. For me, I regret killing that girl. I also regret the way I treated you. I promise that spite, hatred, and deception will never cloud my life again."

"You mean, you have forgiven Helena?"

"Yes. It wasn't easy, but she is the only link I have to my father."

"I have no family left," Isabella said. She sat up and gazed into his fathomless eyes.

Draven stroked her cheek. "You have me."

Her stomach dropped. Was he going to utter the words she desperately wanted to hear?

"Now that my curse has been severed," he said, "we can have as many children as we wish."

Warm tears spilled down Isabella's cheeks. She nodded.

As a broad grin stretched across Draven's face, he dipped forward to catch her mouth with a kiss. Isabella surged against him and she realized that all the barriers between them had been dissolved.

Still smiling, Draven took her hand and led her to where Marga Yavidovich was waiting. The Gypsy woman placed a gnarled hand on his arm. "May you two live in peace."

"Thank you, Marga, for showing me the way," Draven said.

The Gypsy gave him a caring nod and disappeared into her wagon again.

He encircled an arm around Isabella's waist and urged her closer. "You make me the happiest man on Earth."

"And I am the happiest woman," she said through a grin. "Perhaps you and I can enjoy a proper honeymoon now."

"Don't you remember?" he teased her softly before pulling her into a kiss. " 'Proper' is a formality I threw out the window long ago."

Epilogue

A satisfying chain of events took place in the months that followed Morton Farrington's death.

With the staggering fortune Cyril Winthrop had left his son, Draven promised to build the embankments Dunwich was so desperately in need of. He also lavished Thorncliff Towers with renovations while officially setting his shipbuilding business into motion at the same time.

Draven and Isabella bought another house close to Helena's posh London mansion. Rogers, who claimed he was too old to tend to Draven anymore, opted not to go with them. Because Draven continued to have a soft spot for the elderly man, he presented Rogers with a hefty compensation for his faithful service—and for saving his life. Ironically, Rogers and the long-widowed Mrs. Tidwell married a few weeks after Draven and Isabella moved to London. After all, they had been having a torrid affair for years.

Isabella, who still mourned the loss of Gwyneth, had a statue erected in the garden of Thorncliff Towers in the abigail's likeness. The household staff was grateful for the commemoration as it truly captured Gwyneth's charm and resilience.

Because Draven had passionately planned and painstakingly implemented his new business, it was in fine enough shape for him to whisk Isabella away for an exotic trip cum delayed honeymoon.

Before she and Draven left on the exclusive ocean liner they had booked passage on, Isabella had searched for the Egyptian amulet without success. She was downhearted at losing it, but she agreed to Simon Collingsworth's request that she add Amenhotep's bracelet to the Egyptian exhibit at the British Museum. She figured that her father would like to have seen at least one of his discoveries on display.

Subsequently, the remains of Sir Harris Farrington were buried next to Isabella's mother in London's Highgate Cemetery. The burial brought with it a much-needed sense of closure for Isabella.

On a wondrously warm April day, the S.S. *Royal Legacy* slipped through the glassy, languid waters off the coast of Cyprus. Enjoying the eighth week of her honeymoon, Isabella sat sprawled in the bed she and Draven left on rare occasions. She shifted her weight unconsciously with the rhythm of the elegant vessel and marveled that she hadn't left her husband's side during their trip abroad.

Draven slept beside her. She gently mussed his hair and admired the expanse of his shoulders as he lay on his abdomen with his elbows jutted out. Smiling, she raised that same hand in order to gaze upon her filigree wedding band with new meaning.

Draven stirred. Stretching, he turned on his back. His stomach gave a hungry gurgle. "Time for supper, darling."

Isabella scrunched up her nose in refusal, a habit her husband apparently found charming. "I'm not hungry."

He slid closer to her and plopped his head on her chest. He seductively raised his thick eyebrows up and down. "Oh, but I am."

"You're always hungry for *that*," she giggled.

"You're absolutely right."

Urging her head forward with one hand, he caressed her lips with a kiss. She pulled away with a sigh and studied her handsome husband. "Actually, I'm feeling a bit ill lately."

"Seasick?"

She shook her head as she trailed the masculine lines of his face. "I'll be fine, but I'm anxious to return home. And you? How do you think your shipbuilders are getting along without you?"

"I hope they aren't missing too many days of work while I'm gone," he quipped. Reaching up, he slipped a finger through one of her auburn curls. "I, for one, am dreading going back to Thorncliff

Towers. I know we agreed to divide our time between the bloody estate and our London house, but I feel as if bad memories await us on the coast."

She smiled tenderly. "It won't be so bad, you'll see. Thorncliff Towers is a part of you, Draven. Besides, it's a place I intend to freshen up with a more feminine style. I have excellent taste, you know."

"I know. You married me, didn't you?" His lips spread into a dazzling grin.

She swatted his arm.

"Very well." He yawned lazily. "Change the damned place as much as you like."

"I know the very room I'll start with." She squared her shoulders excitedly.

He supported his head with his hand. "Which would that be?"

She blushed. "My previous bedchamber. After all, in six months' time we will need a nursery."

"A nursery?" His pupils dilated. "We? Us? I mean, you and I are going to have a baby?"

"Yes."

He sprang up with joy. "This is incredible!"

"It happened the night you sent me away from Thorncliff Towers. When your sheath broke . . ."

He scratched his head. "Why did you wait so long to tell me?"

"I wanted to be sure you truly wanted a child," she said gently.

He leapt to his feet. "Do you feel all right, darling? Would you like an extra pillow?"

She grinned. "I'm very comfortable. I just want you to come here and hold me close."

Draven did so with zealotry.

The light of a full moon streamed through the window and illuminated their tender lovemaking that night. Afterward, the redeemed nobleman fell asleep with one hand on his wife's belly. At the same moment, the rosebush he'd planted with his own hands began to blossom in the garden at Thorncliff Towers. It signified the emergence of spring but more than that, it represented the beautiful baby girl he and Isabella had created.

* * *

Less than a mile from Thorncliff Towers, deep in the woods by the Gypsy camp, Marga Yavidovich came upon something shining on the ground. Smiling, she picked up the object and carried it to her wagon. After she locked it away, she hid the key in a secret place.

Tousret's amulet would be safe with her. For the time being.

Author's Note

I have always been fascinated with fairy tales, delightfully mesmerized by their timelessness and their magic. It seems that whether readers are young or old, they, too, never cease to be amazed by spells that seem unbreakable—and by the power of true love. I know that altering a classic fairy tale is a bold move, and that changing a "Prince Charming" into a tortured werewolf is even bolder, but I believe today's romance readers are ready for their heroes to be less perfect and more flawed. Somehow it adds to their allure. Besides, turning a prince into a doomed immortal provides a chance for the princess to shine as the unexpected heroine.

If you liked *Beauty and the Wolf,* I hope you'll look for *Snow White and the Vampire,* the next Cursed Princes romance, in December 2013.

About the Author

Although **Marina Myles** lives under the sunny skies of Arizona, she would reside in a historic manor house in foggy England if she had her way. Her love of books began as soon as she read her first fairy tale and eventually led to a degree in English literature. Now, with her loyal Maltese close by, she relishes the hours she gets to escape into worlds filled with fiery—but not easily attained—love affairs. She's busy being a wife, a mother, and a member of Romance Writers of America, but she is never too busy to hear from her amazing readers. Visit her at www.marinamyles.com.